Z-BURBIA 5
THE BLEEDING HEARTLAND

JAKE BIBLE

CHAPTER ONE

Meetings are fun! SO FUCKING FUN!

Sorry. Sorry. I really shouldn't knock meetings. I mean, meetings are what has saved us from the zombie hordes all these years during this fucking apocalypse, right?

NO, THEY HAVE NOT!

Fucking meetings ...

"Jace?" Stella asks. "Did you hear me?"

"Huh?" I reply. "Oh, yeah, sure."

"No, you didn't," Stella grumbles.

"Sorry, I was just thinking about how much I love meetings," I smile.

"None of us love meetings, Long Pork," Critter snaps. "But what the hell else are we going to do when we're camped at night? Play fucking charades? You have one hand, you moron. You can't even tap your wrist to mime two syllables!"

"Mimes, man. Mimes," I respond.

"Let's call it a night and get some sleep," Stuart sighs as he stands up and stretches. "We have a long haul tomorrow. And if it's like the past few weeks, we have a lot of actual hauling too."

"Ha!" I snort. "I see what you did there! Because we have to haul all the stupid fucking trucks and cars out of the way just to get down the road!"

"Honey?" Stella asks, looking worried. "Are you feeling okay?"

"What? Yeah, I'm fine," I say. "Super fine. Super-duper fine. Ain't nothing but a chicken wing here!"

I puke. All over Stella's lap.

Shit. Those don't look like chicken wings. I think that's squirrel.

"Goddammit, Long Pork!" Critter yells. "This is my RV! Now it's gonna smell like Stanford puke!"

"My bad, Critter. I'm just a little- BLERGHUCKHOOOPBLUG!"

"Son of a bitch," Critter mumbles as he walks away from my growing puddle of sick and into the back of the RV. "You're cleanin' that up."

"Doesn't really matter," Melissa says. "These RVs stink like hell already."

33 days. That's how long it's been since we left Knoxville and Cannibal Road. 33 motherfucking days.

It wasn't so hard to get from Knoxville to Nashville. But Nashville was a nightmare to get past. Need to stay awake for the rest of your life? Just picture a bunch of Zs dressed as rhinestone cowboys chasing your ass. Well, not so much chasing, as sort of shuffle skipping after your ass. It's like the gayest cowboy chorus line from Hell got turned into Zs, and still remembered their choreography.

So, Nashville sucked balls.

Then getting out of Nashville sucked more. Instead of heading straight for St. Louis as planned, we had to go up to Louisville because of washed out roads and massive Z herds.

"Jesus, Jace, you're burning up," Stella says as she puts the back of her hand to my forehead. John hands her a couple of towels. "Thank you. Maybe we should get Dr. McCormick in here and check him out."

"No needles," I mumble.

What? I don't like needles. Or maybe I don't like blood... No, it's needles. Is it? Fuck if I know right now.

I feel poopy.

I look around the RV at the worried faces and give everyone a thumbs up. And puke again for good measure. Hey, is that a bucket? Who grabbed a bucket?

"Where'd the bucket come from?" I grunt.

"Pee bucket," Buzz says. "Don't worry, it's clean."

"Not anymore," I reply, then heave-ho.

I can hear voices and sort of see the worried faces in a swimmy-vision kind of way. Phew, whatever has my innards by the short and curlies sure is messing with my head. I feel funky. Funky poopy. Funky poopy- BLARFGUGHHUEK!

Okay, so I have mentioned lots of names. Buzz, Stella, Critter, Stuart, John, Melissa. If you don't know these people by now then fuck you. Why do I even bother ...

You want a recap? Again with the fuck you, you stupid fucking- HURKGLOPPPPPPP-PPP-PPPft.

Recap: used to live in Asheville, NC in a subdivision called Whispering Pines. Z-Day hits, and we turn the neighborhood into a locked down sanctuary. Then I blew it up. Didn't want to, but there were bad guys. After that we tried to fix it. Guess what? More bad guys. Then more bad guys. And a dirty bomb. Asheville is a radioactive yuck zone. Left North Carolina and barely made it through Knoxville, TN and the oh so fucking fun Cannibal Road. There was a guy named Barfly there. He was a dick, bro. Got out of there, made it through the Dead Ole Opry in Nashville, nearly got our asses handed to us in Louisville, KY (ha ... KY), and now we are trying to get to Kansas City even though Dr. Kramer says it's scorched earth.

Fuck Kramer. He's an asshole mad scientist. Fuck mad scientists.

Oh, and fuck the Consortium, who are probably coming after us. Fuck, they may have even sent some super skilled, brainwashed, killing chicks to wipe us out.

Luckily, we have our own super skilled, not so brainwashed (more brain addled? Don't tell her I said that. Oh, God, please don't tell her I said that!) killing chick named Elsbeth. She rocks. She's family.

"Jace? Baby? What are you saying?" Stella asks, lifting my face from my personal puke bucket. "What's that about Elsbeth?"

Was I talking out loud?

"Was I talking out loud?" I ask.

"Yeah," everyone replies.

"Hey, we have a problem," my son Charlie says as he steps inside the RV. "Half the fucking camp is throwing up right now."

"And shitting themselves," my daughter Greta adds as she shoves Charlie out of the way and steps into the RV. "Jesus! What's that smell?"

"Uh-oh," I grumble. "Incoming! I mean, outgoing!"

The eyes in the swimmy-faces go very wide, and I feel several hands lift me up and pretty much eject me from the RV right before the unthinkable happens.

Motherfucker. I just totally pooped my pants.

"Awesome," Greta smirks.

I am puking and shitting myself, yet that smirk shines down on me like an evil beacon in the night. Teenagers, man. They have sarcasm superpowers.

"I don't feel good," I say.

"No shit, Dad," Charlie says.

"Lots of shit, actually," Greta replies. "Just so we're really clear, I am not wiping his ass. That's all you, Mom."

"Thanks, sweetheart," Stella replies. "Your kindness is so overwhelming."

Let us not discount the sarcastic abilities of a mother of teenagers, either.

"More poopies," I mumble. "Sorry."

"Outta here," Charlie says.

"Me too," Greta agrees.

"Greta!" Dr. McCormick shouts as she runs up to us. "I'm going to need your help. Oh, shit. Jace has it too?"

"Bad," I say.

"How many are we looking at, Doc?" Lourdes asks from the back of our little crowd.

I don't even remember seeing Lourdes in the RV. Was she at the meeting? When did she show up?

"I was there the whole time, Jace," Lourdes replies.

"Talking out loud again?" I ask Stella.

"Yeah, baby. Best to just not open your mouth," she says.

4

"Not in the cards," I say as I barf up one kidney and half my pancreas. How my pancreas split in two, I have no idea. Pancreases are silly that way. Silly splitting in two pancreas.

"Shit," Lourdes says as calls for help ring out from our little RV camp.

We started with fifteen RVs, but we're down to ten now. A couple broke down, a couple were overrun by Z hordes, and one just disappeared in the night. No fucking clue where it went. All the people inside, all the supplies, everything was gone in the morning. No one heard a thing, no one saw a thing. Fucking bizarre.

So, ten RVs circled like pioneer wagons, with our few flanking vehicles spaced out around them. Way out past our little camp is the canny camp. I think I see a campfire flickering, although we aren't supposed to have campfires. Lourdes ordered that since out here they can be seen for miles. But the cannies aren't exactly beholden to our fearless military leader (Critter is the civilian leader and technically he outranks Lourdes, but I'll leave that between them), so there are campfires.

"You know, there're other people that can help with the medical stuff," Greta snaps at Dr. McCormick. "Why do I have to always help?"

"Because you have a knack for it," Dr. McCormick says. "And everyone else that even has a fraction of your skills is already helping. Reaper is overrun with cases in half the RVs."

"Food poisoning?" Lourdes asks.

"I don't think so," Dr. McCormick says. "With the little rations we have, we'd all be sick right now. It has to be some bug."

"That hospital in Louisville," Stuart says. "We probably picked it up there when we scavenged supplies."

"Jesus," Dr. McCormick sighs. "We'll need to gather all of that back up and quarantine it. We can't afford to throw the supplies away, so just bag them up and keep them away from everyone else. I'll figure out how to sterilize them later. But, for now, I need all hands on deck."

"Poop deck," I laugh. Then poop.

"This is not good," Dr. McCormick says.

"Ya think?" I ask just before spewing bile all over the ground. Spewing bile is good, it means my stomach is almost empty. Uh-oh. "Uh-oh."

My bowels are still plenty full, though. Well, not so much anymore after this last blast from the ass.

"We need to clear the RVs," Dr. McCormick says. "Anyone not sick will need to sleep outside tonight so we can separate those stricken from those not stricken."

"It'd be a whole lot easier for clean up if the pukers and shitters were outside," Critter calls from the window of his RV. "We could just hose them down once they're done."

"It's dropping into the twenties," Lourdes counters. "People will freeze."

"Sick in the RVs, well outside," Dr. McCormick orders in a voice that even Critter doesn't argue with. He just shuts the RV window and pulls the drapes closed.

"He realizes that means him too, right?" Lourdes says.

"I'll let you break it to him," Dr. McCormick says. "I have other problems."

"Let's get tents set up, and boost the perimeter watch," John says. With this many people outside, there is bound to be noise, and that'll bring the Zs."

"My people will handle the perimeter, if Melissa can handle the tents," Lourdes says.

"I got it," Melissa nods, then looks at Buzz. "Rally the boys, we got tents to set up and people to piss off."

"We won't piss them off if we ask nicely," Buzz replies.

"I'm not in an ask nicely mood, Buzz," Melissa says. "Go get our brothers and round up Critter's men for Dr. McCormick. She'll need help moving the sick."

"Thank you," Dr. McCormick nods. "Greta?"

"Mom?" Greta whines.

"Move your ass, little girl," Stella growls. "We all pull our weight. I'll come join you once I pull your father's pants off, and get him cleaned up."

"I wish that was sexy talk," I mumble as I collapse onto the hard, cold dirt of the abandoned field we stopped in. I press my fevered head into the cool earth and sigh. "That feels good. Oh, crap. CRAP!"

So, my front half is nice and chill against the ground, while my back half is a raging inferno of diarrhea.

"Burn, baby, burn! Poopy inferno!" I sing. "Burn, baby, burn! Burn that mother down!"

"Yeah, I'm going to go help Dr. McCormick," Greta says, and bails.

I feel tugging, then hear gagging. Lots of gagging. I can sort of make out the swear words coming from my wife's mouth, but she's holding her breath, so they aren't super easy to piece together. But I get the gist. It's really about the cadence of the swear. "Motherfucker" sounds way different than just "fuck" or "shit" or "shit fucking cocksucking son of a bitch." I should know, I'm an expert.

"We don't have a huge water reserve," I hear Stuart say. Stuart didn't leave me! "Wipe what you can with the grass and set that aside. We'll probably have to bury it or burn it."

"You want to burn shit covered grass?" Stella laughs. "You really think that's a good idea?"

"No," Stuart says. "But if we bury it and someone else comes along and digs it up then we're spreading whatever this disease is."

"Who would dig up grass covered in shit?" Stella snaps, tugging at my jeans in a not so gentle manner.

"They may think it's a cache of supplies buried," Stuart says.

"Make it look like graves," I suggest then clench. "Back off! Back off! FIRE IN THE HOLE!"

"Oh, for fuck's sake," Stella cries as she scrambles away from me. Just in time too. "I got this, Stuart. You should go help secure the camp."

"I'm not going anywhere," Stuart says. "John and Lourdes have it covered. I'll keep an eye on you and Jace."

"You called me Jace," I sigh as a hot air balloon's worth of gas escapes my ass. "You didn't call me Long Pork."

"I didn't want to kick you while you're down," Stuart says. "Get well, and it'll be back to Long Pork."

Stuart hasn't been happy with me lately. For some stupid reason we have been butting heads left and right. I think the comment I made back outside Knoxville about him being Brenda's trigger man kind of ticked him off. Don't blame him, really. Being connected in any way to that bitch would tick me off too.

Huh, I probably should have thought about that before I said what I said. Live and learn, right?

"Once we get him moved into an RV, you should go help," Stella says.

"Yes, ma'am," Stuart says, and I can hear the smile in his voice.

"Hey!" I growl. "No flirting with my wife, asshole!"

"Jesus Christ, Jace," Stella sighs. "Shut the fuck up."

"Yeah, Long Pork," Stuart grumbles. "Shut the fuck up."

Oops. Back to Long Pork. It all goes bad so fast in the apocalypse.

There's more tugging on my legs, then I hear Stella say a few prayers before she gets to work with the grass. God bless my wife.

***

The zombie apocalypse is certainly not short on sensory stimuli.

From sounds to sights to touch to taste, it can be overwhelming. Especially the smells.

Now, I have smelled some seriously rank stuff since the dead started to walk the earth a few years ago. Things rotting, things burning, more things rotting, even more things rotting, and then there's the things rotting. Rotting things is top of the list. Actually, it pretty much is the list.

Until now.

Being stuck in an RV with people coated in their own puke and poop has just replaced the smell of rotting what the fuck ever.

Rotting things have a smell that's finite. You know eventually it will fade away. But sick folk? Not so much. Each smell is warm and living. Those smells say to your nose, "Hey nose! Don't get too comfortable and used to this because in about three seconds we're going to blast you with a new fresh and funky wave of olfactory annihilation! Huzzah, nose! Huzzah!"

The worst part of it all? The moaning.

Not that I'm a moaning virgin (whatever a moaning virgin might be) since I do live in the zombie apocalypse, and those undead fuckers sure do know how to moan. But, as with the smells, the living are different. Z moans sound empty, hollow, and, well, dead. They tend to all meld together into a monotonous chorus of zombie despair. Whereas, (good word, whereas. Whereas, whereas, whereas, whereas. I could say it all day)…

What was I saying? Oh, right, the sounds of the living. They aren't dead, so they don't tend to meld together. The living have individual voices. Some are high and squeaky, some are low and deep, some are just flat and empty. Many people, many voices.

"Shut up, Jace!"

"Will you be fucking quiet, Long Pork?"

"One more word, and I shit in your mouth!"

"Someone kill me. Just kill me. I can't listen anymore."

Shit. I was talking out loud again.

"No shit, Dad," Greta says from my side as she takes my temperature. "You haven't stopped talking since you got in here."

Her voice is muffled since she has a cloth wrapped around her face. I can almost smell something floral coming from her.

"Lavender," Greta says. "And you're still talking out loud. Maybe just stop thinking, okay? You need to rest anyway."

Rest? Who gets to fucking rest in the apocalypse? I haven't rested since I lost my arm. And that rest was forced on me and boring as all fuck.

"Shut him up!"

"I'm going to rip your tongue out, Stanford!"

"If we all stick to the same story, then no one will know we smothered him to death!"

"Yeah, making friends as always, Dad," Greta says as she looks at the thermometer. Even in my weakened state, and with the towel covering most of her face, I can see her blanch. "Fuck."

"How bad is it?" I ask.

"What? Oh, it's good," Greta says. "You're gonna be fine."

"Liar," I say. "What's my temp?"

"High," Greta says. "I'll be right back. I need to get more alcohol to sterilize this and check on the next person."

9

"You're going to tell Dr. McCormick what my temp is, aren't you?" I ask. "What is it, Greta?"

"One-oh-four," Greta says. "It's going up, not down."

"Open a window," I say. "It's cold as fuck out there. That'll cool me off."

"Speak for yourself, asshole!"

"I'm already freezing here!"

"I say we just bash his head in. Bish bash the little bitch."

Bish bash me? Are cannies in here too?

"Yeah," Greta sighs. "And they can hear you. Whatever this is, it's hitting the whole convoy, including the cannies." She pats my shoulder. "I'll be right back."

"Okay," is all I say. What else is there to say?

"NOTHING!" everyone shouts.

Okay, gonna stop thinking now.

"THANK GOD!" they shout again.

***

Fever dreams, man. Fever dreams.

A person's mind can really make up some weird shit when it's being cooked at one hundred and four degrees. Add the surreal existence the zombie apocalypse affords, and hoo-doggy, you got yourself some seriously fucked up brain magic.

That's what I call dreams now. Brain magic. I just made it up. Like this second. I just made it up this second.

Huh ... no one is yelling for me to shut the fuck up. Maybe I'm actually talking in my head. That has to be a good sign.

My throat is raw as hell, and I push myself up onto my elbows and look around the RV. Pretty much all the furniture has been stripped out to make room for all of us to lie down. All I see are long lumps in the dark that must be my fellow stricken. There are some murmurs and some snores, which tells me it's late into the night. I must have fallen asleep at some point.

In fact, I know I did because of the fever dreams. I'd tell you about them, but they have already faded. All I remember are the sounds. The moans and groans of the undead; the slapping of their putrid hands on the side of the RV; their broken nails and bony fingers clawing at the doors.

I can almost still hear the noises, making me think maybe I didn't dream them. But in my dreams there weren't gunshots. Now that I'm awake there are plenty of gunshots.

Gunshots?

Oh, fuck me…

I hear one of the doors open, and the moans and groans of the undead get louder.

"Wake up, people!" Porky Fitzpatrick yells. "We are under siege and getting out of here now!"

Lights come on as Porky starts up the RV and guns the engine. People pry themselves from their own fever dreams and start looking around, their glazed eyes, and glazed minds barely able to focus on what's happening.

I can focus. It's the blessing/curse of having an active, never fucking shuts up, mind. When push comes to shove, I can push and shove my mind to behave and focus on the crisis at hand.

"What's the situation, Porky?" I ask as I try to crawl my way around the stirring sickies so I can get to the passenger seat. "How bad is it?"

"Bad," Porky says. "Lourdes and the rest are trying to hold them off, but there're just too damn many of them, pardon my French." The Fitzpatricks don't really cuss, so "damn" is a big deal coming from Porky's mouth.

"Which way are they coming from?" I ask as I climb into the passenger seat. I look down and realize I only have a blanket on me. Nothing else. It's a clean blanket, though, so I got that going. Take the pluses where you can.

"They're coming from the East," Porky says as he slides open the driver's window, picks up a machete from the floor of the RV, and hacks away at half a dozen Zs clawing at the door before he pulls his arm back in, and slams the window shut. "Too dark to see for sure, but looks like a pretty big herd."

"That's like the sixth herd we've come across since we left Nashville," I say.

"Eight," Porky says as he switches on the headlights and turns off the interior lights. "You're forgetting the two small ones we dodged after Louisville."

"Right," I say quietly as I look out the front windows of the RV at the swarming Zs. "They're everywhere."

"Yep," Porky nods.

"Who's still out there?" I ask.

"Just Lourdes, her military contractors, John, Stuart, Critter's guys, and Mel," Porky says. "My brothers are starting up the RVs along with some of the cannies."

"The cannies?" I ask. "Seriously?"

"They had to ditch their vehicles," Porky replies. "Nothing smaller than a full size pick up will get through these things now. And they all know how to drive like pros."

"Yeah, cannies are good apocalyptic drivers," I nod. "I'll give them that."

"Your family is in the RV up ahead," Porky says, reading my mind. "Buzz is driving that one." He picks up a radio and puts it to his mouth. "Buzz? You read me?"

"Loud and clear, brother," Buzz replies. "You ready?"

"Ready," Porky says. "Lead the way."

The RV in front of us lurches, then turns to the left and shoves a small pickup truck out of its way as it breaks from our wagon train circle. I watch as quite a few zombies are crushed between the RV and the pickup. More than a couple of rotting heads pop right off their rotting necks and fly up into the air. Guts splatter everywhere, and Porky turns on the windshield wipers as a few squirts of green pus zigzag across the glass in front of him.

"Yuck," he says.

"True dat," I reply, and wrap the blanket around me tighter. I shiver and shudder as a wave of nausea washes over me, but luckily I keep both ends stoppered and just close my eyes until it passes.

"If you need to throw up, best you stick your head out the window," Porky says.

Dead hands reach up and smack against the glass to my right.

"Yeah, probably not gonna do that," I reply. "I'll use a bucket."

"Buckets are all full," someone says from behind us. There's a clunk and a splash as Porky hits the gas and our RV follows behind the first. "Okay, now there's an empty one."

A dripping bucket is handed up to me, and I can see Porky struggle to keep himself from vomiting.

"It's probably safe to crack your window," I say to him.

"Praise Jesus," he mutters as he mouth breathes and rolls down his window a couple of inches.

Porky barely navigates us around a Charger covered in primer and spray paint. He nudges it out of the way a little, then falls in behind the first RV. Everywhere the headlights shine, all I can see are Zs. There have to be thousands of them. Luckily, because of the open land, they aren't all densely packed together like they'd be in a city. There are thick clumps here and there, but mostly they are spread thin.

Except that the movement of the RVs is giving them purpose and direction (other than just the ever-present drive to eat our sweet, sweet flesh), and as we work our way across the rough ground of the field, the density of the Zs starts to increase. Clumps become large groups, which become small hordes, and soon I can see the gauntlet of Zs we are going to have to drive through.

"I know," Porky says, his hands gripping the steering wheel so hard that his skin looks like it's gonna split. He picks up his radio. "Hey, Buzz?"

"I know, I know," Buzz replies over the radio. "We'll need to get side by side until we hit the road. Better protection that way."

"Except for the RVs on the outsides," I say, but shut up as Porky gives me a "gonna tear your lungs out your throat" look. Melissa is the one that's perfected it, but apparently all the Fitzpatricks are versed in the art of that glare. "Sorry."

"I heard him," Buzz says. "He's right, but there's nothing we can do. Come up on my left. Everyone else join, alternating sides until we're lined up."

Porky swerves and thumps over a good eight Zs. We can hear their bodies crunch and pop from under the RV. For a few feet there is a loud scraping, but then it goes away as whatever was hanging on is shaken loose.

As we get up next to Buzz's RV, I give him a wave, but he only scowls at me. I do see Stella in the passenger seat, and I assume Charlie and Greta are somewhere else inside. Stella's hands are gripping the dash as she leans forward and stares out the windshield at the ever growing herd.

"We're climbing up," Lourdes's voice says over the radio. "Don't slow down. We can grab the ladders and ride on top until we get clear."

"Going to be a cold ride," Buzz says.

"Better cold than eaten by Zs," Lourdes replies.

"Amen, sister," I say, and give a thumbs up.

"No one can see that, Jace," Porky says.

"Oh, right," I smile, and return my thumb to its not up position. Which I guess is down. I, uh, put my thumb down. Yeah, I think I'm still a little feverish.

There's a loud crunching noise, then the sound of screaming over the radio, which is quickly cut off.

"Dammit!" Buzz shouts. "We just lost two RVs!"

"We can't leave them," someone yells over the radio.

I get up and slowly wind my way between the people and the puke buckets until I get to the back bedroom. I slide the partition open and see quite a few more people lying on the floor, the bed having been removed. But my attention is drawn to Critter as he stands at the back window, rifle in hand, and eyes locked onto the scene from behind us.

"How bad?" I ask.

"Already over," Critter says. "Looks like one of the cannies turned too fast and rolled his RV. He got rammed by a second one. Both are covered with fucking Zs. The stupid things just crawled over them like ants."

"Slow ants," I say.

Critter turns and looks at me, his face scrunched up with anger, but also something else. Fear? Oh, fuck. It's not good if Critter is scared.

"They ain't movin' as slow as I'd like," Critter says. "In this cold they should be barely shufflin'. They ain't. Some are downright hustlin'."

"Hustlin'?" I ask. "Zs don't hustle. They shamble, they shuffle, they stumble, but they don't hustle."

"These are," Critter says, and taps the barrel of his rifle against the window. "That ain't good."

"What ya see, Uncle Crit?" Porky calls back.

"Just you keep drivin'!" Critter shouts, making some of the sick at our feet moan and grumble. "Ah, shut the hell up."

"You're nothing but love, Critter," I say. He looks at me and shakes his head. "What?"

"You're blanket's open," he smirks. "Not that there's anythin' to see there."

"What?" I snap as I look down. "Shrinkage, asshole. I'm sick, and it's cold."

"Whatever you want to believe, Long Pork," Critter says. "Hold on. Don't think I'll call you Long Pork no more."

"Well, thanks, Crit," I smile.

"I think Short Pork is your new name," Critter cackles. "Maybe even Tiny Pork."

"You fucking suck," I mumble as I turn and leave. "I'm going to go sit with Porky. He's one of the nice Fitzpatricks."

"You ain't gonna be able to just run from your deficiency, Short Pork," Critter calls after me.

"Fuck off!" I shout back as I work my way through the sick and take my seat again.

"What was that?" Porky asks.

"Critter's being a jerk," I reply.

"Is he making fun of your small penis?" Porky laughs.

"It's cold, and I'm sick!" I yell. "Sheesh!"

***

The RVs wedge their way through the Z herd until we come to an old country road, and are forced back into a two by two configuration. The convoy now only consists of eight RVs. A few of the cannies tried to get away with their freaky cars and motorcycles, but the herd wasn't having any of that. They were all swarmed and taken down faster than we could keep track. At least that means no more motorcycle riding, goggle-wearing, post-apocalyptic clichés! Yes!

Okay, that was mean. People died. I'm a bad person.

But, fuck yeah, to no more goggled cannies!

Sorry, there I go again.

Once out on the road, we have it pretty clear for a good couple of miles, which lets us put some distance between us and the Z herd. Stuart's voice gets on the radio, and he starts asking for a roll call in each RV. Even though every life is worth something, I do sigh with relief as I hear all of the Fitzpatrick brothers, Melissa, Dr. McCormick, my family (of course), John, Reaper, Lourdes and her people, and quite a few others I know.

"Boyd's with us," Stella says. "But he's still passed out from that bug."

"Who the fuck is Boyd?" I ask.

"You know Boyd," Porky says. "Everyone knows Boyd."

"I have no idea who the hell Boyd is," I say.

"Where's Kramer?" Stuart asks. "Anyone seen Kramer?"

"Wouldn't mind losing that asshole," Critter says from right behind me, making me jump and let out a little fart. It's dry. Good thing. "Damn, Short Pork. That was a violent one. Smells worse than all this puke. Roll down your window more."

"I'm not rolling down shit if you keep calling me Short Pork," I snap. "And when Elsbeth hears you've changed my nickname, she's gonna be pissed."

"I'm here," a voice croaks from the floor.

"Kramer's with us," Critter sighs as he takes the radio from Porky. "Ain't we lucky fuckin' ducks?"

"You still need me, Mr. Fitzpatrick," Kramer groans. "As much as you may think to the contrary."

"Yeah, yeah, you just keep flappin' yer gums, and we'll see how contrary things get," Critter sneers.

"No need for violence," Kramer replies. "I'm already in a weakened state. I hardly pose a threat."

"You're always a threat," Critter says. "I ain't kiddin' myself about that. So just shut the hell up, and stop annoyin' me. Short Pork is doin' that already."

"Fuck off!" I yell, and then get yelled at by those trying to rest. "Sorry."

Then something hits me.

"Uh, did Elsbeth sound off?" I ask.

Porky looks over at me and then back at his uncle really quick. "I didn't hear her name."

"Give me that," I snap as I reach for the radio in Critter's hand.

He yanks it away and almost punches me, but I think his fear of touching any part of my sick body is all that stops him.

"No way your diseased ass is gettin' this radio," Critter says, then puts it to his mouth. "Hey, y'all, anyone got Elsbeth with them?"

"Maybe she's sick and lying down," Porky suggests. "They could have just missed her."

"She isn't sick," Kramer says.

"I told you to keep your mouth shut," Critter snaps. "Y'all check the sick, she's probably one of them."

"She is not sick," Kramer insists. "You are wasting your time."

"Why isn't she sick?" I ask before Critter can snap at the mad scientist asshole again. "How do you know?"

"Her conditioning does not allow for illness," Kramer says.

"That's bullshit," I reply. "I've seen her sick before."

"I highly doubt that," Kramer says. "But I am intrigued. What was she sick from?"

"I don't know," I say, and look up at Critter. "Ask Dr. McCormick."

Critter shrugs, but doesn't argue. "Hey, Doc? You ever seen Elsbeth sick?"

"Not that I can recall," Dr. McCormick responds over the radio. "But knowing her, she probably wouldn't have come to me if she was. She'd just tough it out."

"She has not been sick," Kramer says. "Please believe me when I tell you this. Her unique physiology does not allow for illness. She may have the occasional stomach upset by tainted food or unclean water, but since she left my facility there is no chance of her contracting any type of virus or disease. She, along with her sisters, are fit as a fiddle, to use one of your quaint colloquialisms. You do know what a colloquialism is, do you not?"

"I know what a colloquialism is, you smug fuck," I reply.

"I was speaking to Mr. Fitzpatrick," Kramer says.

"I know what the hell it means," Critter replies, then looks at me. "And you ain't exactly the one to be callin' anybody else smug, Short Pork."

"I hate you, Critter," I say. "I so fucking hate you."

"Looks like we have a farm with a good sized barn up ahead on the left," Lourdes announces over the radio. "I say we check it out. We need to regroup and assess what supplies we still have. There may be a diesel tank close by if the farm used any heavy machinery."

"We still don't know where Elsbeth is," I say, and Critter relays the message.

"We stop and get secured, then we'll know who made it and who didn't make it," Lourdes says.

"She made it!" I yell.

"I have to agree with Mr. Stanford," Kramer says. "Considering the young woman's history, I highly doubt she succumbed to the undead. More than likely, if she is not on one of the RVs, she is hiding until daylight. Then she'll do her own assessment and catch up to us. It is how she is trained and programmed."

"Call her programmed again, and you're going to get out and walk from here," I snap.

"Considering we are now approaching the barn, your threat is fairly empty, Mr. Stanford," Kramer laughs. "But I understand your intended meaning, and apologize for insulting your friend, despite your misguided belief that a woman such as Ms. Thornberg could ever be a real friend, considering her true nature."

"I'll be sure to mention you said that as soon as we stop and find her," I say. "She'll love to hear you tell her all about her true nature."

"I'd pay money to watch that," Critter laughs.

***

"Nowhere?" I bark. "How can that be?"

"Calm down, Jace," Stella says and looks at Lourdes as we stand by the large doors to the huge barn that currently houses our rag tag bunch of less than able survivors. "Are you sure?"

Lourdes doesn't even glance at the clipboard in her hand. "If Elsbeth was here, then we'd know. She has no reason to stay hidden and keep quiet, even if I thought she was capable of either of those things. Elsbeth isn't exactly an inconspicuous presence."

"I can't believe we left her back there," I say. "What the fuck, people?"

"She wasn't in the camp when the Z herd hit," John says as he walks up to our group. "She took off on one of her recons."

"Then the puking and shitting started," Stuart says from John's side. "So no one was really looking for her."

"So we did leave her back there," I state. "She's out making sure we are all safe, and we fucking ditch her ass at the first sign of trouble."

"Now hold on there," Buzz says. "No one ditched her. Not one of us would intentionally leave that woman behind. You know that, Jace. And that was hardly a first sign of trouble situation. We haven't seen a herd that big in long time."

"Not to mention how some of those things were moving," Reaper adds.

"You saw that too?" Porky asks as he and his twin brother, Pup, lean against the barn. "Something ain't right here."

"You ain't kiddin', nephew," Critter says. "The Zs are changin'."

"How?" Lourdes asks. "It's been years since Z-Day. Why would they start changing now after all this time? I've been in the field for most of these years, and haven't seen them act any differently than they first did."

"Until the past few months," Stuart says. "You have to admit that every once in a while there's been one or two that have gone off book."

"I saw a few more than one or two back yonder," Critter says. "A whole damn horde was crawlin' and runnin', like they were hopped up on goofballs or somethin'."

"Goofballs," I chuckle. "I like that word. Goofballs. Goofballs, goofballs, goof-."

"Shut up, Short Pork," Critter says.

"So what are we going to do about Elsbeth?" I ask quickly, hoping no one else noticed the new nickname.

"Short Pork?" Stella asks.

Dammit.

Critter is smiling so wide his old, craggy face is about to rip in two.

"Asshole," I mutter.

"To answer your question," Lourdes says. "We aren't going to do anything except line the RVs up with these doors, so if we need to leave, we can climb from one to the other without exposing ourselves."

"Don't you worry," Critter says. "Short Pork has done plenty of exposing for all of us."

"Will you shut the fuck up?" I shout. "It was cold and I'm sick!"

All eyes are on me. Then they move to my crotch, which is covered by a couple of thick blankets, then the eyes move back to mine.

"Long pork," I say. "*Long* Pork." I look at Stella. "Tell them, baby."

"I'd rather not get involved," Stella grins.

"Et tu, Stella?" I sigh, and shake my head. "Whatever. I don't fucking care about a nickname right now. I just care about finding Elsbeth."

"That Dr. Kramer was pretty darn sure she'd be fine," Porky says. "I bet she catches up to us tomorrow."

"Porky is probably right," Buzz says. "It's not like it's hard to follow our trail. She'll find us."

"She has until midday," Lourdes says. "Then we hit the road again."

I begin to object, but I can see from the faces around me that I'd be the only one. Apparently, everyone else has more confidence in Elsbeth's abilities to keep herself safe than I do.

"Fine," I say. "Midday. We wait that long."

"We'll have to," Stuart says. "It's gonna take us all night and into the day to get the RVs clean."

"Everyone looks over at the row of RVs. Yeah, you can pretty much see the stink lines wafting off of them.

CHAPTER TWO

It takes a little longer than all night and into the day to get the RVs cleaned up, which is fine by me. Then it takes us all of the next day to scour the vehicles with bleach before Dr. McCormick and Reaper are satisfied that they are sterile. By the time they give the go ahead, the sun has already started to set.

Which is all good since it gives those of us still recovering time to rest up. Whatever we had, it was just a twenty-four hour thingy. Luckily, no one else has started puking and shitting, so score one for the survivors!

I'd be happy about that, but there's still no Elsbeth.

"Don't worry, she'll find us," John says as he sits down next to me on an old wooden bench just outside the barn doors, and offers me an apple.

"No, thanks," I say as I rub my belly. "Still just sticking to water and some of those stale crackers. An apple might do me in."

He nods and takes a bite, then chews slowly. And silently.

"Is that all?" I ask finally. "Don't worry, she'll find us?"

John shrugs. "Not much else to say. You know her better than I do, although I've gotten to know her a little better these last few weeks."

"Yeah, we all know," I say. "El isn't exactly a quiet one."

John shrugs again. "Not like I can tell her to hush. Especially not when I'm exposed like that. I like my junk right where it is."

"Don't we all," I say, then flinch. "I mean, we all like our own junk where it is, not that we like your junk where it is."

"I knew what you meant," John laughs.

"When did you last see her?" I ask.

"Three nights ago," John answers. "She was gone before the stomach bug hit. I remember looking for her most of that day, then gave up when the meeting started. By the time I realized she was really missing, we were neck deep in vomit and Zs."

"That'll be the name of my memoir," I say. *"Neck Deep In Vomit and Zombies*. It'll sell millions."

"To who?" John laughs.

"The people in my head, soldier. The people in my head," I smirk.

The wind whips up around us, and I pull my coat up around my neck. I miss my warm blankets, but there are still some folks recovering that need them more than me. A winter coat, some heavy boots, and a pair of thermal underwear beneath my jeans will have to do.

And a hat. I have a great hat. Found it in Nashville as I was sprinting through a clothing store to avoid the undead yeehaws that were chasing us as we tried to do a little scavenging. The hat is wool felt, pure black with a silver band around it, and fits my head perfectly. It's not a cowboy hat, more like an Indiana Jones hat.

"What type of hat is this?" I ask John.

"A fedora," he says.

"No, no, a fedora is smaller," I say. "This is more like the hat Indiana Jones wore."

"Right, which was a fedora," John replies.

"No, it wasn't," I argue. "A fedora is smaller, like the one he wears at the end of Raiders when he's dressed in a suit."

"There is more than one type of fedora," John says.

"But this isn't a fedora!" I insist. "It's more like a safari hat. No, it's an outback hat!"

"That's not it," John says and shakes his head. "An outback hat has a bigger brim in front. That one is too symmetrical. I'm telling you, man, it's a fedora."

"Believe what you want, man," I say. "But I'm right."

"No, you aren't, but who cares," John shrugs. "It's a nice hat."

"Yeah, it is," I smile. "Don't let it distract you, though."

"Huh? What do you mean?" I ask.

"Like with Indiana Jones," John says. "You know how his hat is always falling off, and he has to rescue it. It's a running gag in the movies."

"Oh, right, that," I nod. "No, I know it's just a hat. If it falls off I'm not going back for it if we are being chased by a zombie horde."

"Or cannibal gang," John adds.

"That too," I nod some more.

"Cannibal gang?" a voice asks behind us. "Anything I need to know?"

I look back and see Mr. Flips, the de facto leader of the cannies that joined our convoy just outside Cannibal Road back in Knoxville. Mr. Flips is an average looking guy, except for the top hat he always wears, which is part of his whole emcee persona he had created back with the cannibal gangs. He found a niche, and a place with a bunch of people that would have carved him up for dinner in a heartbeat.

Not that I'm condoning his complicity in the running of Cannibal Road. That's all pretty shitty. But, at the end of the day, Mr. Flips is a nice guy. And he's kept his promise and not tried to eat me, so that's a plus. I mean, if you're gonna keep a promise, that's the one to keep. He's also kept the other cannies in line, even when I know for sure some of them have been eyeing me like I'm a cartoon steak or chicken leg.

"Hey, Flips," I say, and pat the bench on the other side of me. "Take a load off."

Mr. Flips hesitates. "You aren't still contagious, are you? I hate puking, and it sounds like we're all out of TP."

"We're all out of TP?" John frowns, and looks at his delicious apple which happens to be filled with wonderful fiber. "Son of a bitch."

"Not to worry," Mr. Flips grins as he does sit down. "I have some people working on the problem." He nods towards a far off shape in the night. "They're with Melissa now, and checking out that farmhouse. Stuart's with them, so no need to worry if my peeps try to turn Melissa into a midnight snack."

"Not too worried about that," John chuckles. "She's a Fitzpatrick. Your peeps are the ones that should be careful."

"Let's not say the word peeps, okay?" I suggest. "A little too Barfly for my taste."

"Fair enough," Mr. Flips nods. "Nice hat. That was a good find."

"Thanks," I grin. "Wait! You make your own hats, right?"

"I do at that," Mr. Flips nods. "Or did."

"Okay, then what type of hat is this? What style?" I ask.

"A fedora," Mr. Flips replies. "It's a wide brim fedora. Kinda like what Indiana Jones wore."

"See," John says.

"Fuck off," I respond. "Both of you."

"I guess you thought it was something else?" Mr. Flips asks.

"I thought it was an outback hat," I answer.

"No, the front brim would be bigger," Mr. Flips says.

"See," John says again.

"Haven't you fucked off yet?" I sigh.

"Not lately," John says.

The wind hits us again, and I shiver despite the thickness of my coat. The three of us stare into the darkness, listening to the dry grass rustle in the late fall, almost winter, night.

"Feels like snow," John says.

"Really?" I ask, and sniff. "I don't smell snow."

"No, it doesn't smell like snow," John replies. "Not yet. I bet it will in the morning. It's going to get colder."

"You from the north?" Mr. Flips asks John.

"I'm a soldier," John says. "I'm from all over the place. But I have spent most of my life where it snows. Trust me, snow is coming."

"That's going to make things harder on the convoy," I say. "The roads are bad enough with the abandoned cars and shit. Add snow to the mix, and we won't hit KC until spring."

"We need to get through St. Louis first," Mr. Flips says. "And that may not be so easy. I've heard a few things about St. Louis."

"Really?" I ask. "Like what?"

"Not much," Mr. Flips shrugs. He takes off his top hat and runs his hand through his thinning light brown hair. "Just that there may be some tough survy gangs in a turf war around that area. We had a few refugees stumble into our trap now and then. Doesn't sound like crazies, just like things might be a tad out of hand."

"That would have been good intel to know when we started down this road," John says, his voice turning as cold as the air. "Anything else you want to share there, Mr. Flips?"

"Not at the moment," Mr. Flips replies, and stands up. "Gotta keep a few aces up my sleeve just in case you all decide that me and mine aren't welcome anymore."

"If you are holding back intel and anyone gets killed because of it, then you can be sure I'll end your ass without blinking," John snarls as he stands up quickly.

"Hold on, hold on," I say, and get between them. "Flips has a point. He's just keeping some information as leverage. I'd do the same thing."

"Thank you," Mr. Flips says.

I turn and jab him in the chest. "But if your information can save lives, then I'd advise you spill it. If not to us, then to Critter and Lourdes. You hold back and someone dies, then I'll be in the line to end your ass."

"I understand," Mr. Flips says, and doffs his hat to me. "We walk a fine line between self-preservation and preservation of the species, don't we?"

"Your bunch of cannies didn't exactly fall into the latter category," John says, still pissed.

"I could argue the opposite," Mr. Flips says. "Hard to preserve the species when you starve to death."

"Yeah, this debate is not happening right now," I say. "It's going to go nowhere, and eventually one of you will hit the other one. Or more than likely, you'll try to hit the other one, miss, and end up hitting me. The slapstick writes itself."

I watch John slowly calm down and look at Mr. Flips, who always seems to be calm, my eyebrows raised in an "are we cool?" arch.

"Fine," John says, then nods towards the far off farmhouse. "I'm going to go check and see what's over there."

26

"I was actually going to do the same, but I'll defer to you out of respect," Mr. Flips says. He bows, turns, and walks back into the barn.

I watch him go, then see Greta standing there, looking bored as hell like always.

"What?" I ask.

"Critter sent me," Greta says, then switches into a pretty good imitation of Critter's voice. "Tell Short Pork to get his ass inside the barn so we can close those damn doors. Stupid Short Pork..."

"Did he say the last part or did you add it?" I ask.

"What do you think?" Greta smirks.

"Sounds like Critter," John laughs.

"Sounds like my daughter, too," I say.

"Know what else sounds like your daughter?" Greta says. Then she flips me off with both fingers and walks away.

"Those fingers didn't sound like anything!" I call after her. "That was a lame comeback!"

"No, it was pretty good," John says, and claps me on the shoulder. "You head in and close the doors. I'll go check on the scavenger crew and see what's up there. Hopefully they found TP that is still useable."

"Or sheets or newspaper or something we can cut up," I say. "I may not have had an apple, but the tum tum still isn't one hundred percent."

"Back in a minute," John says, and walks off.

I start to step into the barn when several shouts followed by a gunshot echo across to us from the farmhouse.

"Shit," John says, and pulls his pistol from his hip. "Go get Lourdes."

"Already here," Lourdes says as she comes running up to us, her M4 carbine at her shoulder. "What do we got?"

A few of her PCs, joined by several curious faces, come sprinting over.

"Heard some shouting, and then the gunshot," I say, and point at the running figure of John. "Came from the farmhouse."

"Stay here," Lourdes says, and looks to her people. "On me. We go in fast, but safe. No shooting friendlies."

"That's a good plan," I say.

They take off running, and I'm left with a bunch of people that really want answers I don't have.

"I'll be right back," I say, and turn towards the farmhouse.

"Mom's going to be pissed," Greta says.

"Then don't tell her," I say as I walk off. I get a few feet and realize my daughter is still with me. "What do you think you're doing?"

"Coming with," she replies, all teenage casual like.

"No," I say. "You're going back to the barn."

"To tell mom that you're going against Lourdes's orders to stay put," Greta says. "Good idea. I'm sure she's going to be so super thrilled with you when you get back."

"You scare me sometimes," I say.

"Good," Greta smiles. "That's the plan."

We walk quickly but cautiously across the small field between the barn and the farmhouse. I can see flashlights whipping about through dirty windows, and I slow us both down as we get to the front porch.

"Just us," I call out, not wanting to get shot in the face by a startled PC or scavenger. "No shooty shooty."

"Jace, what are you doing?" Stuart asks as he steps out onto the porch. "Didn't Lourdes tell you to stay put?"

"How would you know?" I ask.

"Because she told me she said it, and also told me she expected you to ignore the order and come along anyway," Stuart sighs, then looks at Greta. "And you brought Greta. Even better thinking."

"She was going to rat me out to Stella," I say. "I had no choice." I try to look past him and into the farmhouse. "What's up?"

"Come see," Stuart says to me, then blocks Greta's way. "Not you. You don't need to see this."

"I don't need to be in the middle of the zombie apocalypse either," Greta says. "But, hey, guess what? Too fucking late. I think I can handle whatever is in there."

He looks at me. "She doesn't need to see this."

"I probably don't either," I say. "But what ya gonna do?"

"Ugh," Stuart moans. "You two are obviously related. Come on."

We follow him into the house, and instantly get hit with the smell of flesh and blood; that sharp, iron tang is impossible to mistake.

"Back here," Stuart says as he leads us through a small living room and down a narrow hall.

We pass a couple of bedrooms and I see some of Lourdes's PCs clearing the rooms, their carbines up as they yank open closet doors and flip over beds. Stuart steps into a wide kitchen and moves to the side so we can get a good look. I wish I had listened to him. Greta doesn't need to see this.

"Not cannies," Melissa says as she leans back from the corpses that are nailed to the kitchen table. "The skin is all that's gone, none of the meat."

"Jesus Christ," I say as I try to push Greta out of the kitchen.

"Stop it," Greta resists and moves around me. "It doesn't freak me out."

"Freaks me out," Melissa says, and more than a few heads nod in agreement.

"What was the gunshot?" I ask. "And all the shouting?"

"Gunshot came from there," Stuart says as he points to a hole in a side door. "We came in fast, saw shapes on the table, yelled at them to stay still, then one of the cannies opened the basement door and triggered a booby trap."

"He get blown away?" Greta asks.

"Nah, I'm good," a young man says from the corner as he holds a dish towel to a wound in his shoulder. "I'm fast."

"And you slipped in the blood, and fell on your ass," Stuart smirks.

"That too," the young man shrugs, then winces. "Ouch."

"It was a shitty booby trap, also," Stuart says. "Line too short and angle all wrong. It was either made by someone that didn't know what they were doing, or it wasn't meant to kill."

"What was it guarding?" I ask.

"Good question," Lourdes says. "That's what we're about to find out."

"If you slipped, then that means these corpses are pretty fresh," Greta says to Stuart.

"That's exactly what it means," Stuart says.

"Stay here," Lourdes says to me and Greta. "I fucking mean it, Short Pork."

"Ah, come on!" I snap. "You too?"

"You're lucky it's only name calling," Lourdes says. "I should beat your ass for insubordination."

"Not a dictatorship, tough girl," I reply, wagging a finger at her.

"Did you just call me-?"

"Knock it off," Stuart says.

"Yeah, knock it off," I echo.

"I was talking to you, Jace," Stuart says. "Stop being a dick, and listen to the professionals. Stay here. We'll sweep the basement, and then you can come down once we know you won't get killed or get one of us killed."

I start to reply, but Greta punches me in the arm.

"Just shut up, Dad," she says.

"Listen to your girl," Melissa says. "And get over here. I want that big brain of yours to tell us what the fuck we're looking at."

"Well, since she asked so nicely, I'll stay," I say.

Stuart, Lourdes, and a couple of her PCs don't even bother responding to me, just open the basement door, and slowly make their way down into the dark.

"Phew, I thought they'd never leave," I say. "What you got, Mel?"

"I know a thing or two about skinning kills," Melissa says. "These are clean." She angles her flashlight towards the neck of one of the bodies. "See? Still some skin there, and there. Also, here, and right there. But it's like a pattern, not a mistake. This was no hack job."

"They look pretty hacked to me," Greta says.

"It's a message," the young canny says. "They were left there as a sign to others."

"Others? What others?" I ask. "And how the hell do you know it's a message? What kind of message is this?"

"It wasn't a fucking invitation to tea," Greta says. The canny laughs, and she glares at him. "Something funny?"

"Yeah," the canny nods. "What you said. That was funny." He steps forward and holds out his hand. "I'm Rafe."

Greta looks at the hand like it's on fire. "Good for you. Or not. What kind of name is Rafe?"

"The one my parents gave me," Rafe shrugs, then winces again. "Ow."

"Your parents were idiots," Greta says.

"That's why I ate them," Rafe replies.

Needless to say, that changes the mood quickly. Not that the mood was all happy-go-lucky in the first place, but it does bring it down a couple more notches on the fun scale.

"Kidding," Rafe says. "I ate them because they sacrificed themselves so me and my little sister could live."

"Okay, well, this has been awesome," I say. "But I'm gonna have to put my foot down on the cannibal family tales segment of the evening."

There's a loud whistle from below, then Stuart shouts, "Jace! Melissa! Come check this out!"

"Perfect timing," I say.

I grab Greta and pull her with me as we make our way down the basement steps, and then stand there, gawking at what we see.

Written in blood on the basement walls are the words, "*Loyalty above all else.*"

"Traitors," Rafe says from behind us, making me and Greta jump. "Sorry. But that's what happened to those folks upstairs. It's a message to traitors."

"How do you know?" I ask.

"He's right," Stuart says. "It makes sense now. The Viet Cong used to do this to US collaborators. They'd skin them with machetes, then write messages on the huts with blood to warn others."

"I thought they burned down the villages," Greta says.

"Nah, that was us," I say. "Yay for war!"

"They burned down villages too," Stuart sighs, his Marine hackles up from my comment.

"This doesn't really answer anything," Melissa says. "We may know why those people are missing their skin, but we don't know who did it or how they were traitors."

"Actually, we don't know anything," I say. "We're just guessing. That message may not be in their blood. It could be from the blood of someone else."

"Could be," Lourdes says, and wipes her fingers across the lettering. "But this is as fresh as the blood in the kitchen." She turns and points her flashlight to pile of towels in the corner. "Then there's that, too."

The towels are sitting in a pool of blood. In fact, there is blood everywhere, splattered all across the basement floor. But most of the blood is on or under the towels.

Yeah, and those aren't towels.

"Total waste of good skin," Rafe says.

"You need to shut up and leave," I say, and point at the stairs. "Go away, little canny."

"Dude," Rafe frowns. "You're an asshole."

"You're the asshole," I call after him as he stomps back upstairs. I turn and see everyone staring at me. "What?"

"You are a piece of work," Stuart says.

"He started it," I snap.

"Dad, just don't," Greta sighs. "You aren't winning this one."

"Okay, you know what? Y'all need to lay off the Jace punching bag, and focus on what the fuck we are looking at," I say. "Me being a dick is not as important as who the fuck did this to these people. Right?"

"He's right," Lourdes says.

"Thank you," I nod.

"You are a dick," she smiles.

"Fuck all y'all," I mutter.

"As much as I hate to say it, we don't have time to rag on Jace right now," Stuart says. "We need to figure out whether this new development means we have to leave or not."

"Then how about everyone shuts up and lets me think?" I snap. "That is the reason you keep me around, right?"

"You want to think? Then think," Lourdes says.

So I do. And it doesn't take long.

"The blood is still fairly fresh," I say. "It's tacky, but not dried out. How long does it take for blood to dry out?"

"That amount?" Lourdes replies. "A couple days."

"That's what I thought," I say. "That means this shit went down while we were here."

"It may have happened just before we found the barn," Stuart says. "We pull up, and whoever did this took off. It's cold, so the blood isn't going to dry quite as fast."

"True," I say. "But either way, I think people know we are here."

"Great," Lourdes says, then grabs a radio from her belt. "Shots?"

"Yeah?" a man replies over the radio.

"Looks like we have more than just Zs in the area," Lourdes says. "Double the patrols, and tell everyone to keep sharp. They could be watching us right now. Be aware of cover, and stay out of the open."

"Will do," Shots replies.

"If they wanted to hit us, then they probably would have by now," I say. "It would have been easier when most of us were still sick."

"Or they didn't want to catch what we had, and are keeping their distance until they know we don't have the plague or something," Greta says. "That would be the smart thing to do."

"Yeah, I was gonna say that next," I say. "You just beat me to it."

"Right," Greta says, then turns to the stairs. "I'm going back to the barn."

"Not alone," Lourdes says. "You wait here until we all go back."

"Then let's all go back," Greta smirks.

"We're still scavenging," Lourdes says. "We aren't going to waste this opportunity because of a couple of corpses. Let's keep searching the house, then we'll head back to the barn and lock it down for the night."

"I was gonna suggest that too," I say.

"Jesus, Dad," Greta says. "Pitiful much?"

***

"The skin was gone?" Charlie asks. "Like all gone?"

"Exactly like all gone," Greta says as we sit, huddled close in one of the corners of the barn.

I'd love to be sitting in an RV, but they are all lined up outside against the barn doors for security. Lourdes's people are in each one to make sure our mystery friends don't try to snag any in the night. Almost makes me wish I was a PC so I could be sitting in a comfy chair instead of on a shitty pile of hay.

And I'm not kidding, the hay smells shitty. Like old manure. As if I haven't had to smell enough shit lately. Joy.

"You think they're still around?" Stella asks me.

"Probably," I say. "I'd stick around if I saw a convoy of RVs come rolling in. Even if I wasn't a people skinner, I'd still want to know what's up."

"But they are people skinners," Stella says. "Which means we are being watched by people that skin other people, but don't take the meat as food. I don't like how that sounds."

"No one like's how that sounds," Greta says.

"How long do we stay?" Charlie asks. "Here in the barn. Are we on lockdown for a while?"

"No, honey, just for tonight," Stella replies. "We'll want to get going in the morning."

"Well, that ain't exactly gonna be easy," Critter says as he crashes our little family pow-wow. He grabs an old bucket, flips it over, and takes a seat. "Looks like we have a bit of a fuel issue."

"How much of an issue?" Stella asks.

"Enough that we would need to leave half the RVs behind," Critter says. "Or we could take them all, and only get a few miles down the road."

"What happened to all the fuel?" I ask. "I thought we had plenty for a while?"

"We lost some of the cargo trucks back at camp," Critter says. "And as far as we can tell, ain't no diesel on this farm. We'll need to do some scouting around the other farms close by tomorrow, and see what we can find."

"The RVs are multi-fuel, right?" I ask. "Maybe there's some kerosene or something else here."

"Oh, gee, Short Pork, I didn't think of that," Critter says as he smacks his head. "Neither did Lourdes, Stuart, John, or any of the other people that have brains bigger than a fuckin' walnut."

"So no other fuel then?" I glare.

"No other fuel," Critter says. "But that ain't why I come over here, as fun as this little talk of ours has been."

"Then why did you come over?" I grumble.

"Kramer," Critter says. "He wants to talk to you."

"Good for him," I say. "Then have him come over here and talk with me."

"He says it has to be private with just you, me, and Lourdes," Critter snarls. "Burns my balls to even say that. Like I'm his damned errand boy. The son of a bitch is lucky I didn't end him right then."

"You'd have disappointed a lot of people," Stella says. "There's a line for slitting his throat."

"Wow," Greta says. "I have such a sweet, loving family."

"Since when?" Charlie laughs.

"Come on, Short Pork," Critter says. "Let's get this over with."

"I'm not going anywhere if you insist on calling me Short Pork," I say.

"I can come up with a hundred worse names, if you'd like," Critter sneers. "Feel lucky ya got the name ya got."

I point at him, and then shake my finger back and forth as I try to think of a comeback. But I'm too fucking tired, and he'd probably have a better comeback, since he's Critter.

"Fucking whatever," I say as I get up from my fragrant seat of nasty hay and follow him across the barn. I look over my shoulder at my family. "Hopefully, I won't be too long."

"Be sure to call if you're going to be late," Stella smiles.

"Will do, sweet thing," I smile back.

"Gross," Greta says.

***

I really just want to punch Dr. Kramer in the face over and over. The asshole sits there, a grin teasing about his mouth like he has the best secret in the world, but refuses to share it. I swear I'm going to rip that secret from his throat and feed it to him one day.

Wait, that doesn't make sense.

"Thank you for indulging me, Mr. Stanford," Kramer nods as I sit down.

"Fuck you," I say. "Just say what you have to say, and let's skip the bullshit."

"I can assure you that I always skip the bullshit," Dr. Kramer replies. "Bullshit is inefficient and gets in the way of true discovery and progress."

"Again, and I mean this from the bottom of my heart, fuck you," I say.

"Jace, let the man speak," Lourdes says.

"Okey doke," I reply, and wave my hand at Dr. Kramer. "Your show, Doctor. Pull that curtain, and let's get this going."

"I am concerned at the absence of Ms. Thornberg," Dr. Kramer says. "While I was not worried before, I am worried now. It seems out of character for her to be gone this long unless she has been mortally wounded."

"Great," I say. "You brought me over here to tell me you think she's dead or dying out there? Did you think that shit wasn't running through my head already? And who the fuck are you to say what is out of character for Elsbeth? You don't even know her."

"Get to the goddamn point, asshole," Critter says.

"I did," I say. "I think that was about as to the point as I can get."

"I was talking to him, Short Pork," Critter responds. "Dumbass."

"Oh. Well, you call me asshole too, so it's hard to keep the names straight," I say.

"I call everyone asshole," Critter says. "I'd think you'd have figured out when I'm calling you asshole, and when I'm calling someone else asshole by now with that huge brain of yours, Short Pork."

"Gentlemen," Lourdes sighs. "Can we get through this, please? I'm exhausted and would like to get a couple hours of sleep before I'm on watch."

"Sorry," I say. "Dr. Asshole? You were saying?"

Dr. Kramer ignores the insult. "While I may not know Ms. Thornberg personally as well as you do, Mr. Stanford, I do know her scientifically better than anyone on the planet. With the possible exception of her mother."

"And? So?"

"So, she has the skills to have easily survived the zombie attack from the other night," Dr. Kramer responds. "She also has the skills to track us to this farm, so I doubt she's lost. Which leads me to think, excluding the dead or wounded suggestion from earlier, that she is staying away deliberately."

"And why the fuck would she do that?" I ask.

"That is why you are here," Dr. Kramer says. "I was hoping you would know."

"So am I," Lourdes says. "Elsbeth is wild, but she is an important asset to this convoy. I am not exactly thrilled with the idea of getting across the plains without her."

"Me neither," I say. "But I have no idea where she is."

"The day before the sickness hit, did she mention anything to you at all?" Dr. Kramer asks.

"You've met Elsbeth, she isn't exactly the most chatty person," I say. "Sure, she has almost no filter, but that doesn't mean she shares her every thought. And I wasn't the last one to talk to her. John was."

"How do you know that?" Lourdes asks.

"Because he told me earlier," I reply. "Last time he saw her was three nights ago."

"Three nights, you say?" Kramer replies, then leans back and looks up into the dark rafters above. "Three nights would give her time to circle back."

"Circle back? Why the hell would she do that?" Critter asks.

"She thinks we're being followed," Lourdes says.

"Followed? Shit," Critter says. "Who the hell is following us? Some of the cannies from back in Tennessee? Ya think they want revenge?"

"No, they aren't after us," I say. "I've asked Flips if that was something to worry about, and he says that the cannies that stayed behind would have no reason to follow us. They're too busy with Cannibal Road, and working out their new pecking order. They couldn't care less about the survivor convoy that got away."

"Then why is she circling back?" Critter asks. "If that's what she's done."

"My theory is she is worried her sisters may be closer than we think," Dr. Kramer responds, still looking up at the rafters. "I believe she is trying to ascertain their location so she can report back to us."

"Wouldn't it make more sense for her to let us in on this idea, and take some of Lourdes's people with her?" I ask. "Why go it alone?"

"She can move faster and quieter by herself," Dr. Kramer says. "Her conditioning and training is vastly superior to any of the soldiers or contractors with us."

"Hey!" Lourdes snaps. "Speak for yourself."

"I'm speaking for reality, Ms. Torres," Dr. Kramer says. "I know exactly what skills Ms. Thornberg has, and as professional as you are, you do not even hold a candle to her. I do not mean this as an insult, I am merely stating the facts as they exist."

"Fuck you," Lourdes says.

"Exactly," I nod.

"Blah blah, blibbety-blah," Critter says. "What the holy hell does any of this mean?"

"It means that if Ms. Thornberg believes her sisters are close enough that she needs to circle back and find them, then we do not have the luxury of staying here another day," Dr. Kramer says. "We will need to get on the road ASAP. If those young women find us, I can assure you it will not go well for any of us."

"Any of us? Or just you?" I ask.

"It will not go well for any of us," Dr. Kramer says. "Especially me. Camille Thornberg has most assuredly co-opted the young women, and activated their full conditioning. That means they are under her orders, and hers alone. I highly doubt she has sent them after us to invite us to tea."

"Jesus, what is it with the tea gag?" I ask. "Greta pulled that one on me earlier at the farmhouse. We really need to get everyone together and have a sarcasm workshop or something."

"Short Pork? Shut up," Critter says.

"If that is all true," Lourdes says, ignoring both me and Critter, "then your only suggestion is we run?"

"That is the only suggestion I can give," Dr. Kramer says. "Especially since there is an unknown element in play as well. We should leave right this minute, if we can."

"But there is still the chance that Elsbeth is just off doing Elsbeth stuff," I say. "The Psycho Sisters may still be in Atlanta. I mean, how could El possibly know if they are following us?"

"She would know," Dr. Kramer says. "You are well aware that she is special in many ways. So are the other women. They have a connection. It is not something I planned nor is it scientifically explainable, although I would love to dissect them and find out if it can be explained." He stops and looks at us. "I do not mean vivisect. I was speaking more psychologically than physically."

"You fucking better be," I say. "Not that I'll let you psychologically dissect El."

"I'd like to see him try," Critter laughs. "That girl will mind fuck you in three seconds, Doctor. Good luck with that."

"Leave now?" Lourdes says. "We'll need to syphon the fuel from half the RVs into the other half. That's going to take most of the night right there."

"Then you should get started," Dr. Kramer says.

"Why are we listening to this assfuck again?" I ask.

"Because if you all die, then I die as well," Dr. Kramer says. "My wandering in the wild days are long gone. I may have had a chance back in the Appalachians, but out here in this hill country? Or when we get out on the plains? I wouldn't last through the winter."

"Shit," Lourdes mumbles then stands up. "Listen up people!"

The pockets of quiet conversations go silent, and people begin waking up those that have already fallen asleep for the night.

"We have a change of plans!" Lourdes announces. "With some new information, it looks like we won't have the luxury of staying here another night! As of this moment, we are prepping to leave! Pack your stuff, and get it piled up against that wall there! We need to bug out fast, so we are leaving some of the RVs behind! Things will get cramped, but we can find new vehicles down the road!"

"Whoa! Hold on!" Dr. McCormick shouts as she comes stomping up to us. "We still have people that are not even close to ready to travel. If we get stuck out in the cold in cramped quarters, and some of them relapse, then we run the risk of another outbreak. Not everyone came down with it the first time. We push this too soon, and I can guarantee that those that didn't get sick before will get sick later."

"That is a risk we have to take," Lourdes says.

"Why's that?" Stuart asks. "What's going on, Lourdes?"

"Yeah, what's up?" Buzz asks, joining the growing throng of worried survivors.

"Jace? You care to fill them in?" Lourdes says. "I need to get the ball rolling on the fuel situation."

"Sure, have me break the bad news," I sigh. "Give everyone another reason to get all up in Jace's face."

"Shut up, Short Pork," Critter says. "No one likes a whiner."

"Just tell us what's going on," Stuart says.

"Fine," I say. "Here's the deal."

And I tell them.

***

We are lucky to get enough fuel to fill up five of the RVs, which means we only have to leave three. Still sucks, but it's better than leaving four. Not that five RVs is really enough space. Even with most of them stripped of all furnishings and pretty much bare, quarters are going to be seriously cramped. We didn't have the addition of the cannies with us before, since they had their own vehicles, but now they are jammed in with us.

"How much do you believe Kramer?" Stella asks me. "And no smart ass response. I want to know what your gut is saying."

"My gut is saying that I better go take a shit before getting on the road," I say. The punch to my chest is fast and hard. "Ow. Okay, sorry, I deserve that."

"Be serious, Jace," Stella says.

I can hear the fear in her voice, and I take a deep breath.

"I think he's right," I say. "As much as I would rather not admit that, my gut says he's right. The only reason El would disappear is if it meant protecting us."

"But why stay quiet?" Stella asks. "She could have told us."

"Would you have let her go?" I ask.

"No, but she's a grown woman,' Stella replies. "She can do what she wants."

"If you had told her to stay, then she would have stayed. You know El and the 'family' thing. Disappointing you is the last thing she wants to do."

"But scaring me to fucking death by going off alone is okay?" Stella snaps.

"Hey, I'm not happy about it, either," I say. "Trust me, when she gets back she's getting quite the talking to."

"LOAD UP, PEOPLE!" Lourdes yells as she shoves the barn doors open. "WE ARE LEAVING NOW!"

"So much for that last minute shit," I say.

"Holy crap," Charlie says as he and Greta walk up next to us. "Is that snow?"

"That's what they call it, genius," Greta says.

"Be nice," Stella growls. "I am not in the mood for your shit."

"Told ya," John says as he walks by us, his sniper rifle over his shoulder, and a smirk on his face.

"So?" I call after him. "You think that makes you special or something?"

"Yes!" John yells back before he hops on one of the RVs that are idling just outside the barn.

We, the Mighty Stanfords, walk out into the cold wind and stare up at the grey sky that is spitting light snow down on us.

"Doesn't look too bad," I say.

"Uh, Dad?" Charlie says, and taps me on the shoulder. "Look behind us."

I turn and gulp.

"Oh," I say. "That's not good."

The sky to the east is filled with nothing but dark, thick clouds. The horizon is hazy with approaching snow.

"Good thing we were ready to go," Critter says, suddenly next to me. "That's one bad storm. If we'd stayed another night we'd be buried by it. Right now we might have a chance of outrunning it."

"If we can find more fuel," I say. "Otherwise, we may end up buried in it anyway."

"That's true," Critter says. "But wouldn't be my first time I was snowbound in an RV with a bunch of people I don't like."

He walks off and finds his RV, leaving us Stanfords to ourselves again as the rest of the survivors file past.

"Dad?" Greta asks. "Doesn't that mean Elsbeth could be stuck in that?"

"Yeah, sweetheart, it does," I say. "But you know El. She'll be fine. She'll be just fine."

Sure. She'll be just fine.

CHAPTER THREE

The snow isn't too heavy as we roll on down the road, our five RVs loaded with equipment and people making them heavy enough to keep from slip sliding away. I'm in the lead RV with Critter, Lourdes, Stuart, and my family, with Buzz driving. There are a few more people in the vehicle, but they're all cannies, and I don't really know them.

Except for that Rafe kid. Who keeps staring at my daughter. I am not liking this Rafe kid. Not liking him at all.

You know the joke about the overprotective dad with a shotgun? Ready to blow away any ill-intentioned suitors that approach his daughter? Well, normally, back in the old world pre-Z, that was just said as jest amongst fathers. But, guess what? This isn't pre-Z. And I actually have a shotgun. A double-barrel, sawed-off shotgun that is fully loaded. And not with rock salt. There is no rock salt in this motherfucker.

"Dad, stop," Greta whispers to me as we all huddle together on the floor of the RV. "You're acting all creepy."

"He's the one acting all creepy," I reply. "He's looking at you like you're a piece of meat. Fucking creepy canny kid."

"Yeah, I don't think he wants to eat her the way you're thinking," Charlie laughs, then sees my face and shuts up real fucking fast. "Sorry."

"You think this is a joke?" I snap, and a few heads look my way. "What?"

"Jace, calm down," Stella says. "He's just a teenage boy."

"No, he's a cannibal teenage boy," I correct. "Teenage boys are bad enough, but when you add the word 'cannibal'? Then we're talking about a father's worst nightmare."

"Dad, I think he's a freak," Greta says. "He can stare all he wants, but he's not getting anything from me, okay? Just fucking relax."

"I'll relax when he stops staring at you," I growl.

"You guys know I can hear you, right?" Rafe asks. "We can all hear you."

"You can?" I ask, looking at the less than pleased faces around us.

"Yeah, Short Pork," Critter says from up front. "So shut that stupid trap of yours! You're giving me a damn headache!"

"We should talk about our next move," Lourdes says as she and Stuart sit down next to us.

A few cannies have to scoot over, but they have learned not to argue or mess with either Lourdes or Stuart over the past few weeks. Not that the two of them have been heavy handed, just that they've proven themselves over and over again during our less than fun times in Nashville and in Louisville. You want to gain canny respect? Rip a few heads off, and wipe out a couple dozen Zs with your bare hands.

The cannies leave Lourdes and Stuart alone.

"The weather is going to get worse before it gets better," Stuart says. "It'll make it harder to scavenge for supplies and fuel."

"I thought we were trying to outrun the storm?" I ask.

"We are," Lourdes replies. "But we need a contingency plan in case we can't."

"A contingency plan would have been staying in that barn," Stella says. "We could have scavenged the area from there and waited out the storm."

"No, we couldn't," Lourdes replies. "You have to remember that it's been years since most structures in this land were maintained. I had a couple of my guys check out the structural integrity of that barn, and they think it had a fifty-fifty chance of holding up against a big snowstorm. Fifty-fifty doesn't work for me."

"Plus we have the issue of whoever skinned those people in that house," Stuart adds. "We could have been sitting right where they wanted us."

"Or it could have just been a dispute between crazies," Stella counters. "And they would have left us alone."

"All possible," Stuart says. "But are you willing to risk everyone's lives by leaning towards the optimistic possible, or the pessimistic possible? Is that what you want then? Maybe safe or maybe dead?"

"I'm just saying that this is something we should have discussed back there," Stella says.

"There weren't no time, Stella," Critter says as he spins the passenger seat around and looks back at us. "I seen some bad storms in my time, and this is a bad storm. The best choice was to high tail it out of there. Crazies or no crazies, that barn wasn't going to hold up against what's coming. We need somethin' a little more solid."

"So what are you guys thinking?" I ask. "We find an exit and look for a Sam's Club or Costco?"

"Those will be too obvious," Lourdes says. "Even if there aren't squatters already, buildings like that are a target just for being what they used to be. No, we need something more municipal."

"Please don't say a jail," Charlie says. "Jails are a bad idea."

"A school might work," Stella says. "Most of them are built with concrete block because of fire code. And this is almost Tornado Alley, so they should have large storm shelters as well."

"A school might be good, but they were also evac points when Z-Day hit," Lourdes replies. "A few may still hold the Zs."

"After all of these years?" I ask. "Even if Zs were trapped in there, they'd be bones by now, right?"

Lourdes and Stuart share a look that none of us miss.

"Might as well spill it," Stella sighs. "What's really going on?"

"You know I send recon scouts out all the time, right?" Lourdes asks. "Well, since we've left Asheville and Tennessee, they are seeing more and more Zs that aren't exactly conforming to the norm."

"Which Norm? Norm MacDonald or Norm from Cheers?" I laugh. No one else does. "I'll shut up."

"You do that, Short Pork," Critter smirks.

"Fuck and you, old man," I mumble.

"The Zs aren't rotting like they did in the first year or so," Lourdes says. "They're also getting faster. It's like their bodies are adapting."

"Adapting to what?" I ask. "I agree with the faster part, I saw them back at the camp when we lost the RVs. There were more than a couple that moved a little too spryly for my taste."

"Spry Zs suck," Charlie says.

"Amen to that," I agree.

"I think Kramer has an idea about what's happening to them," Stuart says. "But the fucker won't talk. That's another reason we want to find someplace secure to hunker down in."

"It's not just this storm, but the Zs we're worried about," Lourdes says. "We get everyone safe, then we sit Dr. Kramer down and find out exactly what he knows."

"And we can send people out to look for Elsbeth," I say. "Good idea."

"We aren't sending people out for her," Lourdes says. "We don't have the resources to search for one woman in a snowstorm."

"She's more than one woman," I say. "She's—."

"She's family," Greta growls.

"Actually, what I was going to say is that she's Camille Thornberg's daughter, and a full on badass that has saved all of our lives more than once," I continue. Kids, man, why they got to be interruptin', yo? "She's also the only person Kramer is even remotely afraid of. Once he learned that his mind control doesn't work on her anymore, he adjusted his attitude faster than a something about prom dresses and virginity."

"Really?" Charlie asks.

"I'm tired," I sigh. "The jokes aren't coming like I want."

"Maybe you should have gotten them drunk," Rafe says. "That's the best way to get a joke to come."

All eyes turn to the canny kid.

"That was funny," Charlie says. "Gross, but funny."

"It was stupid," Greta says, but I swear I see a twinkle in her eye.

Fuck! No twinkle! Twinkle is not good!

"Yeah, it was stupid," I say. "Good call, Greta. This guy is stupid with his stupid dirty jokes."

"Jace, honey, just be quiet," Stella says then looks at Lourdes. "So, we find someplace safe. What about a courthouse? Built to last and be secure, probably not an evac point for any region when there are plenty of schools around, and they always have basements for storage."

"That's what we were thinking," Lourdes says.

"A courthouse is like a jail," Charlie says, shaking his head. "Jails are a bad idea. Easy to get locked up in our own sanctuary."

"Look who's all gloom and doom today," Greta says. "What's with you and jails?"

"I've heard a few things from some of the cannies," Charlie says.

"They make great meat lockers," Rafe shrugs. "Just sayin'."

"See!" Charlie exclaims. "Jails bad!"

"If there is a small jail in the courthouse, then we'll disable the cell doors so they can't be locked on us if things go south," Lourdes says.

"Do we expect them to go south?" I ask. Wow, talk about looks of pity. Tough crowd. "Right, they always go south. Got it."

"Map," Stuart says as he unfolds a map of Illinois and flattens it on the floor. "The next town we'll be coming to is Mt. Vernon. It's not that big and is the county seat, so it should have a courthouse."

"Uh, why do you have a map of Illinois?" I ask. "We're in Missouri."

"Dad, we haven't gotten to Missouri yet," Greta says.

"Oh, I thought we had," I say. "My bad."

"Missouri is close," Stuart says. "Which is another reason to stop soon. Once we hit the true plains, then we'll be sitting ducks. We need to have as much gear as possible, and all of our ducks in a row."

"It's easier to get ducks in a row when they are sitting," I say.

"Hush," Stella says.

"Mt. Vernon is also high ground for the area," Lourdes says. "There's a lot of water and swamp land around, so it'll make it harder for Z herds to get to us, and we'll also have a better view if crazies decide to make a play."

"This sounds like we're going to be there a while," I say. I look over at Critter because I know he will not bullshit me. "Crit? What's up?"

"Winter, Short Pork, that's what's up," Critter says. "Travelin' is one thing, travelin' across the plains in the middle of winter is a whole other."

I look at Stuart. "So, when you meant getting our ducks in a row, you were talking about springtime ducks, weren't you?"

"If needed," Stuart says. "Maybe the winter storms won't be so bad, and we can leave around February. But you saw how long it took to get from Cannibal Road to here. More than a month, Jace. We won't last a month in the plains, not with how things are going. We're down to five RVs, and we've lost a shit ton of people already. And that's without a blizzard nipping at our asses."

We all let that settle for a second. The plan from the start has been to get to Kansas City first, verify if it is a dead zone like Kramer says, then move on to Colorado and The Stronghold. The faster we get there, the more people we'll have left to even make it worth it. We aren't doing so hot so far.

Oh, and there is one more thing...

"What about the sisters?" I ask. "Kramer is pretty sure they are now under Camille's control."

"We'll stand a better chance of defending ourselves if we can dig in," Lourdes says. "Stuart and I have talked about this. We'll lose a lot more people if they catch us out in the open."

"But we'll have a better shot at escaping," I say. "If we are dug in, like you two say, then are pretty much trapping ourselves."

"Jace, they are the professionals," Stella says. "The reason Lourdes is in charge is because of situations just like this. And Stuart has more years as a Marine than almost all the PCs combined."

"Jesus, Stella, how old do you think I am?" Stuart grumbles.

"I spent a bit of time with an M16 in my hand, ya know," Critter says. "And for the damn record, I was put in charge of this group of morons, even though I tried to turn it down and you dumbshits wouldn't let me."

"I'll take the job," Rafe smiles.

"I'd rather Boyd was in charge than a canny like you," Critter replies.

Everyone laughs. I don't get it.

I really wish someone would tell me who the fuck this Boyd guy is instead of everyone always saying that I know who this Boyd guy is. I do not know who this Boyd guy is. I will swear that now. I. Do. Not. Know. Who. This. Boyd. Guy. Is.

"Listen, Short Pork, I don't feel so great about hiding like a bunch of scared ducks," Critter says.

"What's with the duck metaphors?" Charlie asks.

"But," Critter sighs. "The lady soldier here has pretty much shown she knows how to keep us alive."

"Most of us," Greta says.

"Which is why I think we should listen to her, and Stuart, too, since he's jabbering the same thing, and get us to that courthouse," Critter says. "I do have one stipulation, though."

"Which is?" Lourdes asks.

"If we get there, and things ain't as rosy as they should be, then we bust ass and keep movin'," Critter replies.

"There is no way to quantify 'rosy', Critter," Lourdes says.

"I think we'll know it when we see it," Stuart says. "I hear where you're coming from, Crit. If our guts say to keep going, then we keep going."

"And find a new place to settle in to," Lourdes says. "The plan is sound, even if our first choice of location turns out not to be."

"We'll see," Critter says.

I can tell Lourdes is getting frustrated with how the conversation is going, but what did she expect? We'd all just salute, and tell her she's the best thing since sliced bread? Not that we've seen sliced bread in a long time. You never realize what conveniences will be out the window when the zombie apocalypse hits. Turns out it's sliced bread. I miss sliced bread.

All eyes are on me.

"Out loud?" I ask.

"Yeah," Stella says. "And there are a lot better things to have back than sliced bread."

"Are there, Stella? Are there?" I smile.

"Yes," she replies.

"Well ... okay, then," I nod then look at everyone else. "Mt. Vernon, Illinois it is."

No one seems one hundred percent thrilled with the plan, but at least it's a plan. I will admit that maybe staying in one spot and setting up a little bit of infrastructure might not be a bad thing. I sure as hell wouldn't mind figuring out how to have a hot shower each day. Or even every other day. Shit, I'll settle for one a week or even twice a month.

Yeah, we all pretty much stink.

***

Napping in the daytime sure is an interesting thing. It has this surreal quality that totally fucks with your head that nighttime sleeping doesn't. At night, you know you are supposed to be asleep; you know that things should be still; things should be calm.

But daytime? Not so much.

So when I wake up and the RV is skidding all over the road, I actually think I am still asleep and dreaming. I used to always have weird car crash dreams when we would go on long road trips. That was pre-Z, of course. It isn't until the screams start, and Stella's nails pretty much dig their way down to the bone of my left arm (which is my only arm), that I realize I am wide awake, and shit is about to get fucked up.

"Grab on to something!" Buzz shouts from the driver's seat. "I don't think I can pull us out of this!"

With the RV stripped down to the screws, there really isn't a whole lot we can grab on to. Which is why Stella has ahold of me, and the kids have ahold of her. The adrenaline that rushes through my body cuts the pain of Stella's grip and smooths out my nerves enough for me to assess our situation. I look out the window, and see a lot less daylight than I should. In fact, all I see is a blanket of white whipping past the windows.

And I fucking mean it: a blanket of white. Not a flurry of flakes. Not a swirling mass of snow. Those things would be great to see. They would actually have definition and tell me that we haven't been swallowed by the Stay Puft Marshmallow Man. But, alas, the signs of an outside world are not meant to be seen. Instead, we see only that motherfucking blanket of white.

That includes out the windshield as well. Which is why Buzz is still yelling for us to hang on to anything we can.

"So this is a whiteout," Charlie says. "I always wondered."

"Go fuck yourself and your wondering," Greta snaps.

"Kids, shut the fuck up," Stella says.

The RV swerves to the left, then back to the right, and Buzz starts swearing like I have never heard a Fitzpatrick swear in my life, including Melissa, even though she's a Billings since she married my late best friend Jon. I miss Jon. He was a great guy.

Screams bring me out of my head.

Left, right, left, right, right, right.

Okay, we're now sliding across the road sideways. Or I assume we are since I can't see a damn thing other than that fucking blanket of white.

The RV feels like it's up on two wheels then it feels like it's up on no wheels. No wheels is bad.

Bam!

Okay, wheels are back on the ground, but we are still sliding. And fast.

I look about and see everyone hanging onto everyone else. It's an orgy of fear.

Huh, I kinda like how that sounds. Orgy of fear. I'll need to use that again sometime. Orgy of fear.

"Jace! Shut up!" Stella screams at me.

"No one cares about your orgy of fear, Dad!" Greta shrieks.

Man, I really have to work on the talking out loud thing. This is becoming a serious problem. If we ever get someplace that has the right equipment, I may have Dr. McCormick do a full brain scan, or whatever is possible in this shitty world. She'll probably just shine a flashlight in my ear, and tell me I'm fucked. That sounds about right.

We all shout, and scream, and yell, and freak out as the RV hits something and then begins to spin out of control. I have no idea what we have hit, or really if we did hit anything at all. Maybe the tires caught on a not so slippery part of the road. Fuck if I know.

The RV keeps spinning, and I can see Stella about to lose her lunch. She is not a happy camper when things get all spinny-spinny. Not that anyone would be a happy camper in this situation, but spinny-spinny is not her thing in the best of times.

There are definitely impacts against the sides of the RV, and realization hits me regarding what the fuck the impacts are. I focus and listen to the sounds just to make sure, but after a few thumps and splats, I am almost one hundred percent certain of what is happening.

Zs.

Not only are we in a whiteout, but we are in a fucking herd of Zs. Or maybe it's just a manageable horde, and not a full-blown herd. One can hope, right?

A spray of brown, black, and red covers the window across from me, and my fears are confirmed. Yep, it's motherfucking Zs.

More impacts, more spinning, Stella's face is green, more spinning, more impacts, Stella turns and throws up, people shout and scoot away, more spinning, more impacts, more Stella puke.

Then nothing.

The world is floating. Or, more accurately, we are floating in the world. Time slows and I can feel my ass lifting off the floor of the RV. I'm going weightless, bitches! Ground control to Major Tom, motherfuckers!

The weightlessness lasts for a couple seconds before the weight of my pure terror hits me. Not only are we up in the air, but the RV is now rolling, as well as still spinning. This is some real 360 bullshit. Tumbling now, my family rolls on top of me, then I'm on top of them, then that dickhead Rafe is in my face, then I see Critter, then white and red and white, and Stella and Stuart, and white and...

It's all white. And so fucking cold.

But, I have that weightless feeling once more. I'm flying!

Flying through the cold, cold air. Flying through the blanket of white. Flying who the fuck knows where?

And smack, bam, the trip is over.

I hit the ground hard. Dirt and snow are shoved up my coat, down my pants, in my boots, in my eyes, my ears, my nose. There is some more tumbling, but it's all solo now. I am rolling across Illinois and not liking it so much.

My body slows, slows, and stops. I lie here for a second, trying to figure out what the fuck to do.

Do I stand up? I'm afraid to, in case I find out that I'm now missing a leg as well as an arm. But, hey, then Stumpageddon would have a buddy, right? If I am missing a leg, I can call him something cool like Choppy or Da Gimp. More like everyone would call me Da Gimp, not my leg. That's probably not the best name to choose.

I'm really fucking cold!

Okay, no more daydreaming about my unconfirmed new amputation's name.

I reach down and pat myself, and find I'm fully intact (with the exception of Stumpageddon, of course). Intact is good. Still hurts, but better than missing a leg in a snowstorm with Zs all around.

Oh, fuck! Zs!

I have to get up. I have to move some ass. Crashing is bad, but just waiting to become some undead fucker's human snow cone is even worse.

Getting up now. Hurting a lot now. Standing now.

The world is still completely white.

"HEY!" I scream. "HELLO! ANYBODY!"

The wind whips my words away, taking them off to the land of Wind-Whipped Words. Which is not a real place, in case you were wondering. I'd hate for folks to try to book a vacation in the Land of Wind-Whipped Words based on my recommendation.

"Jace!"

Great, now the fucking snowstorm is talking to me.

"JACE!"

Hold on, I know that voice.

"Stuart!" I yell back.

"Jace!" he shouts as I see a shape stumble out of the white towards me.

"Stuart!" I cry as I limp over to him. "Am I glad to see you!"

We get to each other and from the look on his face, I must be in about as bad of shape as he is. He has a nasty gash across his forehead and there is frozen, matted blood covering most of the left side of his head above his ear. He's clutching his left arm up against his chest, and I can see that his left shoulder is drooping way lower than it should.

Oh, and he's missing a boot. His right boot. That's gotta be fucking cold, but it explains the stumbling.

"How bad is it?" he asks as we hunch over and huddle up against the wind. "My head hurts like a bitch."

"You got a little banged up," I say.

"You too, buddy," Stuart says. "That leg has to hurt like hell."

I look down at my left leg. "Huh?"

"The other one," he says. "Better hope that hasn't hit an artery."

I look down at my right leg and see the problem. Right smack dab in the middle of my thigh, a blood coated sliver of shiny RV, about four inches of it, is staring back at me. The blood is frozen and clotted around it, and I know from its position that it didn't hit an artery or vein or whatever would cause me to bleed out. Oh, lucky me!

"I should leave that there," I say.

"Good call," Stuart replies.

"Where is everyone else?" I ask, my teeth chattering so hard I'm afraid I'm going to bite my tongue off.

"I don't know," Stuart replies. "I only found you because you were talking to yourself so loud I could hear you over the wind. Apparently wind-whipped words all lead to Jace."

"You heard that?" I ask. "Shit."

"We can't stay here," he says.

"No shit, Sergeant Obvious."

"That's Gunnery Sergeant Obvious," Stuart grins. His lips look blue, so it's a blue grin.

"Which way?" I ask. "I can't see shit."

"I came from that way," he says, and points, then looks about. "I think. Shit, this snow is so thick I can't even see my tracks anymore. We are going to fucking freeze to death if we don't find shelter."

"The RV," I say. "We have to get back to the RV."

"But which fucking way, Jace?" Stuart snaps. "If we wander off we could end up going the wrong way and be even more fucked."

"We're fucked if we stand right here," I say.

"So we wander."

"We wander."

We wander.

I try to put my arm around Stuart's shoulders for some support since my leg is not in the greatest shape, but he nixes that idea in point zero seconds.

"I dislocated my shoulder," he says. "You're on your own, Long Pork."

Wow, never thought being called Long Pork would be a relief. That's how much I hate the name Short Pork.

We stumble our way through the storm. The freezing cold keeps my leg numb—not that I'd recommend hypothermia as a pain management system. Vicodin is really the way to go. Or whiskey. Mmmm, whiskey.

"I'd love some whiskey, too, Jace, but we don't have any," Stuart says. "So shut the fuck up."

"Gotcha," I nod. "Shutting up."

More stumbling, with a healthy dash of limping, and we both know we are totally lost. I can see the panic in Stuart's eyes as he glances over at me. He has little icicles hanging from his eyelashes, which I would totally make fun of if it wasn't for the fact that I'm having to look through my own eyelash icicles. Plus, my lips are frozen shut. Hey, at least I can't accidentally talk out loud now. Neither can Stuart, since I can see his lips are just as blue and frozen as mine.

Which makes me wonder what I'm hearing.

The wind has slackened some, but the snow is coming down so hard that visibility is still shit. Yet, with the lessened wind, I can almost make out other voices. Maybe it's Stella and the kids!

I try to yank Stuart along, desperate to get to my family, but he grabs my arm and holds me back. I look at him, and he shakes his head then nods forward. I squint into the white and make out some shapes coming for us. They are people shaped, but the way they move tells me they are not people. Not anymore.

Fuck.

There are close to a dozen shapes that we can see. There could totally be more, but well, you know, the snow.

Stuart eases his pistol out of the holster on his hip then looks at me and holds it out.

"What?" I ask, or try to with my frozen mouth.

"Slide," he shouts. A few moans respond.

I'm completely confused when I realize he is one arm short because of his shoulder and can't rack the slide on his pistol. I give him a thumbs up, grab onto the top of his pistol, and pull back as he holds the grip as hard as he can. I can tell his fingers are losing feeling because he almost drops the pistol when I pull, and that is not like Stuart. The slide does go back, and I see the hammer cock into place.

Stuart lifts the pistol and keeps moving forward, taking aim at the approaching Zs. I pat myself down and realize I have no firearms on me. Nothing at my hip, just an empty holster, and of course, I lost the shotgun I had in the RV when, well, I lost the RV. Or did the RV lose me? Toe-may-toe, toe-mah-toe.

But, and this is a good thing, a great thing, an amazing thing, I do have a collapsible baton inside my coat. I remember tucking it away there in one of the bajillion pockets the coat has. It's one of those swanky snowboarding coats that has a pocket for your phone, your iPod, your flask, your mini-fridge, your vacation house, the Holy Grail, and even a pocket for a collapsible baton if you happen to find yourself stuck in a snowstorm with a dozen Zs coming for your ass.

So, in conclusion, the coat is almost as good as sliced bread.

(No, it's not.)

Baton out and at my side, ready for some Z killin'. Which is how I can describe Stuart, too, since he's at my side and ready for some Z killin'.

The Zs finally get close enough to see us and they lunge. The first three fall right on their rotten faces because their feet get hung up in the ever-deepening snow, but the rest of them use their fallen friends as launching points and come at us.

A Z reaches for me, and I crack its skull open with my baton. But the thing doesn't stop. You see, since the monster isn't all warm and squishy, my skull crack only brakes bone and doesn't really go all the way into the brain. This is going to be harder than I thought.

I decide to change tactics, and instead of going for the kill, I go for the cripple. I bring my baton down on the fucker's knee and it shatters that bastard's leg like a twig. The Z falls forward, and I step out of the way as another comes for me.

I try to pivot in the snow, but there just isn't enough good footing, and I almost fall on my ass. But I keep myself upright, and slam my baton into the Z's thigh. I can almost hear the femur crack. Down goes that one.

The shots from Stuart's pistol are loud as fuck, which is surprising since I'd think they would be muffled by the falling snow. But maybe it's the crisp air that's making them seem louder. I don't know. Gonna have to ignore the science right now.

The snow around us is soon covered in black blood and bits of Z brains. The ones I take down but don't kill thrash around on the ground for a bit, then start to slow until they are barely moving. I'm guessing the temperature is finally getting to them. I don't waste the opportunity and go from one to the other and bash, bash, bash until I finally crack their skulls to get to their chewy brain centers.

Stuart and I stand here, sweating and freezing, hurting and lost. He points weakly with his pistol at the way the Zs came from, and I nod in agreement. If our RV hit a bunch of Zs while spinning out of control on the road, then it makes sense the Zs came from the general direction of said road. Unless the spinning RV sent them flying all over the place, then we are fucked. But that shitty thought is gonna have to take a backseat to the more optimistic thought of the road being straight ahead.

More stumbling and limping, then we finally come to the road.

No, that's not quite true. We finally come to *a* road. But it isn't *our* road. Not the road we were on with the RVs. It's easy to tell from the ramshackle farmhouse we walk past and the rows of collapsed single wide trailers across the road. This is some country road, not I-64, which is what we should have been on.

Jesus fuck, we are so lost.

Stuart grabs me by the arm and steers me towards the farmhouse. Good idea. It doesn't fucking matter what road we are looking at since the snowstorm could give a fuck. It's gonna bury us in a couple minutes if we don't find shelter.

We get to the steps and pitifully make our way up onto the front porch. Stuart stops me before I reach for the door and points at a couple spots by the front windows of the house. Footprints. The snowstorm has blown enough snow to cover any tracks that may have been on the steps and right in front of the front door, but the overhang shelters the windows just enough that some prints are left, telling us that someone was just on this porch before us.

Stuart glances down at his pistol then up at me, and taps my arm three times with the barrel of the pistol. I hold up three fingers to indicate that I think he's telling me he only has three rounds left, and he nods.

Okay, so let's hope there aren't more than three people inside this house. Or if there are, they are all friendly people. Because that's so likely. Nothin' but friendly people in the zombie apocalypse, right?

Fuck.

Stuart braces himself and is about to kick in the front door when it is yanked open. There staring at us, with my motherfucking shotgun in his hands, is Rafe. Fucking Rafe has my motherfucking shotgun. That shotgun is my kill-Rafe-because-he-was-looking-at-Greta shotgun. Not his shotgun to be pointing at me. Fucking canny named Rafe.

"Hey!" Rafe shouts, but not at us. He shouts over his shoulder. "It's Stanford and the old Marine!"

"Get them in here, you dumbass!" a very familiar voice shouts from inside. "Hurry up and shut that fuckin' door! We're gonna fuckin' freeze to death!"

We don't need any more invitation as Rafe lowers the shotgun and steps aside. Stuart and I hurry inside as fast as our numb legs will carry us. Rafe slams the door behind us and scoots an old couch up against it. He moves to the front window and peers out, then turns and looks at us.

"Hey, there," he smiles. "We weren't sure if anyone else made it."

"I ain't surprised it's you two," Critter grins from a recliner stuck in the corner of the small front room of the farmhouse. "Stuart's got the brains to survive. And everyone knows Short Pork is just fuckin' lucky as all hell."

"Yeah, Crit, I am so fucking lucky," I stutter as I pull my frozen lips apart. I look down at the sliver of metal sticking from my leg. "I'm a regular walking lottery."

"You're alive, ain't ya?" he sneers.

"Yeah, but I have no idea where my family is," I say. "So I'm still gonna have to argue against the lucky part."

"They're out there somewhere," Critter says as he stands up. "And that wife of yours is way smarter than you, so I'm sure she'll get your kids someplace safe. Have a seat before you fall down, Short Pork. I don't want to have to be steppin' over your body all night when I want to go take a leak."

"You already sweep the place?" Stuart asks.

"Who the fuck do you think you're talkin' to?" Critter frowns.

"Just asking," Stuart replies.

"Yeah, I swept the place with the kid here," Critter says. "Two corpses upstairs. I'm guessin' it's Mr. And Mrs. Farmer. They ate their shotguns a long while back from the looks of 'em. You're welcome to go get one, Short Pork."

"One what?" I ask as I stumble and fall into the recliner. My leg is warming up and I can tell the pain is gonna hit me soon.

"One of them shotguns," Critter replies. "It'll be easy to snap their fingers and pluck them from their dead hands."

"Charming," I reply. "But I have a shotgun right there."

I point at Rafe, and he looks down at the weapon in his hands.

"Is this yours?" he asks. "I found it in the snow, so I'm going with finders keepers."

"The fuck you are," I say. "Give me my fucking shotgun!"

"Or what?" Rafe grins. "You'll get up and take it from me?"

"How about you give me the shotgun?" Stuart asks, making sure the canny kid pays attention to the pistol in his hand. "How does that sound?"

Rafe looks from the pistol to Stuart, the pistol to me, the pistol to Critter, and I can tell he realizes he's not exactly amongst friends.

"Sure, sure, here," Rafe says as he walks the shotgun over and hands it to me. "I was just fucking with you."

"Whatever," I say. I rest the shotgun across my lap then look out the front window at the never-ending snowstorm. "We're gonna need heat."

"You're gonna need a lot more than heat," Critter says as he nods at my leg then looks over at Stuart. "What the fuck's wrong with you?"

"Shoulder," Stuart says.

"I can fix that," Critter says.

"I figured you could," Stuart sighs. "Let's get this over with."

"Then it's your turn," Critter says to me, and points at Rafe. "Go find whatever you can. Bandages or old sheets. Alcohol would be good."

"Gotta keep things sterile," I say.

"Fuck that," Critter smiles as he grabs onto Stuart's wrist. "I just need a fuckin' drink."

He pulls and twists, and Stuart cries out then falls to his knees.

"Thanks," he mutters, and sort of crawls his way to the couch blocking the front door. "I'll be right over here if anyone needs me."

"Move ass," Critter snaps at Rafe. "You want to hang with the big boys, then you better listen, and do what I say when I say it."

"When the fuck did you become my boss?" Rafe asks.

"The second you handed your shotgun away, dumbass," Critter grins. "Because that was a stupid as fuck thing to do, and the stupid ain't in charge around here."

"Could have fooled me," Rafe mumbles as he leaves the room. "All I fucking see is stupid."

"That's yer eyelids!" Critter calls after him.

He looks out the window at the snow, and I do the same.

Shelter is good, but we'll need more than that really soon, or we'll be dead in hours. The cold isn't as bad in here as out in the storm, but it is still fucking bad. Really bad.

CHAPTER FOUR

So, what are three men and a teenage boy to do when there's no heat, and you're stuck in a snowstorm?

If your answer is "cuddle," then I fucking hate you.

But, you're right.

We have to cuddle.

Well, more like we restrain ourselves from killing each other while under a pile of moldy blankets. At least I'm on the outside so my leg wound doesn't get bumped. This is both good and bad. Good for the non-bumping of the leg, bad for the Critter HOGGING ALL THE COVERS!

Fucking asshole.

Yet, it's not like we have another choice. No power means no heat. We can't use the small wood stove because we have zero idea if the chimney is clear or not. Last thing any of us want to happen is die during the zombie apocalypse because of motherfucking smoke inhalation. That'd just be the shittiest way to go out.

So ... we cuddle.

"Critter, I swear to god if you don't stop rolling over and taking the blankets with, I'm going to gut you like a tauntaun and sleep in your split open carcass!" I shout.

"I ain't got a goddamned clue what you just said to me, Short Pork," Critter replies from across the cuddle pile. "But you are more than welcome to try and split me open. I'd love to see how that turns out for ya."

"Will you two shut up," Stuart says from next to me.

I draw the line at sleeping next to Rafe. Gotta have standards and shit.

"I'll be quiet if Short Pork is quiet," Critter says. "But I ain't gonna let no one-armed jackass talk to me about no Star Wars horsey things without givin' him a piece of my mind."

"See! You do know what I'm talking about!" I snap. "You are such an asshole, Critter! Why the fuck do you have to constantly bust my balls? What the hell did I do to deserve that?"

"You blew up your subdivision," Critter replies.

"*My* subdivision, Critter," I growl. "Not yours."

"It was mine too," Stuart says.

"And are you always busting my balls?" I ask. "No."

"Because if I busted your balls right now, they'd get all over me," Stuart grumbles. "Stop spooning me."

"I have to lay on my side or there's too much pressure on my leg," I respond. "Have a heart, dude."

"You killed the President of the United States," Critter continues.

"You hated that guy as much as I did!" I exclaim. "And I didn't have a choice! He'd kidnapped Elsbeth and was going to kill Charlie!"

"You brought down the Consortium on us and ended up getting Asheville nuked," Critter says.

"Dude! That is not on me! The Consortium was coming anyway!"

"So you say," Critter says. "But you're the only one that talked with that Thornberg lady. No way to know if you're lying or not."

"No way to know-?" I sputter. "Lying? Lying! Are you out of your fucking mind?"

Then the jerk begins to chuckle. It starts small and builds until Critter is laughing so hard that he pulls the blankets all the way over to his side.

"Dammit!" I shout, and painfully get to my feet. "What the fuck is wrong with you, Critter?"

"Lie down, Jace," Stuart says. "He's only fucking with you."

"I know he's fucking with me!"

"No, I mean he's playing," Stuart says. "Critter busts your balls because he thinks it's fun. He laughs about it all the time when you're not around."

"He what?" I ask, stunned. "He's just doing it for shits and giggles?"

"Ain't much else to do in the apocalypse, Short Pork," Critter says between chuckles.

"Stop calling me Short Pork!" I scream so loud my voice cracks. This, of course, makes Critter laugh even harder. "Fucking knock it off!"

"Will you old men be quiet?" Rafe mumbles. "You're gonna bring the dead to the door."

I shut up and turn to look at the couch-blocked front door. Yikes. I totally forgot about the Zs outside. Not that they can hear much with the snowstorm still raging, but it's always better to be safe than sorry, and right now I'm being sorry.

"Fuck this," I say. "I'm gonna go sleep upstairs with the corpses. You fuckers suck."

"Ain't no more blankets," Critter says.

"I'll figure out something," I snap and stomp off.

Okay, I don't exactly stomp so much as I limp with extreme prejudice. My point is made, either way.

I get upstairs and stumble around for a bit until I figure out that one of the bedroom closets will fit me just fine. It's an interior closet, so all the walls are insulated by the rest of the house. I find some old, dusty towels and cover myself with those. It's actually not too bad, really. I shut the door and the closet warms up pretty fast.

It takes me a long while to drift off to sleep because I'm so pissed at Critter, but after a while good ol' sleepy time comes knocking and that sweet, merciful sleep takes me.

***

The dreams come in fits.

Screaming, fire, vehicles crashing, bullets whizzing by, explosions. All of it. And Zs, plenty of Zs. They swarm about us, come at us like a tsunami, sweeping us away into their rotten world of the undead. Teeth gnash, claws rip, the smell overpowers.

So, my dreams are pretty much business as usual in the zombie apocalypse.

What isn't business as usual is the shouting from downstairs.

Well, yeah, I guess people shouting is pretty normal in life nowadays, but the fact it's Stuart and Critter shouting isn't so normal. I listen closely, and can hear a few other men yelling, plus the very distinct sounds of pump-action shotguns being pumped and actioned. Critter keeps yelling, but Stuart quiets down. Then I hear the thud and Critter's voice is cut off.

Motherfucker. Do I have to go save that old pain in the ass's life now?

And where the fuck is that Rafe kid? I didn't hear his voice in the chaos of shoutiness.

I slowly push open the closet door and there is the kid, his finger to his lips, his eyes wide with fear. He shakes his head slowly, and I get the idea that making noise is bad. Not that I intended to make any noise, but I nod at the kid, hoping he'll chill out. He looks jumpier than shit.

We both huddle there next to a stripped single bed, and wait as the voices grow quieter and quieter. Then there's the sound of a door slamming and boots stomping on the front porch. A lot of boots. My guess? Six, maybe seven guys. If they all have guns, then there's not a fucking thing Rafe or I can do to stop them from taking Critter and Stuart.

Neither of us move. We wait. And wait. And wait. Then we hear the far off sounds of engines. But even as the engines slowly fade away, we still don't move.

One of the things you learn in the apocalypse is that no one trusts a damn thing.

Which is why after waiting through a good ten minutes of silence, I am not surprised by the sound of boots on the stairs slowly making their way up to us. Whoever the guys with the shotguns are, they know how to play the game. They left one of their guys behind to see if maybe there are some stragglers. Which there are. We also happen to be unarmed stragglers, since all of the weapons were left below with Stuart and Critter.

Well, almost all of the weapons.

Rafe slips a seriously sharp looking knife from his boot while I pull out my collapsible baton. We look at each other and nod, and slowly get to our feet, each taking an opposite position by the bedroom door. He flattens himself against the wall and looks over at me, then down at the still collapsed baton. His eyes go wide, but I shake my head since the baton will make a very loud clunkety-click sound when I extend it, and it locks into place.

Grumbling a bit, Rafe holds his knife at the ready as the boot steps reach the second floor landing and start to make their way down the hall. They stop, and then there's a loud crash as the man kicks in the door to the bedroom next to us. There's even more crashing as—and I'm guessing here—he rushes into the room, and just goes hog wild on the furniture. He's probably tossing the bed aside and shoving the dresser over.

Which is a good technique if you only have one room to search, but a shitty technique if you don't want anyone in the other bedrooms to hear you. I should seriously write a fucking apocalypse manual on how not to be a dipshit. This guy could use the advice.

The rock star level room trashing stops, and the boot steps start up again as the guy moves out of that room and comes for ours. There's a slight pause, and then our door comes flying open.

I pretty much miss everything that happens, because the door slams into my face and knocks me against the wall. I stagger a bit, but stay on my feet as I hear Rafe and the guy struggle with each other.

"Short Pork!" Rafe yells. "I could use some help!"

I rush from around the door and extend the baton just as the guy turns and sees me coming. He tries to whip his shotgun around, but Rafe has it gripped by the barrel and the stock with both hands, his knife lying on the bedroom floor at their feet. I raise the baton and start to bring it down, but the guy elbows Rafe in the face, and then yanks the shotgun free. I barely have time to dodge out of the way before the shotgun blast rips a huge hole in the door.

Tumbling out of the room and into the hallway, I scramble up onto my feet and sprint-limp to the stairs as the guy flies out of the bedroom and fires again. Old plaster and wood explode by my head as I get to the stairs and basically fall all the way down.

"Hey! Get back here!" the guy yells.

Seriously?

I do not get back there, and head straight for the front door. I rip it open and then freeze.

Zs. A holy metric shitload of Zs. There have to be a couple hundred of them. They are all knee to thigh deep in the fresh snow, which should lock them in place, but damn if they aren't looking motivated by the sight of my pink, tasty flesh.

The storm is over and the sun blares down on the snow, making it almost impossible to see a damn, fucking thing without an instant migraine. I squint into the bright light and try to look for a path through the herd of Zs. They may be moving, but they aren't even close to moving as fast as if they weren't all half buried in snow. If I can spot even the slightest of gaps, then I can get through them and away from shotgun guy.

But the glare from the snow is too much, and the Zs keep shifting, stumbling, falling over in the snow.

The shotgun blast ends my idea of going through the herd, and I jump over the porch railing and land around the side of the yard as buckshot tears into the boards where I was just standing. I land in about six feet of nice, soft snow, and instantly start digging out of the drift and crawl my ass across the yard towards the back of the house.

More Zs.

The farmhouse is surrounded by them, and now that my eyes have semi-adjusted to the glare, I can see that my first estimate of a couple hundred is way off. We're talking a good six or seven hundred of the fuckers. Probably more since I can't really see the back of the herd.

Awesome.

"Hey! Get your ass back here, boy!" Shotgun Guy shouts just before firing again and again.

I do some more diving and get behind the house, but not before some of that buckshot finds its way into my leg. Yes, the same leg that I wounded in the crash. The leg that hasn't been hurting so much because of the adrenaline pumping through me and the little bit of sleep I did get. Yeah, now it is hurting like a mother fuck all over again.

And news flash! A Jace with a wounded leg moves in deep snow about as well as the Zs do! So it's a slow race.

"Hey!" Shotgun Guy shouts. "Where the fuck ya think you're going?"

Really? Does he expect me to listen? This guy is ten kinds of stupid, believe me.

Or is it believe you me? What the fuck does that even mean, anyway? Believe you me? I have never gotten that saying. I just say believe me. Believe you me is what some Gatsbyesque doofus would say.

"Why that's a fine sailboat you have there, sport," Gatsbyesque Doofus says. "That is sure to impress the dolls, believe you me!"

Did they say dolls back then? Or was it dames?

"What the hell is wrong with you?" Shotgun Guy asks from behind me as I try to limp/hop through the snow and around the back of the house. "Who are you talking to?"

I stop in my tracks and throw up my hand, turning around slowly.

"Was that out loud?" I ask.

"Yeah, it was," Shotgun Guy says.

"Sorry about that," I say, then glance at the house. "Uh, where's my friend?"

"I clocked him good," Shotgun Guy replies. "Knocked him cold. He'll be out for a long while."

"Okay," I nod. "Well ... uh, what now? Are you going to shoot me?"

"Depends on you," Shotgun Guy says. "You make a break for it again, and I will shoot you. Do as I say, and forget the funny business, and you might live."

"Hey! Up here!"

Shotgun Guy whirls around and fires behind him. A couple of Zs get torn apart, but that's it.

"No, you stupid fuck, up here! Look up!"

I look up even though I don't normally answer to the name of "stupid fuck," and see Rafe leaning out of a second story window, knife in hand. Shotgun Guy whirls back at me, and I flatten myself into the snow as he fires again. What the fuck is wrong with this guy? Does he not understand what up means?

There's a thunk, and then the shotgun goes off once more just before I hear a soft thud. I wait a second, and then push up out of the snow. I notice the spray of blood on the white before I notice the indentation in the snow and Shotgun Guy's body.

"Grab that shotgun before it gets too wet," Rafe yells. "I'll be right down."

I hobble over to Shotgun Guy and see a lot more red than I was expecting to. Carefully, I get closer until I can snatch up the shotgun. I put it to my shoulder, and limp back a step or two and wait. Rafe comes barreling out of the house's backdoor and jumps into the snow, then scrambles to the man and flips his body over. He pulls his knife from the guy's left eye socket, and wipes it on the man's coat, then looks over at me and grins.

"That wasn't a lucky shot," Rafe says as he slides the knife into his boot. "I can make those all day. Easy way to take down meat, right through the eye."

"We are not eating this guy," I say, and fight the urge to turn the shotgun on the kid. "I don't give a fuck how hungry I am, we are not eating this guy."

"Fucking relax, Short Pork," Rafe says. "My people eating days are behind me. We'll leave him here for the Zs. It'll buy us some time." He glances at my bleeding leg. "Which it looks like we'll need."

He's right, we do need some time, because my leg hurts like hell, and the Zs are closing in on us. Rafe hurries over to me, takes the shotgun, and then throws my one arm over his shoulders. He points with the shotgun at a decent sized gap in the herd, and we both head for it.

"Where's that baton of yours?" Rafe asks. "We may need it in a sec."

"Dropped it somewhere," I say. "I was sort of busy running from Shotgun Guy."

"You were busy leaving my ass behind, is what you were doing," Rafe says. "Good thing I know how to play possum. He smacked me hard, but not hard enough to knock me out. Takes a lot to turn off my lights."

"Not me," I say. "I've been knocked out by pretty much everyone in the apocalypse. You look at me the wrong way, and I go unconscious."

"Uh, that can't be good for you," Rafe says, glancing at me. "You probably have some brain damage."

"Nah, I'm good," I say.

"How many times have you been knocked out?" he asks.

"Jeez, close to eight or nine times in the last couple of years," I reply. "I think I've been knocked out by cannies at least three times. Then there have been a couple of explosions I've been too close to. I'm actually surprised I can still hear. Mondello's people knocked me out at least once, maybe twice. Three times?"

"Mondello?" Rafe asks.

"Wannabe POTUS," I say.

"POTUS?"

"President of the US."

"Why would the President want to knock you out?"

"Long story," I say. "Doesn't really matter, since I never considered him the real POTUS anyway."

We get through most of the Z herd without much issue, and find ourselves out on a road. I know it's a road, because the snow isn't quite as deep as it is in the field we just crossed. Gotta love the warming properties of asphalt. Except in the summer, then you gotta hate the warming properties of asphalt. I have a love/hate relationship with asphalt, as you can tell.

Rafe is looking at me like I'm crazy.

"I think all those concussions are why you talk out loud all the time," Rafe says.

"What? That's crazy," I laugh. "I don't talk out loud all the time. Just some of the time. I wasn't talking out loud right now, was I?"

"You have a love/hate relationship with asphalt," Rafe says.

"Oh," I frown. "Huh. Well, maybe I do talk out loud a little more than I intend to. But lots of geniuses have talked out loud."

"Geniuses?" Rafe asks. "Uh, no offense, man, but I'm not sure you fit in that category."

"Hey, kid, listen up," I snap. "I've been tested. I'm a certifiable genius."

"You're certifiable," Rafe says. "That's not exactly a secret."

"Lame joke, dude," I say. "Don't try to be funny if you're gonna recycle old humor. Go for something original. Life's too short for stale laughs."

"Yeah, okay, whatever," Rafe says as we stop in the road. He looks down and shakes his head. "Those aren't tire tracks."

"Nope," I say as I look at the road. "Those are snowmobile tracks. Shotgun Guy's friends were ready for the snowstorm."

"Guess you'd have to be if you live around this place," Rafe says.

Tracks are good since they are easy to, well, track. But these go in both directions, which makes me think the people that took Stuart and Critter just happened by our hidey-hole and weren't out looking for us specifically. The problem is, I have no idea which way they went. The snowmobile tracks don't exactly have arrows pointing us in the right direction. They just look like tracks in the snow.

"What the hell is that?" Rafe asks, squinting into the bright glare. He points to our left. "Do you see something coming?"

I squint too and do see something coming. It's a couple more minutes before I realize what that something is.

"RVs!" I shout, and then flinch as several Zs moan from behind us. I glance over my shoulder and see that the herd has turned itself around and is trying to come for us. "Oops."

"Don't worry," Rafe says. "The RVs will get to us before the Zs do. But maybe we should cross the road."

"Good idea," I say, and limp across the road so we can face the herd instead of having it at our backs. I stick my thumb out and smile. "Nothing like the freedom of the open road."

"You are one weird motherfucker," Rafe says.

"Says the canny kid," I reply.

My arm tires out quickly, so the whole sticking out my thumb for a ride thing gets old pretty fast. We both just stand there calf-deep in snow and wait for the RVs to get to us. I really fucking hope my family is in one of them. Please, please, please let Stella and the kids be alright.

I shield my eyes from the glare of the sun off the snow and off the shiny RVs. The vehicles get closer and closer until they are only a couple hundred yards away.

That's when I notice that we are fucked.

"Shit, shit, shit," I say. "We gotta go."

"What?" Rafe asks. "Why? Those are our RVs."

"They *were* our RVs," I correct. "They're the ones we left back at that farm! Unless our people went back to get them, then whoever is driving probably isn't a friendly face."

"Oh, fuck, you're right," Rafe says and frantically starts looking this way and that. Then he stops and his shoulders sag. "There's nowhere to go. We are so screwed."

"Hand me the shotgun," I say. "They'll think twice about messing with a one armed guy with a shotgun."

"Why? How are you any different than a two armed guy with a shotgun?" Rafe asks.

"I look scarier," I say.

"No, you don't," Rafe states. "Trust me, Short Pork, you do not look scary. I look scarier than you do."

"Yeah, well, that's a matter of opinion," I snap. "And don't call me Short Pork. That's just dick, kid."

"Don't call me kid," Rafe replies, refusing to hand me the shotgun.

"Give me your knife," I say.

"No way! I love my knife!"

"I need some kind of weapon!" I yell. "I can't stand here with my dick in my hand!"

"Make a snowball!"

"Ha ha!" I growl. "Tell the one armed man to make a snowball! Real fucking nice, you canny asshole!"

The RVs are almost on us, and there is no doubt we look like Dumb and Dumber standing on the side of the road arguing.

Oh, well, nothing we can do about it now.

"I know," Rafe says.

"Was that out loud too?" I ask.

"Yep," he replies as the RVs slow and then stop about five yards away.

We're on the opposite side of the road from the side doors, so we hear the doors open and close, then the sound of boots crunching on snow well before we see anyone.

Guess what? Guys with shotguns.

"Uh, hey there," I say, and wave. "Nice RVs."

"You boys lost?" a man asks from the front of the pack. And there is a pack. About eight of them in all. "Don't think I've ever seen you around here before."

"We're passing through," I say. "On our way to Kansas City."

"KC is gone," the man replies, his shotgun aimed right at my belly.

"We heard that," I say. "But you can't always believe what you hear, right?"

The man doesn't respond, just keeps pointing the shotgun at my belly.

"Nice RVs," I say again.

"You boys want a ride?" the man asks. "We aren't going to KC, but we can give you a lift part of the way."

To say I'm a little surprised is an understatement.

"Uh, yeah, that would be great," I say. "How far are you going? St. Louis?"

"No, not that far, either," the man says. "No point. St. Louis is gone too. The biters took that place over from the gangs a long time ago."

"Oh," I nod. "So how far then?"

"Far enough," the man says.

"Right," I smile. "But, let's say we were playing some type of game where telling the other person the actual distance was how you win. You'd probably score some serious points if you actually told me how far you could take us."

The man looks past me and at Rafe.

"What's wrong with your friend here?" he asks.

"I have no idea, mister," Rafe shrugs. "I barely know the guy."

"Gee, thanks," I say.

"Well, when you think about it, it's true," Rafe says to me.

I start to protest, but realize he's right. We do barely know each other. I probably know more about Boyd than I do about Rafe. Boyd...

"Get in the RVs," the man orders.

"Small talk is done, I guess," I say.

"You're wasting time," the man says. "There's another storm on the way, and we need to get to ground before it hits. We've got a couple hours of traveling to do before that."

"Can't move as fast as the snowmobiles," one of the men says, and gets a stern look from the lead man. "Sorry."

"Oh, you know the guys on the snowmobiles?" I ask.

"Are you fucking kidding me?" Rafe sighs.

"Shut the fuck up, kid," I snap. "People with snowmobiles are good people. We like to keep snowmobile people happy, right?"

Everyone, including Rafe, looks at me like I've lost my mind. Which I probably have, but that is beside the point.

"Which RV?" I ask, resigned to our fate.

"This one here will do," the man says, and steps aside.

The whole shotgunned group steps aside also, and several of the shoguns start waving us on, as if we needed help figuring out which RV was which.

"Hey. Hi. How's it going? Nice gun. Ooh, that one's shiny. You polish it yourself or is it new? Howdy. I'm Jace. You guys brothers?"

"Shut the hell up," the lead man says. "Just get in the damned RV."

"The RV is damned?" I ask. "Like cursed? That would explain a lot, trust me."

A shotgun is jammed in the small of my back, and I shut up as the RV side door opens. More shotguns greet me and move aside so Rafe and I can step up into the vehicle.

The first thing I notice is the bleach smell from the RV being cleaned after Pukeapalooza. The second thing I notice is that we aren't the only hitchhikers.

"Daddy!" Greta shouts, but doesn't move as several of the shotguns get racked and pointed at my face. "Daddy?"

"Daddy's here to save you, sweetheart," I smile. "Just as soon as I figure a few things out."

"Daddy?" the lead man asks as he steps up into the RV behind me. "Too bad."

"Why's that?" I ask as I turn to look at him.

All I see is the butt of his shotgun flying at my face.

I guess I'm adding one more concussion to the list. Night night.

***

Not a fucking clue how long I'm unconscious. Could be a couple hours, could be a couple days. All I fucking know is my head hurts, and the stink of bleach is burning the fuck out of my nostrils.

"Yeah, it stinks," Greta says.

And apparently I'm talking out loud again.

My eyes pop open at the sound of my daughter's voice, and glance about. She's sitting right next to me, her arm looped in mine.

"Hey, baby," I smile, then wince from the pain in my head.

"Hey, Daddy," she frowns. "How are you feeling?"

"Like someone clocked me with the ass end of a shotgun," I reply.

"Good thing," Rafe says from my other side. "Because that's how you look."

"Where are we?" I ask.

"In our RV," Greta replies.

I glance about and sure enough, it really is one of the RVs we left behind. But since we didn't have to make room for a bunch of extra passengers and supplies, all the furniture is still inside. I am not on any of the furniture. The guys with shotguns are on the furniture, while I'm on the floor with my daughter and Rafe. Furniture hogging assholes with shotguns can suck my balls.

"Dude," Rafe says. "You seriously need a filter for that brain to mouth thing."

"Was the furniture hogging assholes with shotguns suck part out loud too?" I ask.

"Yeah, it was," the leader of the shotgun people says as he swivels in the passenger seat and points his oh so holy weapon at me. I think these guys sleep with their shotguns, that's how attached they look to them. "That was out loud also."

"Son of a bitch!" I snap. "What the fuck is wrong with me?"

"It's been getting worse," Rafe says more to the guys with shotguns than to me. I think he's worried my mouth is going to get us killed. Which is a completely valid worry, since I have no idea what I say in my head, and what I say outside my head.

I look around and wait. No one responds. Good.

"We have a doctor back at the Tomb," the leader says. "He can look you over. You taken a lot of hits to the head?"

"I don't know," I reply. "There have been a few over the years."

"Concussions add up," the man nods. "I used to coach football. I've seen my share of head trauma."

"You ain't seen shit, Maury," another man says, his eyes locked on me. "I was in Iraq and Afghanistan. That's some serious head trauma shit there, man."

"You should probably shut your mouth, Cole," Maury, the shotgun people leader, says. "Ain't a good thing to talk shit in front of the captives."

"By captives, I'm hoping you don't mean dinner," I say. "Rafe used to be a canny, so karma says he should totally be barbecued, but my daughter and I have never eaten of the human flesh. Sure, they call me Long Pork, but that's a, well, long story."

"They call him Short Pork now," Rafe says, glaring at me. "And thanks for throwing me under the bus."

"It's an RV," Cole says. "Recreational vehicle. Not a bus."

"Figure of speech, Cole," Maury says. "He wasn't talking about this as the bus."

"Although you could probably use the short bus, eh, Cole?" I say.

"Daddy, hush," Greta whispers.

Yeah, probably not the best thing to say to a big guy with a shotgun, but that damned filter part of my brain really, really isn't working so hot right now. Maybe this Maury guy is right, and all the lumps to my skull have finally caught up with me. Although, I seem to be thinking fine. I can reason and figure shit out. My only problem is my internal voice is becoming my external voice.

Maybe I should just stop thinking to myself, and then I wouldn't have to worry?

Hahahahahahahahahahahahahahahahahahahahahaha!

"Your bud has lost his shit," Maury says to Rafe.

"He's fine," Greta snaps.

"I ain't so sure about that, little girl," Maury says.

"Why's he laughing?" Cole asks. "Is it because he thinks that short bus crack is funny? I know what the short bus is asshole! My brother had to ride the short bus!"

Then Cole is up and coming at me fast. Yet, I'm still laughing. I can't seem to stop.

He shoves Greta away from me as his fist hits me square in the jaw. That stops the laughs pretty fucking fast. This Cole guys is built like the proverbial brick shithouse. Although, was there ever a proverb about brick shithouses? I guess I can't really call it proverbial unless there is an actual proverb involved.

"Get off my daddy!" Greta screams, but Rafe holds her back as she tries to lunge at Cole. "He doesn't know he's talking!"

"Shut him up!" Cole shouts as he grabs me by the neck, and then brings his fist down so hard and fast that I don't even see it coming. All I see is a pinkish blur, then stars.

So many stars. Lots and lots and lots of stars.

"Shut the fuck up about the stars!" Cole yells, and both of his hands are around my neck. Even if I wanted to cough up a couple more words or laughs I can't because I am quickly losing air.

"Let him go, Cole," Maury orders loud enough to drown out my daughter's pleas. "I won't ask again. I'll count to five, and if you're still strangling that man, then it'll be your time in the pit."

Cole's hands loosen, and he slowly lets me go, then backs up and takes his seat. There are even more stars now, along with spots and streaks of lights that blur my vision. I feel Greta wrap her arms around me, and I try to soothe her, but I can barely stay conscious.

When I can finally see well enough to trust my eyes, I notice that no one is looking at Cole. Not Maury, and not any of the other shotgun guys. I have a feeling the threat of the "pit" holds some serious weight with these folks.

"What's the pit?" Rafe asks.

"You'll see," Maury replies.

"Not even a hint?" Rafe asks. "It doesn't sound good, and the way Short Bus here backed off Jace when you threatened him with it, I can only guess it's probably the worst punishment you all have."

"Who's Jace?" Maury asks.

I raise my hand and try to speak, but Cole has done a job on my throat, and I only croak a couple of sounds before I stop trying. I glance at Rafe, and can tell he's trying to be brave, but since he used my real name and not Short Pork, I know he's scared shitless right now. So am I. So is Greta as she clings to my chest and weeps quietly.

Maury unhooks a canteen from his belt and throws it to me. "Drink some. You're croaking worse than a retarded bullfrog."

"Thanks," I reply, but it comes out more like "thghs."

"Care if I have some?" Rafe asks Maury, and the man nods.

"Keep it," Maury says. "I don't know what bugs you three have, so I don't want it until it's sterilized again."

"Thanks," Rafe responds.

Oh, sure, it sounds easy when he says it. Fucking kid and his working larynx.

Rafe and I pass the canteen back and forth until it's empty. I try to give some to Greta, but she refuses to pull her face away from my chest. I set the empty canteen down, and we just sit there and watch our captors. I can tell Rafe is sizing them up just as I am. There's five, not including the driver, and they all have their precious shotguns ready to blow our heads off. I'm almost afraid to fart, they all look so jumpy.

We drive for at least another hour before Maury turns and looks at us again.

"How many were in your party?" Maury asks. "Your girl here wouldn't tell us a thing. But I know there were more of you because she waved us down, just like you did. She wasn't surprised to see two RVs coming along that road at all."

"Just us," Rafe says.

"Really?" Maury smiles. "Just you three? So the babbling idiot here drove one RV while you drove the other?"

"Yeah," Rafe says.

"Huh," Maury nods. "Seems like a big waste of fuel to drive two RVs when there are only three of you."

"You never know when you'll need a spare," Rafe says.

"That's true," Maury says. He pulls a radio from his belt and holds it up. "But the bullshit you're telling me isn't even close to true. Know how I know that? You folks like to chat. We heard you coming yesterday from miles down the road. Couldn't quite tell how many of you there were, but we know it was at least three or four RVs. Only found the one all busted up over off 64. That's when we picked up the girl."

Rafe doesn't say anything, just keeps his eyes locked on Maury. I'd really like to get in this conversation. I have a way of getting assholes to reveal all kinds of information. I like to think it's my charm, but both Critter and Stuart have told me it's more because people just want me to shut the fuck up so they start talking instead.

"What's that?" Maury asks, and leans towards me. "What the hell are you gurgling about?"

Gurgling? I have to sound way cooler than gurgling. You get your windpipe crushed, and you have a deep rasp, right? That's how it works. No way I sound like I'm gurgling.

"Man, that's annoying," one of the other men says.

Son of a bitch.

"Just tell me how many other RVs you have, will ya?" Maury asks Rafe. "Don't even have to tell me how many people, just how many RVs."

"I'm sure experienced guys like y'all could tell by the tire tracks," Rafe replies.

"Snowstorm covered all the tracks," Maury says.

"Did it? Bummer," Rafe grins.

"Listen, kid, I'm going to find out what I need to find out," Maury sighs. "Everyone talks. Information is all you have to bargain with."

"So I better wait, and bargain with the guy in charge then," Rafe says.

"What makes you think I'm not in charge?" Maury glares.

Ooh, that pissed him off! Way to go, Rafe!

"It's obvious," Rafe says. "You had to use that pit threat to get Short Bus to behave. If you were the man in charge, then all you'd have to do is bark, and he'd heel. You had to use a stick."

"You train a lot of dogs, have ya?" Maury asks.

"In a way," Rafe smiles.

"In a way?" Maury chuckles. "Kid, you're more full of shit than your buddy here."

"Probably," Rafe nods. "But I'm right. You're not in charge. So who is?"

"You'll find out," Maury says. "And you won't be happy when you do."

"Scary," Rafe says.

"Yes, he is," Maury nods, then turns away from us.

I glance about and see the reality reflected in the other guys' eyes.

I have a really bad feeling that Rafe may have overplayed his hand. I should know, I overplay my hand all the time. But, hey, I'm still alive, so maybe things won't be so bad when we get to the Tomb. Yeah, yeah, I heard it.

CHAPTER FIVE

Apparently there are coal mines in Southern Illinois. Who knew?

These guys do, since that's where they are taking us. I have no idea of exactly where we are, but I do know we are still in Illinois. That has been made obvious by the way the shotgun guys start talking about "Illinois this" and "Illinois that". I tune out most of it.

Mainly I tune it out because I am afraid that if I start listening to them, then my internal dialogue will become my external dialogue, and I really don't want to piss them off by making some stupid joke about Illinois.

See? I know restraint when it comes to my mouth.

No, wait, that doesn't sound right at all…

"I guess you don't have to worry about fuel for power," Rafe says after a huge gate is opened and the RVs are waved inside a compound that is easily as big as two football fields. At the end of the compound is the gaping maw of some mine. "You still pulling coal out of there?"

"They shut the mine down in '97," Maury replies. "But there is plenty of good coal in there for our needs. Also, plenty of good space. A small town's worth of folk can live down there comfortably."

"That how many you have here?" I ask as I look out the window at the buildings in the compound. Several single wide trailers are set up in clusters here and there with men (and shotguns) mingling about, their eyes watching the RVs with suspicious interest. "Did you move your old home town here when Z-Day hit?"

"Something like that," Maury says. "You'll see."

"They said they had a use for me," Greta whispers, her mouth close to my ear. "You don't think they mean...?"

"No, sweetheart," I say. "I'm sure they didn't mean that."

The looks on some of the shotgun mens' faces tell me they mean exactly what my daughter and I think they mean. This is not going to be good.

"Well, thanks for the ride," I say as I slowly get to my feet, making sure I make deliberate, non-threatening motions so there's no misunderstanding. "I hate to ask it, but is there any chance we could get a backpack with some water and a little food? We've got a long walk ahead of us."

As you may guess, there are a lot of confused stares.

Maury clears his throat and motions for me to sit back down. At least, I assume that's what he's trying to convey when he points his shotgun at my nuts then at the floor. Either way, I sit my ass down.

"You aren't walking anywhere," Maury says. "Except inside the Tomb."

"Yeah, about that name," I say. "Do you call it that because it's a deep hole in the ground and resembles a tomb? Or is it because it holds a bunch of corpses?"

"Yes," Maury says.

"Yes, what?" Rafe asks.

"Oh, he answered the question," I say. "It's pretty clear what's up."

"It is?" Rafe asks.

"Sure," I say as I watch a small group of shotgun-toting men wheel a supply laden cart into the huge mouth of the mine. Or Tomb. I should get used to calling it the Tomb. "Like our new friend said, the mine still has plenty of good coal for their needs. Except it takes plenty of good labor to extract that plenty of good coal. Hard to defend against Zs and the less than honest human contingent when you're busy with a pickaxe down in the dark. So they are enlisting our help with the process of keeping the lamps lit and the heat on."

"So we're slaves," Rafe says.

"Exactly," I nod.

"Why didn't you just say that?" Rafe growls.

"Because he likes to hear himself talk," Maury smiles. "You must not know each other very well if you haven't figured that out yet. I've known plenty of smart guys like him. They always like to hear themselves talk."

"I like to hear him talk too," Greta glares. "He sounds a lot more interesting than a moron like you."

Awesome. Now she gets her spirit back. While we're in an RV with shotguns pointed at us. In a compound surrounded by ten foot high fences with razor wire. And about to be shoved into a deep hole for forced manual labor. But, hey, at least she's ready to rumble, right?

I check everyone's faces, and I'm very pleased to say that all of that was inside my head. Good. I call that progress.

"That's what Kelvin calls it too," Maury says.

"Excuse me?" I ask.

"Progress," Maury says. "Kelvin considers our arrangement progress. He believes we lost a part of our foundation as a country when we decided that ditch diggers could dream of not being ditch diggers. The world needs ditch diggers."

"You have no idea how many times I've expressed that very thought and been chastised for it," I say. "I am a firm believer in the ditch digger principle. However, I also believe that there are those suited for digging ditches, and those suited for designing the ditches to be dug. I am in the latter category. You don't want me anywhere near a shovel. I'm more than likely going to totally screw up and fill the ditch."

"Kelvin believes that you can never know your true nature until you have tried all others," Maury says. "That's why you start in the Tomb."

"Start?" I ask.

"You'll see," Maury says as he stands up and opens the side door. "Kelvin will fill you in on everything you need to know."

"Looking forward to it," I smile. "This Kelvin guy sounds like a dynamic personality. Can't wait to share a beer and rap a while."

"Daddy, don't say rap," Greta sighs. "This isn't the sixties."

"No, I meant I want to share a beer and work on some sick rhymes," I reply. "I have some mad beatbox skills, and a way with words."

"Not a good way," Rafe says, and gets a couple chuckles out of the ever stoic shotgun gang. He brightens up a bit, and I get a sinking feeling in my gut that maybe we just lost Rafe to the other side. Cannies are known for being opportunistic bastards that way.

Maury leads us out of the RV, and the frigid air is a serious shock to my system. My leg hasn't stopped hurting since we left the farmhouse, but that pain is nothing compared to the sheer agony that stabs me when the freezing wind hits me. It's like my whole leg has been dipped in glass.

"Son of a fuck," I grumble as I pull my coat around me.

"Told ya there was another storm coming," Maury says as he glances up into the grey sky above. "Gonna be a lot worse than that last one."

"Great," I say as Greta huddles close to me.

I look about and scope the scene. It's a fenced off compound that butts up against a huge hole in a hillside. There's some old, rusted machinery around, but mainly the compound is full of a bunch of single wide trailers that are set up in about six or seven clusters. A few of our shotgun guards head to one cluster, while I watch as some less than healthy looking people push a loaded cart towards another cluster. Smoke and steam are coming from a third cluster, and I'm not surprised when one of the doors opens, and a woman steps out with a heavy apron on. She empties a bucket of something into the dirt, glances at us, sneers, then goes back inside.

I don't have time to study the other clusters as a booming voice echoes across the compound, coming from the mouth of the Tomb.

"Visitors!" the voice cries. "How delightful! We always need fresh faces and strong backs to do the Lord's work around here! Praise be!"

A couple of the shotgun guards reply with their own praise be's, but mostly everyone just stops what they're doing and watches with what can only be described as suppressed awe as the man comes bounding towards us. Yes, he bounds. His voice booms, and his legs bound. He's a regular bounding boomer. Or booming bounder. I may call him BB.

"Daddy, quiet," Greta whispers at me.

"Out loud?" I ask.

"Very," Rafe says.

The bounding, booming man is around my age, maybe mid-forties, with shoulder length, light brown hair, and bright blue eyes. He's average height and build with long fingers on his hands, which he holds out in front of him towards us in an exaggerated welcoming jester. As he gets closer and closer I realize he's the likeness of someone we are all familiar with.

"Jesus..." I start.

" ... Christ," Rafe finishes.

So ... BB looks just like the Anglicized version of the Lord and Savior. He is the spitting image of every white washed Jesus Christ I have ever seen.

Uh-oh.

"Maury, look what you have brought me," the man grins, almost splitting his perfectly complected skinned face in two. "Two healthy men, and a beautiful young woman that looks to be close to child bearing age."

"Hold on a fucking second," I growl. "Child bearing are not words I want said when describing my daughter."

"And why is that, sir?" the man asks, looking truly perplexed. "God's work is to be fruitful and multiply. Heaven knows we can use more Christian soldiers in our war against Evil nowadays. The demons have killed too many of our Lord's disciples, and we must do God's work and replace them as quickly as possible."

"Yeah, you do that," I say. "Just leave my daughter out of it."

"Show some respect," Maury barks. "This is Kelvin, and he has saved us all. Without this man, the biters would rule the Earth, not man. He has brought us back from the brink of extinction, and you will thank him for it."

There are a few things wrong with what Maury says, yet I decide not to argue with him. Not because I think I'll get myself hurt, nor because I think they'll hurt Greta, but because the way Maury talks about Kelvin, and the way everyone looks at him, puts it all into perspective really fucking fast.

We've got a cult on our hands.

Charismatic leader? Check.

Armed followers willing to use violence to carry out said charismatic leader's orders? Check.

Compound that is eerily similar to a prison? Check.

Obvious misogynistic vibe? Check.

Class system with a promise of rising in the ranks if one were to perform whatever duties and obey whatever orders? Check.

I'm guessing food and water are rationed perfectly, so those that need to be controlled have just enough to survive and work, but never enough to gain any strength and rise up against the charismatic leader and his shotgun acolytes.

"Shotgun acolytes," Kelvin laughs. "I like that."

"Shit," I mumble to Greta. "How much of that was out loud?"

"Just the shotgun acolytes part," Greta replies.

"Oh, thank God," I sigh.

"Yes, let us thank Him," Kelvin says, and bows his head.

Everyone, and I do mean everyone, bows their heads as Kelvin starts to bellow out a prayer.

"Oh, Lord! We thank You for the wisdom to bring these fine folks onto our path," Kelvin says. "A path that is righteous and true, caring and kind, just and powerful! We thank You for Your gift of brotherhood and sisterhood! We thank You for showing me the way in the darkness! A way that was clouded by the demon hordes, blocked by the wicked men and women whose sins brought this plague of death upon us! But You Lord, You took me by the hand and led me from my own wickedness and into the light that only You can shine! We thank You for giving us the strength and vision needed to be the new Ark, one built around a flood of undead instead of a flood of water! Behold!"

And he whips about and points at the mine.

"It is the Tomb from which we will all rise in Your image! Praise be to You, Lord! PRAISE BE!"

"PRAISE BE!" the compound echoes.

"That was a nice one, Kelvin," Maury says. "One of your best."

"It was, wasn't it?" Kelvin smiles, then walks right up to me and offers his hand. "I'm Kelvin and you are?"

"Jason Stanford," I say as I offer him my left hand.

He seems to recoil from it, and I see a brief flash of disgust and anger flit across his face. He quickly composes himself and steps back to me, switching from his right hand to his left. We shake, and I instantly want to throw up. His grip is strong, but there's a sliminess to it. Not a literal sliminess, but more the mythical snake sliminess where it felt like muscles rippling over bones under his skin.

He's the Reptile Jesus!

I panic for a second, but can tell that I kept that one inside the noggin. Phew.

"They call him Short Pork," Maury says.

"Long Pork," I say. "But I prefer Jace."

"Long Pork?" Kelvin asks, amused. "Is that what happened to your arm? Did one of the wicked sinners get hungry?"

"No, I had to cut it off after a Z bit my hand," I reply.

Shotguns go up fast and all turn on me.

"Really?" I sigh. "Do I look like I'm a fucking Z? Chill, boys."

"Jace, please refrain from cursing while a guest here," Kelvin says. "It lowers you to the level of the wicked and the demons."

"So the wicked are the bad folk, and the demons are the Zs?" Rafe asks.

Kelvin turns his attention from me and onto Rafe. I give the boy credit for not flinching considering the look of disdain Kelvin slaps him with.

"The wicked are sinners and the demons are what are also known as biters," Kelvin says. "And children do not speak unless spoken to. Do you understand me, young man?"

"Rafe," Rafe says, and offers his hand. His left hand, not his right. "And you should refrain from calling me a child. It lowers you to the level of a Z."

"Maury," Kelvin says quietly then turns his back on Rafe as Maury hurries forward and cracks Rafe over the head with his shotgun.

Rafe crumples to the coal dusted dirt. Greta cries out, and I start to move towards him, but the barrel end of Maury's shotgun is up my nose before I can take a single step.

"Get the kid out of here," Maury says. "His first night is in the pit."

A couple men hesitate, then sling their shotguns and pick up the kid. They drag him by the arms across the compound and are soon lost from sight inside the Tomb.

"If he is deserving, then he will rise again," Kelvin says. A loud work whistle pierces the air. "Lunch time. Perfect. I would be honored if you and your daughter would join me for the midday meal, Jace. It will give us a chance to talk more and get to know each other. With your handicap, I'm not sure you are situated for the Tomb. Perhaps you can convince me to place you elsewhere in our little slice of Eden. Come."

"Okey doke," I reply as Kelvin turns on his heels and starts to do that bounding thing towards the far cluster of trailers.

"Move," Maury says. "We don't keep Kelvin waiting."

"Yeah, I'm guessing we don't," I say as I take Greta's hand and follow the bounding Reptile Jesus.

***

So, Reptile Jesus likes velour. Like *really* likes velour.

Velour covers the upholstery of the chairs and couches that fill the trailer we are led into. Red velour, green velour, purple velour, you name it. And, in the center of it all is a chase lounge covered in black velour. Yep. Black velour.

That's where Reptile Jesus plops down. On a black velour chase lounge.

It is so fitting since velour is the trailer trash version of velvet. And who doesn't want to see Reptile Jesus on black velvet? I know I do!

"Sit, sit," Kelvin says as he stretches out on his velour lounge throne thing. He claps his hands. "Tea and biscuits!"

Oh, yeah, this is gonna be great. Reptile Jesus just clapped his hands for tea and biscuits. I'm pretty sure I caught the hint of a faux British accent for a split second. Who the fuck is this guy?

"Daddy, you're mumbling," Greta says as she sits down on a red velour couch and pulls me next to her. "Please try to stay quiet."

"I'll try," I say. "No promises."

"Maury has informed me that you may be in need of medical attention besides your leg," Kelvin says. "Something to do with your head? I hope it wasn't because of our treatment."

"Well, there may have been an extra knock I could have done without," I say. "But the problem started before I met you fine folks."

"Fine folks," Kelvin grins. "Yes, we are, aren't we? Very fine folks. Very fine indeed."

"Super fine," I say. "The finest of fine. Finetastic. Finaliscious."

"Daddy, stop," Greta says.

"Stopping," I smile, then tap my head. "The apocalypse hasn't been so kind to my brainpan."

"The apocalypse?" Kelvin asks. "Oh, no, Jace, we are not in the apocalypse. This is merely a test of our faith in Him. If it was truly the apocalypse, then the signs of the End of Days would be at hand. The Anti-Christ would call his forces to Armageddon, and the battle for our souls would begin. This, Jace, is not that."

"That's debatable," I reply. "But I'm not a religious man, so I have zero desire to debate it. Apocalypse, no apocalypse, whatever. Doesn't matter to me what we call it, it all sucks balls in the end."

"Yes, how colorful," Kelvin says. "While technically not a curse, it does border on one so I will ask you not to use that turn of phrase again, please."

"What turn of phrase?" I ask. "Suck balls?"

"Yes, that phrase," Kelvin says.

"You don't want me to say suck balls?" I ask again.

"Yes, I have made that clear," Kelvin replies.

"Okay, fair enough," I nod. "No more saying suck balls. I promise, from this moment forward to stop using the phrase suck balls. Suck balls has been wiped from my lexicon. If I say suck balls one more time, then God Himself is more than free to strike me down with a bolt of lightning. Or a plague of frogs. Or is it a rain of frogs? A frog storm? Doesn't matter, the point is I will no longer say those two words ever again. Scout's honor."

Maury's eyes, the two shotgun guards' standing in the corner eyes, and Reptile Jesus's eyes are locked on me. They aren't happy eyes.

"I believe I have been hospitable up to this point, Jace," Kelvin says, his voice matching his sliminess a little more than the forced joviality. "Do not test me. Tea and biscuits are not offered to all that arrive here. Your friends were not offered tea and biscuits."

Uh-oh.

My friends?

"Yes, your friends," Kelvin grins, picking up instantly on the fact I did not intend those words to be spoken out loud. "Did Maury not tell you that our scouts brought in some of your friends earlier?"

"Scouts? Oh, right, the snowmobile brigade," I say. "And where are my friends?"

"They are safe," Kelvin says. "Very safe. The impertinent young man that accompanied you will be joining them shortly."

"The pit?" I ask. "You have Stuart and Critter in the pit? Who else do you have?"

"Are those their names?" Kelvin asks. "They haven't exactly been forthcoming with the personal information. My followers have used every means they can think of, short of mutilation, to extract information, but those two are obviously cut from a wicked cloth."

Reptile Jesus leans forward, and I struggle not to shiver.

"The question is whether you are cut from that same cloth, Jace?"

"Is that the question?" I ask. "Because I can say I am cut from the same cloth as Stuart and Critter. It's not fancy cloth like all this velour, but I wouldn't call it wicked."

I smile at Reptile Jesus. He smiles back. I wait for his tongue to flick out at me. It doesn't. I'm a little disappointed.

A door opens and a young woman carries in a tray holding a teapot, cups, and a pile of cookies. Cookies, not biscuits. Unless you're British, then they'd be called biscuits. Reptile Jesus is not British. So what the fuck is up with calling them biscuits? The apocalypse is so fucking annoying. Does everyone have to recreate themselves?

Kelvin eyes me again, and I'm worried I'm talking out loud, but Greta doesn't nudge me, so I just smile and nod. I probably look like a nodding idiot, but who fucking cares at this point?

"Please serve my guests first, Tara," Kelvin says.

"Yes, sir," the young woman replies, her eyes cast down and away from Reptile Jesus. "Thank you, sir."

"Tara has been with us since the very first day we found our sanctuary," Kelvin says. "She was a teeny little thing, just a speck in God's eye, but hasn't she grown up to be such a beautiful young woman? Just like your daughter here. I believe I will have Tara show your daughter the ways of our world. That way I know she will be led from the darkness and towards the light."

"Yeah, you've sort of used that line already," I say as Tara hands me a cup of tea. "Away from the darkness, go towards the light, Carol Anne."

"Carol Anne?" Kelvin asks, watching Greta closely as Tara hands her a cup of tea. "I'm sorry, but are you quoting Poltergeist?"

"It was a play on words," I say.

"I don't think that would be considered a play on words, as much as just a movie reference," Kelvin says. "I would know, as I am trained in the art of words."

"They have an art of words class in messiah school?" I ask as I sip my tea. Bitter, needs milk and sugar. My eyes watch Kelvin carefully. "Or did you learn the art in the drama program at your local community college?"

Kelvin's eyes narrow, then blink a few times before he turns them on Tara as she hands him his tea. "Thank you, my love," he says. "I'll call you back soon to take these, and Miss Stanford, once we are done. You may wait in the back until then; no need to return to the kitchens."

"Thank you, sir," Tara says, and bows her head as she sets the tray down on a small table, then hurries from the room and back through the door.

All the men's eyes are on her ass as the door slowly closes behind her.

"I'm sure you can believe me when I say there is quite the line waiting to ask that young woman's hand in matrimony once she is of age," Kelvin says. "That is not going to be an easy decision to make."

"I can only bet," I say as I take another sip of the bitter, really needs milk and sugar tea. "These guys all look like such great catches. How will she ever decide?"

"She won't, Jace," Kelvin says. "I will. It is my place to make sure the perfect unions are created here. God did not put me in charge to just let the carnal whims of my followers rule who we are to be fruitful with. It takes careful consideration to ensure the future of the human race and the power of the worship given unto Him."

"If you say so," I smile.

"I do," Kelvin smiles back and nods his head. "How do you like your tea?"

"It's great," I reply. "Why? Did you drug it? Am I going to pass out and wake up in some torture chamber?"

"Drug your tea? That would defeat the purpose of inviting you for tea," Kelvin says, and takes a long, loud, exaggerated sip from his cup. "See? Mine was poured from the same pot."

"You could have drugged the cups," I say.

"You are a very suspicious man, Jace," Kelvin says. "It must be hard being you out there in the wicked world."

"What makes the world out there more wicked than in here?" I ask.

"Do you really need to ask that question?" Kelvin responds.

"Uh, yeah, I do," I say. "Because I haven't exactly seen the picture of piety and compassion here at Reptile Jesus headquarters."

"I'm sorry? Did you say Reptile Jesus?" Kelvin asks. "I'm not following. What does that mean?"

Huh, even when I mean to say things out loud I still stick my foot in my mouth. Story of my life, folks. Story of my life.

Kelvin looks about. "Who are you talking to, Jace? Are you addressing me? Am I the folks? And what story? You know, there is only one story, and that is the greatest story ever told."

I set the tea down and slap my leg. My bad leg. I have to bite my tongue to keep from crying.

"Are you alright?" Kelvin asks.

"Dandy," I say, and take a deep breath. "Okay, Kelvin, how about we cut to the chase?"

"Again, I'm not following you," Kelvin replies.

"I'm just a guy trying to survive out in the world," I say. "Same as you. Except I have friends and family, and you have a cult. But, in the end, we're alike in lots of ways."

"Daddy," Greta warns, sounding a lot like her mother. I should heed her warning, but I don't and press on.

"We have people that depend on us," I continue. "You brainwash yours into following you because of some myth about being a leader and talking to God and all that mumbo jumbo. Whereas I have proven myself time and time again by getting our band of survivors out of one deadly situation after another. Sure, I blew up our subdivision, and, yes, I may have started a war with a powerful group of old world movers and shakers known as the Consortium, but hey, what's a guy gonna do in the apocalypse, right?"

Kelvin leans forward and suddenly the reptile side of Reptile Jesus is the complete and totally dominant personality. The man is all viper and predator, his eyes boring into mine.

"Did you say the Consortium, Jace?" he asks.

"Doesn't matter," I reply, waving him off. Then I point my finger at him. "You know what? It does matter. Yes, I said the Consortium. We're running our asses off from those whackjobs, and the last thing we need is to deal with a minor whackjob like you. They have dirty bombs and tanks and bulldozers and helicopters and herds of Zs. What do you have? Tea and biscuits.

Oh, and they're called cookies, dipshit! Cookies! This isn't London, dude. This is bumfuck Illinois. Cookies!"

I stop and take a breath and think I'm done, which would be the smart thing to be. But, I'm not.

"And, by the fucking way, we *are* smack dab in the middle of the apocalypse, okay? Your little End of Days manual is wrong. This is how the world ends, and there's no reaping of souls or Rapture happening to take the worthy up to Heaven. Just a bunch of dead people walking around looking for a munchy or two. Apocalypse, dude. Apocalypse."

"Jesus, Daddy," Greta sighs. "I wish Mom was here."

"I'll forgive your daughter's blasphemy since yours is so much greater, Jace," Kelvin says, those snake eyes of his watching my every move. "I'll also forgive her blasphemy if you tell me more about the Consortium. In fact, Jace, how about you tell me everything you know about that organization? You do that, and I think I can make things very comfortable for you here."

"That's the thing, Kelvin old pal," I smile. "I don't want things to be comfortable here. I don't want to be here at all. I want our RVs, and I want my friends, and I want to get the fuck out of this shithole. Because that's what it is—a shithole. You have taken a hole in the ground and shit in it by creating some throwback to Biblical slave times. I mean, what the fuck, man? You think you are the new messiah, and that gives you the right to force people to mine your coal so you can have all this?"

I start pointing at all the velour. All the goddamned velour.

"What the fuck? Reptile Jesus on velvet? Is that where you're going with all this? Some cheesy, divine single wide? The trailer to Heaven? I mean, come on!" I look at Maury whose eyes are wide and not so pleased with me. "You actually listen to this yahoo? Why, dude? Look at him! He's nothing! Just an actor in a play of his own making! If you ask me, you should bail on his ass. Or, better yet, kick him the fuck out and all just live free. Your compound looks secure enough, so why keep the freak around? You don't need him, trust me. False messiahs of the reptile persuasion are bad news, brother. Bad, fucking news."

I grab a cookie and jam it in my mouth, then lean back against the oh so soft velour, pretty fucking satisfied with my little rant.

As rants go, it was a good one. Some nice points, well placed jokes, just the right smattering of offense, yet not so far that I got my head shot off with a shotgun before I could finish. Yes, it was a fine rant.

"Daddy, close your mouth," Greta says, he face white with fear. "You're spitting crumbs everywhere."

"Have one also," Kelvin says, offering the plate to Greta.

"Yeah, have one, G," I spit, sending crumbs flying everywhere on purpose, coating half the velour within two feet of me. "They aren't half bad. Plus, he's probably going to kill us both, so why not enjoy a last cookie?"

"You are a bizarre man, Jace," Kelvin sighs as he continues to hold out the plate of cookies to Greta.

"No, thank you," Greta says. "I'm not hungry."

"Are you sure?" Kelvin asks. "You may not get a chance to eat again for a while."

Greta shakes her head.

"Fuck it, dude," I say. "I'll have hers."

Kelvin nods and holds the plate closer to me. I snag two more cookies and jam those in my mouth.

"Fanks," I say, barely able to speak around the globs of flour and sugar and chocolate chips. And something else.

With three cookies crammed in my mouth, I can distinctly taste something not so cookie like. I didn't notice it before when I only had one cookie, but now with three? Yeah, these cookies are a little off.

Then it hits me. I'm a complete dumbass. A total moron. A fucktard of epic proportions.

I rake him over the coals and he just sits there and offers more cookies? He doesn't tell Maury to give me a buckshot enema or toss me out into the freezing ass wind? Why?

Because the tea isn't drugged, the cookies are.

Hunks and chunks of cookie fall to the floor as I lean over the arm of the couch and try to get every last crumb out of my stupid, out of control mouth.

"You aren't a stupid man, Jace," Kelvin says as he sets the plate down and leans back into his chaise lounge, a very smug and satisfied look on his face. "That will make things much easier. I have found over the years that the stupid ones are the hardest to interrogate. They get confused by the questions. They lose track of their thoughts. They tell lies and misinformation without even knowing it. The smart ones? You guys are easy as pie. All you smart ones are so used to hearing yourselves talk, and so used to correcting everyone over and over, that the truth just flows from between your lips like wine."

"That'd be some gross wine," I say as I stick my fingers down my throat. Maury is suddenly by my side and slaps my hand away from my face. "Ow."

"I'm glad you spit out what you did," Kelvin chuckles. "You would have been useless if you'd swallowed those three cookies. As it stands now, you should have ingested enough to be more than cooperative."

"What about the girl?" Maury asks.

"Touch her, and I'll rip your balls off and feed them to the first Z I see," I growl. The grin on Maury's face tells me I don't sound as threatening as I'd like. It might be the bazillion giggles that are lining up in my throat. Uh-oh, Jacey is seriously stoned out of his gourd.

For the record, I'm Jacey. I don't want any confusion there. We good?

"Yes, Jace, we are more than good," Kelvin says. He looks past me to Maury. "Take the girl to the women's quarters. Tell Jobeth to have Dr. Stenkler give her a full work up."

Maury looks towards the other two guards, and points his shotgun at the door. "Out."

He waits until they are gone. The mood in the trailer turns instantly and I see a change come over Reptile Jesus. He drops the "Jesus" act all the way, but holds onto the reptile portion of his personality with relish.

Mmmm, relish. I could totally go for a hot dog right now. Man, I miss hot dogs.

"Shut up," Maury says, and thumps me on the back of the head with a finger. I roll my head on my neck and look up at him as he turns his attention to Greta. "If Stenkler gives her a clean bill, then what?"

I may be whacked out on goofballs, but I can hear the implication in his voice.

"I think that depends on our new friend here," Kelvin says, reptile eyes back on me. "His behavior will determine the exact fate of his daughter. If he gives me the information I want, then she will be allowed to work in the Tomb along with the others. If he resists me, then I'll send word to ready her for marriage. I can see quite a few of our more than able bodied followers lining up to get a chance to woo this one."

"Don't you fucking touch her!" I shout, and jump to my feet. My leg cries out in pain, but the goofballs are having a nice numbing effect, so I ignore the agony and reach for Maury.

He probably gets in at least three, maybe four, punches before I even realize I'm getting the shit kicked out of me. But to my credit, I stay standing.

No, wait, that's not true. If I was standing then my face wouldn't be buried in this cheap Berber carpet that feels like sandpaper. What the fuck is up with that? Berber? Everyone knows that if you decorate with velour you have shag carpeting. That's just basic interior design, people.

"Damn, he never shuts up," Maury says as he stands over me. I know he's standing over me because I can see his boots about two inches from my face.

"I am hoping that is true," Kelvin says. "Take the girl, and clear out my trailers. I'll be in the center. Let everyone know I am in deep prayer with our new guest and could be absent all night long. I am not to be disturbed, Maury. We can't afford another Deirdre issue. It took me two weeks to smooth that out with the followers."

"Don't worry, I'll make sure you have all the time you need," Maury says. "Come on."

"No! You fucking let go of me!" Greta screams. "Daddy!"

"Daddy's coming, sweetheart!" I shout into the carpet, unable to even pick my cheek up from the scratchy floor covering. "I'm so gonna fuck these bitches up! You hear that, bitches? Gonna fuck you up! Get ready for the fucking up of your lives!"

"Better you than me, Kelvin," Maury says as he taps me in the temple with the toe of his boot. "I don't think I could listen to this idiot all night."

"We all have our roles, Maury," Kelvin says. "Yours is the dutiful soldier while mine is the savior of the new world."

"Yeah, we need to really talk about that dynamic at some point," Maury laughs. "I think you're getting the better deal."

"Except for the celibacy thing," Kelvin sighs. "How'd I rope myself into that one?"

"The messiah never took a wife, Kelvin," Maury laughs again. "You chose the role, not me."

"Yeah, yeah, I know," Kelvin replies. "Get the girl out of here and over to Stenkler. No hurry to get me the health report until the morning. I'll be busy, and I'm sure she could use a good night's rest. Just make sure Jobeth keeps her from wandering."

"The holy restraints?" Maury asks.

"That should do it," Kelvin replies.

"DADDY!" Greta screams, then her voice is muffled as either Maury stuffs a rag in her mouth, or covers it with his hand. I have no idea since I really can't move. Seriously, I'm totally paralyzed.

I hear the trailer door open, and the cold wind smacks me in the face, then it's gone. And so is my daughter.

"I am so going to fucking kill you," I say.

Kelvin kneels down so I can see his face. The messiah act is completely gone now. All I see is the look of a determined man. And trained professional. I've been around enough sketchy military types to know that look. I am beginning to think he isn't some actor from the local community college drama program. Oh, he's an actor alright, but not the spotlight type.

I am so fucked.

"Not if you are cooperative. Which, considering your inability to filter your thoughts, is a very likely possibility," Kelvin laughs as he reaches out and touches my nose. "Can you feel that?"

"Yeah," I say.

He taps my shoulder, or I think he does. I can't feel that.

"Good," Kelvin says. "Miracle stuff, I have to say. I developed the formula during my time at a rendition facility in Germany. They have some amazing chemists in Germany, Jace.

The government was more than willing to loan a couple to our country's cause. It took about a year to get the paralytic to anesthetic ratio right so subjects could still speak, but not be able to struggle. If you really concentrate you can wiggle your fingers and toes, but I would advise against it."

I ignore him and try to wiggle my fingers and toes. Pretty sure I bust a lung screaming.

"Hurts, doesn't it?" Kelvin says as he stands up. "This stuff just lights the nerves on fire if you try to fight against it. My advice is you don't fight, Jace. Stay calm, stay relaxed, and answer my questions when asked. This scenario could end up working out in your favor."

"Suck a donkey dick, Reptile Jesus," I snap.

Barely, like a far off thought, I feel my feet being lifted. Then the rough Berber carpet is scraping against my cheek, and I realize that Reptile Jesus is dragging me somewhere. I watch as velour covered piece of furniture after velour covered piece of furniture slides by. There's a pause as a door opens then I'm being dragged again.

My face is the last part of me through the door, so it's not until then that I realize that my velour and Berber carpet days are over. My cheek hits cold vinyl, and sort of sticks and stutters as I'm pulled into the center of a new room. The dragging stops and I watch, helpless, while Kelvin closes the door and locks it. From the amount of clicking and clacking I'd say there's more than one deadbolt on that door.

"You aren't going to touch me in my swimsuit area, are you?" I ask.

"No point," Kelvin says as he hooks his arms around my chest and under my armpits.

With one heave he has me up and falling into a chair. It's a dentist's chair. Or maybe an orthodontist's chair? How does one tell the difference?

"One doesn't," Kelvin replies. "And you're wrong about both. It's a barber's chair. Maury found it for me in a beauty school he scavenged from back in our early days."

"Was this before or after the Reptile Jesus gig?" I ask.

Kelvin straps my hand to one arm of the chair, then straps my legs down to the foot rest.

"It was after," Kelvin says. "And what is all this Reptile Jesus stuff, Jace? You have to let me in on how your bruised brain came up with that."

"You look like Jesus, and you act like a fucking snake," I reply. "Just without the warmth and cuddliness."

"Well, I've never been known for either of those," Kelvin laughs. "But I do work at it. The followers wouldn't stick around if they thought I was the cold-blooded mercenary that I am. They like to think I'm an actor from Chicago that found the Lord, left my wicked ways behind, and am now here to do His bidding. People are suckers for the Arts."

"So, this whole messiah act really is just some con?" I ask. "You don't actually believe God is working directly through you, right?"

"Oh, no, Jace," Kelvin says as he pats me on the cheek, then is lost from my sight. "My background story is the con, my belief is not."

I can hear the sound of metal on metal, and what little feeling I do have is focused in my balls wanting to scrunch up and hide near my spleen. Kelvin returns to my view, wheeling the proverbial tool laden torture cart (that's a proverb, right?). There's a single, bare lightbulb above me, and the light glints off a plethora of things, most of them dental in nature, but a few just good old hardware from Home Depot.

"I am the instrument of God," Kelvin continues as he picks up each tool and shows them to me, one by one. "I have always been a true believer, ever since I was a small boy and my mother took me to church every Wednesday and Sunday. I became who I am to fight the Muslim heathens, and wipe them from the Earth. My superiors never knew my true intent, which is good or they would have removed me from my duties and put me on a desk job. But God has always known. And he has guided me on my righteous path."

Kelvin's hand hesitates over a good, ol' X-ACTO knife. Looks like we're starting with a classic.

"Is it safe?" Kelvin chuckles.

I laugh. Dammit! I'm a sucker for Marathon Man humor.

"It is not safe!" I reply. "It is not safe!"

"You aren't going to pee yourself, are you Jace?" Kelvin asks as he sets the blade back on the cart, pushes the cart aside, and pulls up a stool right next to my head. "If you need to pee, please tell me. I can insert a catheter." He looks down at my crotch. "In fact, I may just go ahead and do that. You think you might defecate? I have adult diapers ready."

"You have got to be shitting me," I say. "Are you serious?"

"Serious as Job," Kelvin says.

"Is that even a thing?" I ask. "Being serious like Job?"

"If you're Job," Kelvin replies, and gets up from his stool. "Now, where is the catheter? Oh, here it is. Time to get to work." Oh, fuck me. Fuck me!

CHAPTER SIX

"You know, as torture sessions go, this really isn't so bad," I say to Kelvin after he sets the cup of water aside he's just given me. There's been a lot of talking, so my throat is a hair parched. "It's more like a really shitty and uncomfortable conversation."

"That's because you are a talker, Jace," Kelvin says. "If you weren't, I'd have removed several of your toes by now and shown them to you."

"Why show them to me?" I ask. "I think just the removing them would be motivation enough."

"Because of the paralytic and pain killers in my cocktail," Kelvin says. "You wouldn't feel the removal, so showing them to you would be the motivation."

"You know, you could totally show someone somebody else's toes if you wanted to," I suggest. "Never actually cut off your subject's toes, then later show him his intact feet. That's when you start cutting. Really bring the fucked up mind fuckery. Talk about motivation."

"I think you missed your calling, Jace," Kelvin chuckles. "You would be an excellent interrogation specialist."

"Nah, I'm more a generalist," I reply. "I hate specializing in anything. I get bored too easily."

"Well, I have to say our conversation so far has been anything but boring," Kelvin says, and picks up a pad of paper. He flips through a couple of pages, then looks me in the eye, all snakey snake and shit. "Okay, so you killed Mondello, and then tried to rebuild Asheville, correct? That's when your troubles with Camille Thornberg and the Consortium really began, is that it?"

"Yeah, I guess," I say. "But I think those troubles were always there. I mean Vance was sort of in her employ. Or some business partner. I'm not quite sure what was going on with their business relationship, but I know he was connected."

"True enough," Kelvin says.

I catch the confidence in his voice.

"Uh, did you know Vance?" I ask.

Kelvin composes himself nicely, but I can tell my question has rattled him. I think he let his guard down for a second, and I caught him in it.

"I haven't ever heard of the man until you told me about him," Kelvin replies. "He sounds like he was a small player. I didn't mix in circles with small players."

"You don't now, either," I say. "You got the direct hook up to God, yo. Ain't nothin' small in that, am I right? High five!"

"You can't lift your hand to high five," Kelvin says.

"Do it for me, will ya?" I ask. "Humor a torture subject, man."

Kelvin stares at me for a second, then unstraps my hand and gives me a high five. He lets my arm flop back on the armrest, and straps me down again.

"You are such an interesting person, Jace," Kelvin says. "I may keep you in here forever just to study that brain of yours. I have seen people deflect before, but you are extraordinary. It's not just your brain damage that causes you to make light of everything traumatic, I honestly think you are wired this way."

"Copper and gold, baby," I smile.

"What?" Kelvin asks, honestly puzzled.

"My wiring," I say. "It's copper and gold. I'm filled with precious metals, that's why everyone keeps me around. I got the pimped out brain."

"Incredible," Kelvin says, and flips a couple more pages on his pad. "But I think we need to get back to business. Tell me what you know about Camille Thornberg."

"Not a lot really," I say. "She was some rich bitch pre-Z, and is now some rich bitch post-Z."

"Z," Kelvin says. "Just Z. Post-Z would mean after the undead have gone away. I don't think that's likely to happen anytime soon."

"I mean, like post-Z-Day," I respond. "But it's faster to say post-Z than post-Z-Day. That's just awkward. And life is too short to worry about awkward phrasing. We are only given so many days on Earth, Reptile Jesus. Or didn't your big Daddy in the Sky tell you that? Come on, man, if you're gonna have the Batphone to God then you should use it more often and get the details. Awkward phrasing is out, just like grammar Nazis. The world has no need, man. No need."

"Yes, well, we'll agree to disagree," Kelvin says.

"See! That phrase right there," I state. "There is no need to say we are agreeing to disagree. There is no need to agree to that. We can just disagree, and leave it as it is. When people disagree about disagreeing, then that's called a fight, and by that time things are way too far to fix. So, one should always assume that agreement is implied with a disagreement unless it devolves into an honest to goodness throw down. It's that simple."

"I don't believe there is anything simple when it comes to your way of thinking, Jace," Kelvin says. "So let us get back to the subject of Camille Thornberg. Tell me what you know of her *post-Z*."

"Everything I know of her is post-Z, and thank you for using my term, because I had never heard of her pre-Z," I say.

"You had never heard of Camille Thornberg?" Kelvin asks.

"You sound suspicious," I say. "Why are you suspicious? Why the fuck would I have heard of Camille Thornberg?"

"The Thornbergs were once one of the richest families in this country," Kelvin answers. "They had power and influence like you couldn't believe."

"The Thornbergs," I laugh. "Wasn't that a miniseries in the eighties?"

"That was the *Thornbirds*," Kelvin says. "And stay on topic, please."

"If I had a nickel for every time someone told me to stay on topic," I sigh, "I'd have a fuckton of useless nickels. Who needs nickels in the apocalypse? That shit just weighs you down."

"Like this conversation," Kelvin mutters. He stands up and starts to pace back and forth. "I won't bore you with the details of Camille's influence. I will say that I am not surprised she is the head of the Consortium and already making a push to take over more than just the eastern region. She's probably gotten her grip on the South and is about to come after the Midwest. That is going to put a damper on my mission."

"By mission, you mean like the Blues Brothers, right?" I ask. "Your mission from God? Not some secret CIA mission?"

"Who said I worked for the CIA?" Kelvin asks.

"You did," I reply. "Or I think you did. Didn't you?"

"I never said that."

"Huh. Then I must have guessed it," I say. "Probably all that talk about rendition stations and advanced interrogation techniques. That's spook talk."

"Spook talk?" Kelvin laughs. "You are a colorful character, Jace. Let's move on from Camille. I am getting the feeling you know less than I do about her and her organization."

"Really? What do you know?" I ask, honestly interested. "Come on. Sharesies!"

"No," Kelvin states. "This is not a two-way conversation."

"Is it a three-way?" I ask. "Because I've never had one of those. They seem awkward. And a lot of work. Who wants to work like that?"

"Are you talking about conversation or sex?" Kelvin asks.

"I don't know," I say quietly. "My head hurts."

"Does it?" Kelvin asks, then looks at his watch. "That's good to know. I meant to ask you to instruct me as to when you started to feel any discomfort, especially in the form of headaches, but you are such a distracting person that I honestly forgot."

"If I had a nickel for every time someone said-."

"Please stop," Kelvin sighs. He picks up the X-ACTO blade and sticks the tip into my arm.

"Ow! Hey, motherfucker! That hurt!" I shout. Then I realize a lot of me hurts, not just my head, or where he poked me. "Looks like it's time for my medicine."

"No, Jace, it is not," Kelvin says. There's a sadness on his face like I've thoroughly disappointed him. "The formula works differently on every subject. Your system has burned through it faster than most. Unfortunately, I can't give you more without risking serious damage to your nervous system. You could fall into a coma, and end up a vegetable. Or you could have a major seizure and die. Neither of those scenarios helps me."

"So, it's just regular torture, then?" I ask. Using then at the end of my question makes me think of Stuart. I really hope he's okay. And Critter. I hope Critter is okay too.

"They are both fine, I am sure," Kelvin says. "I have instructed my men to let me know if they are overwhelmed in the pit. I doubt they will be if they have both survived in this world this long. The pit will be uncomfortable, but not insurmountable."

"Well, that's nice to hear," I respond. "So ... about that normal torture thing?"

Kelvin glances at his cart of shiny, scary tools. "I may have to go that direction, but I would rather not since pain is rarely a true motivator. Fear of loss is what really drives people. And I am fairly confident that I know what you fear to lose."

I stay quiet. Not even gonna come close to taking that bait.

"Carly Thornberg," Kelvin says, startling me. "Tell me what you know about her."

"Who?" I ask, but I can tell my delivery is less than convincing. "Is she related to Camille?"

"There it is," Kelvin says as he pushes the cart of tools over to the wall. He walks back to me with a particularly nasty looking pair of metal snips. "There is the defiance and deception I have been waiting for. You have been incredibly honest with me all night, almost a little too honest, if I may be honest as well. But now you have told me your very first bald-faced lie. Good. That means progress might actually be achieved."

"I don't know what you are talking about," I reply.

Kelvin sits down next to me and makes sure the metal snips are the center of my attention. "These can cut through sixteenth inch sheet metal without a problem. Can you guess what they can do to flesh and bone? While you ponder that question, let me be more specific. You see, Jace, I can use these to cut off all kinds of body parts. Fingers, toes, ears, of course. Those are extremities and easily accessible. But, a true artist, uses these for other body parts. The tongue, love handles on those that have them, breasts. Ah, breasts. Young, supple, vulnerable breasts."

"You motherfucking asshole," I growl. "Don't even think about it."

"Oh, I have been thinking about nothing else since I dragged you into this room," Kelvin says. "It took us a while, but we are finally where I thought we'd end up. Now, tell me about Carly Thornberg, or whatever you call her."

"Fuck you," I snap.

Kelvin taps me right between the eyes with the metal snips. "What do you call her, Jace? I won't ask again. Tell me the name she goes by, or your beautiful little girl loses her left breast in the morning. She will be stripped naked and made to stand for everyone in the compound to see. Then Maury will take these very same snips and slowly, carefully, agonizingly, cut off her breast. How old is she? Have her breasts even finished growing and forming yet? How sad for a girl to be mutilated like that before she even reaches womanhood."

I turn my head and puke. It's only bile and water, so it doesn't make much of a mess, but the act itself is quite the statement as to my mental state.

Kelvin stares at me, I stare at Kelvin. He gives the metal snips a quick squeeze and they pop open to show me just how sharp the blades are.

"Elsbeth," I say. "She goes by Elsbeth."

"Elsbeth? Really? Why is that?" Kelvin asks. "Is it because of Foster? Did that woman name her that?"

A cold chill runs up and down my spine, and I shudder suddenly.

"I can see you've met the woman," Kelvin laughs. "Did she give Carly her new name?"

"No," I say. "Some cannibal molester did. His name was Pa, and he brainwashed El into becoming like him. They hunted a whole bunch of survivors before I stumbled across them."

"Yet you survived," Kelvin nods. "You left that out of your earlier narrative. In fact, you left out Elsbeth altogether. I am guessing she had a lot more to do with your successes than you did. Any reason you didn't mention her?"

"I'm holding out for a hero?" I say. "Holding out for a hero that is larger than life?"

He presses the tip of the snips to my right eye. "Funny. But answer the question. I have no problem mutilating you, then mutilating your daughter. Oh, and did I forget to mention that I'd brand her a sinner, and that I would declare her presence to be an affront to God? Do you know what happens to pretty, teenage girls that are branded as such? All bets are off. My followers can do what they want with her without worrying about it being a sin. In their eyes, and in the eyes of God, she will deserve every moment of her humiliation and defilement."

"I was being serious," I say. "Elsbeth has an uncanny way of pulling my ass out of the fire. I didn't mention her because there is a distinct chance that she'll track me down and save me. Along with my daughter, Stuart, and Critter."

"And Rafe? Will he be saved as well?" Kelvin smiles. "Or is he the sacrifice in this chapter of your life? I have a sneaking suspicion that there are quite a few sacrifices along the path you have walked, Jace. Not that I see that as a bad thing. God asks for sacrifices all the time."

"You got that right, brother," I nod. "That God is all about his sacrifices. Sacrifice this and sacrifice that. In fact, I think what he really wants, more than anything in the world, is for you to take those metal snips and shove them as far up your nose as you can. Now that would be some sacrifice, am I right?"

"No, you are not," Kelvin says. "I know what God wants from me, and that idea is as far from the truth as you can get."

"When you say truth, do you mean with a big T or a little T? I only ask because it helps me know just how whackadoo you are. People that use the big T are kinda off the charts with the whackadooness, so-."

"Elsbeth," Kelvin interrupts. "What makes her special?"

"I don't know," I say. "I'm not a scientist. Kramer is the guy you want to talk to. He can give you the lowdown on Elsbeth and her sisters."

"Sisters?" Kelvin asks. "So you know about the other girls that were part of that program?"

Son of a bitch.

"Isn't exhaustion a wonderful thing?" Kelvin asks as he reaches between my legs. "It makes you sloppy. Sloppy enough that even the most guarded bits of intel start to come spilling out."

He yanks the catheter out of my dick, and I scream, scream, scream. Oh, do I scream.

"I'm going to let you leak on yourself for a couple minutes while I go freshen up and check in with Maury," Kelvin says. "I'll let you sit here and wonder if I am ordering him to start prepping your daughter or not. When I get back, I expect no more stalling and no more omissions. Is that clear, Jace?"

"Crystal," I croak as I feel warm piss wet the chair and pool around my ass.

"Good," Kelvin says. "Sit tight."

Yeah, I think I'll do that.

***

I drift in and out of consciousness as I wait for Reptile Jesus to return. I don't exactly sleep, since that really isn't possible when strapped to a barber's chair and sitting in your own piss. It's more like when you are watching TV, and you don't want to fall asleep, so you keep snapping awake every few seconds.

You know what I forgot to ask Reptile Jesus? Why he insisted on calling cookies biscuits. And why he had that lame British accent for a split second there. What the fuck was that all about? If the guy is CIA, then what was up with that?

Unless maybe he isn't CIA, and it's all some elaborate rouse. The fucker could totally be faking the whole not faking the actor thing. What if this guys is actually some Second City wannabe? Wouldn't that be the shit?

Except that doesn't make sense. He knows too much about the Consortium and Camille Thornberg. He knows about Ms. Foster and the sisters. I think he knows about Kramer, but I haven't confirmed that yet. Maybe that's where his whole line of questioning about Elsbeth was going. Maybe, just maybe, it's Kramer he's after.

Nah. Nobody wants that asshole. He might be a mad scientist, but after three seconds with the jerk everybody wants to fucking kill him. He's bigger slime than Reptile Jesus is.

Which means I have zero answers to any of my questions. I have plenty of piss, though. Not a problem in that department. I think I heard somewhere that when they remove catheters, the ureter stays expanded and you pretty much leak from your dick for a while. I'd like to know how long that while is, because this is really growing uncomfortable. Each time I shift I leak a little more.

It's been a great few days, huh? Shitting and puking and pissing. I really know how to party in the apocalypse.

The door opens, and Kelvin comes in. He looks tired and frustrated. I'm about to ask him some smart ass question when I see the metal snips in his hand. He tosses them on the cart, and the blood that coats the blades splatters across the rest of the shiny torture tools, instantly making them less than shiny. Kelvin just stands there and looks down at the cart, his eyes kind of glazed and far off.

"Uh, everything alright?" is what I want to ask, but I can't get the words to form. Strange, I know, since it's me, and I seem to have zero problem saying whatever comes to mind no matter what the moment may be. But those bloody snips. They freeze my throat, and I start to feel like it's hard to breathe.

Why are they coated in blood? Whose blood is it?

Dear God, please don't let it be…

Kelvin turns around and meets my eye. The look on my face must convey all the thoughts in my head because he rolls his eyes and takes a seat on the stool next to my chair.

"No, no, that's not your daughter's blood," Kelvin says. "One of my followers decided that now was the time to challenge my authority. Which means he was challenging God's authority. I couldn't allow that."

"Oh, thank fucking God," I say. "Uh, I mean, praise Jesus. Even Reptile Jesus."

"Shut up, Jace," Kelvin says. "I no longer have the patience for your mouth. Just stay quiet for a minute while I gather my thoughts and get myself centered and right with God, please."

Oh, crap. This guy just asked me to stay quiet. How the hell am I going to do that? It was easy when he was interrogating me because my obvious natural inclination is to blabber away. And the fact that my internal filter is shot to shit didn't make a damn bit of difference then. Now? Yeah, it makes a huge fucking bit of difference!

Please, please, please don't let me start talking out loud. Please.

I watch Kelvin closely, my eyes locked onto his face, looking for any sign that what is in my head is coming out of my mouth. But he doesn't even flinch, just sits there, his head hung, his eyes closed, as he 'centers' himself.

What does that even mean? Sure, I know all about yoga and meditation, but that's positive stuff. What does a religious crackpot like Reptile Jesus do when he needs to center himself? Picture burning lakes of fire? Think of pits of damned souls roasting in flames for all eternity?

"I think of a small meadow near where I grew up," Kelvin says. "And please don't call me a religious crackpot. That's disrespectful and will lead to my order to mutilate your daughter."

"Sorry," I say. "I didn't know that-."

"I do not care, Jace," Kelvin says. "Your neurological affliction is not my concern."

He looks up, and I know everything has changed. This next session isn't going to be a hearty chat like last time.

"Tell me about Elsbeth," he says. "Hold nothing back. If you do, I will know. If I know, then you pay. If you pay, your daughter pays. Then we start again. Are we understood, Jace?"

"Yes, sir," I reply. I don't know why I call him sir. It just slips out.

So, without hesitation or any sort of editing, I start in and tell him everything I know about Carly "Elsbeth" Thornberg. From the first moment I saw her in North Asheville, to the last time I saw her a few days ago before she went missing on the road. He gets it all. Not one small attempt at subterfuge or misinformation. He gets the real deal.

Yet, when I'm all done and watching him expectantly, he doesn't look pleased. He doesn't look anything. It's like the life and will has been drained out of him.

"That is quite the story," he says finally and stands up. He stretches and looks about the room as if it holds better secrets than the ones I just told him. "I was told you interacted with Cole on your journey back here."

"Cole?" I ask.

"The man that assaulted you on the RV," Kelvin says.

"Oh, right, that guy," I nod. "Yeah, we had an interaction. It was a bit one sided."

"Yes, that does sound like Cole," Kelvin says. "Or did." He glances at the bloody tools. "Nothing except eternal silence sounds like the man now. I hope he finds peace in the afterlife that he couldn't find in this one."

"You killed him?" I ask.

"I ended his existence on this plane," Kelvin says. "But his journey doesn't end yet. He is now a part of the pit, as are all that are deemed unworthy of a final death."

"Wait, he's in the pit now?" I ask. "As a zombie? You killed him and let him come back?"

"Only the truly righteous are allowed a final death," Kelvin says. "Cole was far from righteous."

"Yeah, but didn't you say that my friends are in the pit?" I snap. "Are you fucking telling me you killed them too?"

"No, Jace, they have not been killed," Kelvin says. "At least, not to my knowledge."

"Then I don't understand," I say. "How can you have zombies in the pit and also have my friends there too?"

"The pit is not some simple hole," Kelvin says. "It is one of those great mysteries that God likes to tease us with. Over millions of years, water seeped down into the mine, the Tomb, and carved out a place that is vast and terrifying. A great underground depression that threatens to collapse the entire mine structure. It's one reason this mine was shut down. The wrong use of the wrong machinery, a buildup and sudden release of gas, an engineer's miscalculation on drill depth. Any one of those things could have caused the mine to collapse into the pit."

"The mine can collapse into the pit? How fucking big is this pit?" I ask.

"Were you not listening? I said it was vast and terrifying," Kelvin frowns. "Listen up, Jace. I do not enjoy repeating myself."

"Sorry. My bad," I say quickly. "The place is vast and terrifying. Got it. So, if my friends work hard enough, they can avoid the Zs you've stuck down there with them, right? Is that what you are saying?"

"Yes, exactly," Kelvin replies. "Many people have been put in there to pay their penance, and then come out unscathed. There are nooks and crannies they can hide in. There are boulders and rock outcroppings. Pillars of stone they can climb. In fact, there are stones of all sizes everywhere. In the right hands, there are more than enough weapons at the ready."

"Oh, okay," I say. "Critter and Stuart are good with their hands. They know how to kill Zs. I'm sure they are fine."

"Yes, I'm sure they are," Kelvin sighs. "So, where were we?"

"I don't know," I say. "I just told you everything I know about Elsbeth. What else do you want to know?"

"Why the Stronghold?" he asks. "Why are you going there?"

"Because Kansas City is scorched, apparently," I reply. "Kramer says it doesn't exist anymore. Your guy Maury says it doesn't exist anymore. Same with St. Louis, but we had no intention of going there. We were just going around it."

"Why did you want to go to Kansas City?" he asks.

"We don't care where we go," I say. "We just needed to get out of Asheville because of the radiation, and because the Consortium was going to come for us. Kramer seems to think that Camille has control over the sisters. That is quite the motivation to get the fuck out of Dodge."

"Control? Like how?" Kelvin asks, and the depression seems to lift like a curtain. Suddenly, the old Reptile Jesus is back and staring right at me. "Tell me all you know about how to control the sisters."

Great. Here we go again.

So, I tell him. It's a much shorter conversation than what I told him about Elsbeth, mainly because I don't really know shit about the sisters. He figures that out in seconds, and the mood goes back to sad Reptile Jesus. This guy is all ups and downs. Kinda getting tired of it. I miss the crazies like Vance who was all bluster and confidence. Or Mondello. That guy had a big enough ego to actually think he could be President and everyone would go along with it. Hell, I'm sure Camille Thornberg doesn't go from happy sappy to grumbly bumbly in point zero one seconds like this guy. Psychopaths rarely do.

Which is what is troubling me. This guy is obviously psycho, but is he a psychopath? I don't know. I can't tell. True psychopaths don't tend towards these types of manic/depression mood swings. They are so narcissistically self-centered that this kind of back and forth depression is beneath them. That's for regular people. For victims.

"Yes, it is," Kelvin says quietly. "Regular people. Am I not a regular person, Jace? Just a man trying to be right with God? A man called upon to do the impossible? To be the Word of God on Earth? I believe you would feel the weight of all Creation if you had the burden on your shoulders that I have on mine."

"I'm missing an arm, so that burden would be even harder for me," I say. "Trust me on that one."

"Your jokes are sad, Jace," Kelvin says as he places a hand on my forehead. It's cold against my hot and clammy skin. "They are a pitiful attempt to ward off the inevitable."

"Which is?" I ask. "Death? I don't joke to ward off death, dude. I joke because I want to live."

"Same thing, Jace," Kelvin sighs. "Same thing."

"Hardly," I snap. "One is running away, while the other is walking towards. I've never been the running away type. Well, unless I'm running from Zs. Or cannies. Or crazies. Or soldiers. Okay, okay, I run away from lots of things. But not metaphorically. Metaphorically I run towards stuff. Life, love, family, friends, the sheer will to exist."

"The sheer will to exist," Kelvin laughs. "That is not what God wants from us, Jace. He wants us to bring back Eden. He wants us to live in His grace and light. Just existing is for the wicked and unjust. But, in talking with you, Jace, I see that is exactly the man you are—wicked and unjust."

"Sticks and stones, brother," I reply. "Sticks and stones. And trust me, I'm not wicked. I'm pretty fucking boring."

"Not very convincing when you curse, Jace," Kelvin says. He looks down at the torture tools then picks up what looks like an ice pick, but way sharper than any ice pick I've ever seen. More like a diamond pick with that fucking point. "If you cannot see God's intentions for you, then what is the point of seeing at all?"

"Whoa there, Hoss," I cry. "I can see God's intentions! I totally see them! He's intentioning all over me, dude!"

"I don't think so, Jace," Kelvin sighs again. "I don't think so."

He pulls up his stool and leans in close. I start to thrash about, but the dope in my system is still working enough that all I do is twitch a bunch. But I know it's worn off to the point where I'll feel that ice pick's point. Too many points! TOO MANY POINTS!

"Hush," Kelvin cringes as my words echo in the dark room. "It'll be over before you know it."

The ice pick starts moving in slowly, deliberately, as Kelvin keeps his hand steady and calm. I think he's done this before. The little light in this room glints off the metal of the pick, and I realize that glint is the last thing my right eye will ever see. Fuck me.

The ice pick is less than a millimeter from my cornea when a loud knock at the door makes me scream. Okay, I was already screaming, I'll admit that. The knock really just turns my scream into a startled squawk. Kelvin hesitates as another knock comes, even louder. He rolls his eyes, like this is some joke between us. It's not. Not a joke. I know jokes, as we have established, and this is not one of those.

"What?" Kelvin calls over his shoulder as he leans away from me, taking that ice pick with him.

I stop screaming. It's the courteous thing to do when someone removes an ice pick from your cornea.

The door opens slowly, and a man peeks in.

"Where's Maury?" Kelvin snaps. "He should be coming to me, not you."

"Sorry, Kelvin," the man replies, his eyes going to the ice pick in Kelvin's hand. "I, uh, well, Maury sent me."

"For a specific reason, I assume," Kelvin says.

"Yes, exactly," the man nods. "The storm is about to hit us hard. The snow is coming down fast, and the wind is picking up. Maury suggests we all seek shelter in the Tomb for the night until we know how bad it is. He's moving supplies in there now. Most of the women are inside." The man's eyes finally leave the ice pick and meet mine. "His daughter is still with Dr. Stenkler. Maury wants to know if she should stay up top or if he can move her as well."

"He can move her," Kelvin says. "Is the storm really that bad?"

"Yes, Kelvin, it is," the man replies. "I've lived around here my whole life. I don't think I've ever seen it look this bad. We could be down in the Tomb for a couple days."

"Well, then, thank Maury for me, and tell him to plan accordingly," Kelvin says as he sets the ice pick on the cart. "Also tell him I will need some men to help transport Jace here to the pit."

"Oh, you so suck," I say. "Sending a one armed man into the pit? You just can't play fair, can you?"

"There is nothing fair about our destiny, Jace," Kelvin says. "Fair is a concept created by man to argue against the Will of God."

"Tell that to a two year old," I say.

"With you, Jace, I think I may be," Kelvin says.

"Funny," I smirk.

"I'm not joking," Kelvin says. "You are a child, Jace. A spoiled child that refuses to listen to the Father."

"I also hate broccoli," I reply.

"Do you?" Kelvin asks.

"Uh ... no, not really," I respond. "That was a joke."

"In so many ways," he says, which makes no sense to me.

Kelvin looks at the man at the door. "Anything else, Jeffrey?"

"No, Kelvin," the man says, and ducks out of the room pretty fucking fast.

"I can't put my finger on that one," Kelvin says. "He has been around for as long as I can remember, but has never warmed up to me. Too much fear, and not enough faith."

"Kids, man," I reply.

"Shut up, Jace," he grumbles. "Our time is done, and your usefulness is at its end. I'll place you in the pit, and you can decide your own fate, although we both know it is up to Him and not you."

"Again, I'm going to have to call dick move on sending a one armed man into a pit filled with zombies," I say. "Bad form, sir, bad form."

"Perhaps," Kelvin shrugs. "But you may get lucky and bump into your friends down there. I have a feeling your strange brand of luck might shine in that darkness."

His last few words echo in my mind, but I can't quite grasp why. We just stay as we are, him sulking, me trying to not freak out. Then a sudden realization slams into my brain, and I gasp so loudly that Kelvin jumps a little.

"Dear Lord, what is wrong with you?" Kelvin asks, taking a step back. "You are truly troubled."

"You said my light may shine in the darkness," I say. "Exactly how dark are we talking about when we talk about this darkness you talk about?"

"You do ramble so," Kelvin says. Then that Reptile Jesus smile comes back with a vengeance. "But, to answer your question, I am talking about total darkness. It is a coal mine, after all. And I see no reason on wasting energy on lighting a place where the unjust are sent to contemplate their actions and behavior. That would not be a good use of resources."

"Son of a bitch," I say. "How the hell can anyone fight Zs if they can't see them?"

"People figure it out," Kelvin says. "Many do survive."

"Many?"

"Well, perhaps not many. More like some," Kelvin replies. "A few. A handful. Now and then."

"Now and then," I whisper. "Awesome."

"Being in the presence of God's plan is always awesome, Jace," Kelvin nods, that Reptile Jesus smile like a blinding strobe light of assholeness. "As you shall see very soon."

***

Fucking A, it's motherfucking cold! Holy shitballs, people! I thought I knew cold, but when a couple of Maury's goons yank me from Kelvin's holy cluster of anointed trailers, I fucking learn what cold really is. Shit fuck!

The wonder dope has my muscles all wobbly, so I can't really walk on my own, and since Maury's men won't give me a piggyback ride, I'm sort of dragged along between the two guys. The snow is several inches thick from the first storm, and is coming down so hard and fast that it's piling up as we cross the compound towards the mouth of the Tomb. I have snow in my boots and it sucks.

"You ever fought biters in the dark?" one of the men asks.

"Sure" I reply from between chattering teeth. "Not pitch dark, but I've had more than my fair share of midnight encounters with Zs."

"This ain't no full moon fight, mister," the other man says. "You can't see your hand in front of your face down there once the lights are turned off."

"Well, I only have the one hand," I say.

"What's that got to do with it?" the first man asks.

"I have half the chance of seeing a hand when I only have one," I say.

"That's not right," the other replies. "It doesn't matter how many hands you have."

"Really? Oh, okay, then I should be able to see just fine," I chuckle. "Thanks, guys. Good talk."

"What the hell are you babbling about?" the second man asks. "We just told you that you won't be able to see a thing once the lights go out."

"Right, sorry, I'm a little confused," I respond.

"Yeah you are," the first man says. "You won't be confused when the biters get ya, though. You'll be dead."

"Or undead," the second man says. "They only eat ya until you die, then they walk away and let you comeback as one of them."

"How nice of them," I say. "Those Zs are so gracious. But instead of walking away, they should work on maybe a gift basket or welcome sign. I have been around this apocalypse since the beginning, and I have to say that the Zs' social skills are sorely lacking. It's common courtesy to do a little something for newbies. A friendly note on a plate of cookies, or even just a big smile and a pat on the back. I'll see what I can do when I get down there. This could be good for everyone involved."

"This guy has lost his fucking mind," the first man says.

"Hey, no cursing," the second man says. "It's foul and goes against God."

"Oh, don't give me that crap," the first man says. "You know Kelvin is just playin' us, right? Not that I care. We get a warm bed, plenty of food, and a little slice of sweetness when we're good. Better than that dead end job I had before the biters came along."

The second man stops, forcing us all to stop, and looks past me at the first man. I wouldn't mind if they addressed each other. That way I could have a couple names to use instead of "first man" and "second man," but, alas, they do not let me in on their monikers.

"Shut up," the second man says to me before turning his attention back to the first. "You know I should report you to Maury for saying that, right?"

"What? You're buying Kelvin's Voice of God crap?" the first man asks.

"I am not buying anything," the second man says. "I am just receiving the truth from a man that has shown us the way in this wicked world."

"A thesaurus is what you guys need," I say. "You all keep using the word wicked like it's the only one available. There are plenty of other words that mean the same thing-."

"Shut up," both men say.

I do. Mostly because it is becoming hard to talk while my teeth chatter. I wouldn't mind if they started walking again, even if it means getting closer to my time in the pit. But the pit sounds like a warm blanket compared to this motherfucking cold snow that is all down my back and in my pants. Did I mention I no longer have my heavy coat? Nope. That puppy is long gone.

"Shut up!" the second man shouts, and clocks me in the face with his elbow.

"You weren't supposed to hit him," the first man says. "Maury said not to hit him. I'll keep quiet on that if you keep quiet on what I said."

"There is no keeping quiet in the eyes of God," the second man says. "But I won't tell Maury. Your faith is between you and the heavenly Father."

"Are you Mormon?" I ask.

"What?" the second man responds. "Mormon?"

"Yeah, they call God the Heavenly Father," I say. "That's like their official handle for Him and shit."

"I'm not Mormon," the second man replies. "I'm Methodist."

"That's totally not the same thing," I say.

"No, it's not," the second man says, and starts walking again. Yay for movement!

The first man falls in step, and the mouth of the Tomb gets bigger and bigger as we get closer and closer. Soon it looms over us, and then we are swallowed whole, like slimy oysters down a yuppie's throat.

No, wait, I don't like that analogy.

Soon we are swallowed whole, like tadpoles in a snapping turtle's jaws.

Nope, that one sucks too.

Soon we are swallowed whole like krill in a baleen whale's, uh, baleen. Is that what you'd call that? Baleen? Or is there a name for the filter stuff those whales have? There has to be. No way it would just be called baleen. Maybe it is. I don't know, really. I'll need to look that up when-.

"SHUT UP!" the two men roar, and I get an elbow from each of them.

So, we get inside the Tomb, and it is all I have ever dreamed it would be. Black and dirty and dark and miserable. Woo-fucking-hoo. Can't wait to see the pit.

CHAPTER SEVEN

I could have totally waited to see the pit.

No, seriously, I could have waited my whole life to see it. Or, better yet, I could have gone my whole life without seeing it. That's the best scenario, right there. Just not seeing the pit.

Once inside the Tomb, the men aren't as gentle as when we were out in the feet deep snow and freezing wind. I'm made to stand on my own, which takes pretty much all of my willpower, and navigate the swirling bustle of activity that is the main entrance to the Tomb.

People are scurrying about left and right, carrying boxes and mattresses, bags of food, and stacks of blankets. Men are shouting at women to hustle, and the women are just taking it, keeping their heads down, going about their work with deep frowns on their faces, and their eyes averted. More than a few of the women keep to the sides of the mine, making sure there is plenty of room between them and the men. I don't blame them; I can see how the men are leering at them.

You see, this is what happens when you separate the genders, man. The men get all worked up, and then as soon as they are around the ladies all they do is think with their dicks. Like that guy there. He's totally staring at that young woman in the ugly white sweatshirt with cats all over it. He might as well just whip out his wang and announce he wants to put it in her.

Hold on, I know that young woman.

"GRETA!" I shout, and her head goes from being bowed to snapping upright, her eyes searching for me in the throng. "GRETA!"

For one split second, Greta almost drops the bundle of towels in her arms, and rushes at me. Her left foot is moving forward, and I can see the tension in her shoulders start to give. But the sudden attention my yells bring on us means that pretty much everyone is watching to see what we'll do.

What I do is fall flat on my face as I catch a shotgun butt to the middle of my back. What Greta does is control herself and move closer to a group of women that are closest to the mine wall. She burrows between them, and they close ranks quickly, whether to shield her from her wicked, wicked father that is bleeding from a gash on his forehead (I'm talking about me) or to shield her from the increasing amount of attention she's getting from some of the men. Either way, I am almost grateful for that little slice of protectiveness, even if it means absolutely nothing in the grand scheme of this crazy place.

"Get your ass up," the first man says as he kicks me in the ass.

"That's not helping," I say as I try to push up with my arm, but my muscles just don't want to behave. Reptile Jesus's whacky juice is still doing a number on me.

"Get up," the second man says. "Get up, or we make you get up."

"Uh, you guys making me get up might speed this along," I say as I kind of scooch my knees under me so my ass is in the air. Only problem is it makes me dizzy, and I end up with my forehead pressed against the coal black ground. And that's not just a description, that's the truth. My forehead is actually on ground that is truly coal black. Funky. I thought that color only existed in boxes of crayons.

"The way I'm going to make you get up is by going over to that new girl and taking her right in front of you," the first man says. "Is she your daughter? Is that it? She's pretty. Kelvin hasn't promised her to anyone yet, has he? I should probably try her out and let the other guys know what they're in for. It'll be good for the rest of the women to see. They need reminding about who is in charge here. It sure ain't them."

"Go fuck yourself instead," I say. "The whole post-apocalyptic rapey thing is old, man. Did all you crazy fucks forget how to masturbate or something? Just whack off, and let the ladies alone, okay? None of them want your hairy, little wieners anywhere near them. I bet you haven't washed down there in like months. You probably smell like old bologna that's been set out in the sun. Hey, that's it! I'll call you Oscar and your buddy here I'll call Meyer! I love it when inspiration hits! Now the bologna dicks have two names!"

Then I focus all my strength into my right leg and kick back as hard as I can. Meyer cries out as my boot nails him right in the shin. Then Oscar's boot nails me in the ribs, and I'm tumbling over on my side.

I look about quickly, and see the women pulling Greta away from the violence as fast as possible. There's a young woman at my daughter's side that looks familiar, but I can't quite place her. Is she one of ours? Are there more of the Asheville convoy folk here than just Critter and Stuart? That would be good and bad. Good, because misery loves company. Bad, because that means I have to figure out how to save more people than just Greta, Stuart, and Critter.

"You ain't saving shit, asshole. Her name is Tara," Oscar says as he grabs me by the neck and yanks me up on my feet. Oh, right, Tara. The tea and biscuits girl. "You're going to the pit and that's that, motherfucker."

There are quite a few gasps from the people around us, but no one vocally objects to Oscar's cursing. That's probably wise since the guy is just a hair ticked off at the moment.

So, the pit. Let's move right along to that fun hole of funny fun fun.

Oscar single handedly carries, drags, pushes, shoves, and kicks my ass through the winding tunnels of the Tomb and down to a weird, ramshackle set of stairs. The stairs just sort of show up in the side of one of the tunnels. They twist and turn in on themselves as they take us down deeper into the Tomb. Before I know it, the world is plunged into pure blackness. A blackness I have never experienced before. Oscar and Meyer weren't kidding about that.

We finally stop, and Oscar shoves me against the wall, his hand clenching my throat in a way that says, "Move, and I snap your fucking neck, Chatty Kathy."

"What the fuck are you talking about?" Oscar growls. "I'm the one that tells you not to move, you stupid idiot."

"Ignore me," I say.

"That's the plan," Oscar says as suddenly I'm blinded by light so bright I think I feel my skin start to photosynthesize. Wouldn't that be a trick?

After a few blinks, I'm able to see that the pit is exactly as Kelvin described it. It's this vast depression in the floor of the mine that goes on forever. There are boulders and stone columns, piles of various sized rocks, and more than a few Zs. Hell, why be modest? There are a fuck ton of Zs!

"Kelvin wants to give you a shot at surviving," Oscar says. "I'd rather see you get your face eaten off right now. Guess which option you get?"

"While your scenario is so welcoming, I'm hoping for Kelvin's," I say. "A shot is way better than getting my face eaten off. But that's just me. I can't speak for everyone you toss down here."

"Yeah, you're getting your shot." Oscar grins, then punches me in my bad leg.

That's an official ow, right there. Like some serious, serious ow. In fact, the ow is best expressed with this poem: MOTHERFUCKING ASSHOLE PRICK FUCKING DICK FUCKER BITCH TURD NICKEL!"

I'm rather proud of ending with turd nickel. That's creativity, bitches!

"Shut the fuck up," Oscar yells as he shoves me off the steps' landing and into the pit proper.

Needless to say, the Zs take a liking to my presence, and all come to greet me with open arms. And open mouths. Open mouths that drip gooey gunks and stuffs.

I try to scurry back from them, but between the Reptile Jesus cocktail, which is still hanging on tight, and the ow in my leg, I'm not doing so well with the scurrying.

Not that I have to.

The pit gets really fucking warm, really fucking fast, as a jet of fire roars above me and streams down on the approaching Zs. I look up, and see Oscar with a flamethrower attached to a large barrel, tucked away in the corner of the stairs' landing. He works that hot magic back and forth, back and forth, until only a couple of Zs are left standing. Those two just kind of bump up against each other as hot bits of dead flesh drip from their bodies.

Good times.

I can see a few more Zs stumble out of the darkness, drawn by the action, noise, and amazing aroma of cooked Z, but Oscar doesn't bother with them. He just sets the flamethrower aside, and glares down at me.

"That's your head start, asshole," he says, standing at least six feet above me. "Better get your gimp ass up and use it. Those new biters are gonna be all riled up by the time they get to you. And once the others stop burning, it'll be darker than a witch's colon in here."

"Is that a thing?" I ask. "A witch's colon? I haven't heard that one before. Oh, and I doubt it's a good idea to use a flamethrower in a coal mine. Coal burns, ya know."

Oscar just shakes his head, glances at the moaning, shambling Zs coming my way, then slams a gate closed on the landing, pretty much blocking any chance I might have of climbing out. He looks down at me and flips me off, then turns, and is gone from my sight. I guess setting the mine on fire really isn't much of a concern for him. Oh well.

"I'll miss you, bologna man!" I call after him. "Don't forget me! I won't ever forget you!"

Okay, well I'm sure glad he's gone. He was such a fucking bummer, right?

Then the lights go out, and all I'm left with are burning Z corpses to see by. I kinda wish Oscar was back now. I'd call for him, since I have no pride, but that would just bring more Zs. And I have plenty to deal with as it is.

Okay, Jace, time to get up off your ass, and get to work.

I get up off my ass. No, I don't. I do try, though. Oh, how I try.

One arm, bad leg, no weapon, and hopped up on goofballs is not how you want to be when thrust into a pit where there seems to be an endless supply of hungry Zs coming out of the dark. Add the oppressive stench of the still smoldering Zs, and it just keeps getting better.

You can do this, Jace. You can so fucking do this. You've been in worse situations. You've been captured by cannies. Stuck in a dump truck with Zs crashing through the window. Chased by motorcycle crazies (oooh, how I hate motorcycle crazies!). Nearly blown up, lost an arm, again with the captured by cannies, made to run some psycho gauntlet. Oh, and I can't forget the Whispering Pines HOA. That was probably the worst of the apocalyptic experiences. Zs, cannies, and crazies are one thing, but I draw the line at bureaucrats.

I get my one hand under me and push, which gets me to my knees. Okay, knees are good. I push again and favor my good leg, and actually get upright. If you count hunched over and gasping for breath because of the daggers of fun shooting through my bad leg. I count it. They're almost the same thing.

I can hear more Zs coming. The fires still flickering from the Z corpses cast shadows across the infinite black of the pit's walls behind me. It's like shadow puppet theatre, just with things that want to eat my face. And my guts. And my legs. And my ass. Okay, they want to eat all of me. But who can blame them?

I'm one tasty Jace.

So ... the Zs.

I straighten up and clench my teeth against the pain. First thing to do is try to maintain my light. I hobble over to one of the Zs that's been burned down to almost nothing, and wrench off a leg. With the right amount of twisting and force with my good leg, I'm able to get the blackened femur free. I snag some strips of cloth from a different Z, rub those in bubbling fat from a whole other Z right next to it, wrap the strips around the femur, and stick it into the flames of yet another Z.

Zs are our country's greatest resource! And they're renewable!

The Zs moan and groan, and I realize I've been talking out loud again. Not good when dealing with flesh-eaters attracted by sound.

First thing accomplished (Z-fat torch), now for the second thing. A weapon!

One problem: I only have one hand. Gonna be hard to carry the torch and wield a weapon. Some might say impossible. I would be one of the some that says impossible. Shit, I can't hold a book and wipe my ass at the same time when I go to the crapper, how the fuck can I carry a torch and fight off Zs?

So I scrap the second part of my plan, and learn to be happy with the first part. At least I'll see the Zs coming before they overwhelm me and devour my succulent, supple, oh so delicious innards.

What? It's my story so I'm gonna sell myself. No one wants to hear about a guy that tastes like one of those savory Jell-O molds with celery and green olives in it. Yuck.

I raise my torch and limp my way to the right, hoping to flank the oncoming undead. But after a few dozen yards I realize that they don't call this place the pit for nothing. I'm not reaching a side wall. I keep going and going and going. Still no side wall, just more of that inky black darkness.

Now, for the silver lining. The Zs aren't gaining on me. I know they can see my light, which attracts them, but not as much as sound, yet they don't seem to be in a hurry. They just shamble along, taking a nice, leisurely stroll through a coal mine. No worries, no hurries. This is good.

I clench my teeth as my foot hits a large rock, and pain reverberates up and down my bad leg like a cymbal crash from a middle school band. Middle school band parents will understand that reference. It's painful. Trust me.

The torch keeps burning, but I know it's gonna give at some point. Little drops of Z-fat follow behind me like the Devil's breadcrumbs. I'm not exactly covering my trail as I go. But I am hoping I'll find one of those outcroppings Reptile Jesus talked about. If I can scramble up onto one of those, then I can take a second and figure out exactly what my situation is.

(Spoiler alert: my situation is Grade A fuck-a-rooni.)

Hey, what's that?

I stop for a second and hold my torch out ahead of me. Hmmm, could that be more Zs? Why, yes, it is more Zs! Lucky fucking me!

Zs in front of me, Zs behind of me, and I'm stuck in the middle with no idea where I should go. I turn and face the ebony expanse of unknown that is the great vastness of the pit. I can't go back, I can't go forward, so I guess I'll just have to go deep (that's what she said).

One step. Two steps. Three, four, five, and I'm off, heading straight into the middle of the pit. No clue how far across it is, or if there will be anything except for Zs, and possibly old bones. I'm sure there have got to be old bones everywhere. I doubt they send a janitor down to clean up after the less fortunate folks that don't make it out. Or maybe they do. I wouldn't put anything past Reptile Jesus and his culty goodness. That guy will surprise ya.

Even at my limping speed, I get ahead of the Zs hankering for my tasty yum yums. After a few near falls, I figure out a weird balance between looking where I'm walking, and staring straight ahead into the nothing. I have to watch out for the stray rocks, chunks of coal, and random holes in the ground, but I also can't just look at my feet because every once in a while I come across the stray Z. Not sure why, but the farther I go into the center of the pit (I assume I'm going towards the center) the fewer Zs I find.

Maybe the Zs have learned to stay close to the stairs because that's where the food is. Or maybe most of them do that wandering herd thing that Zs like to do, and end up bunching up by the wall because they can't go any farther. That would explain why some were so close, and I ran into others while moving parallel with the wall.

None of it explains why they are moving so slowly. Sure, up on the surface they are getting faster, but down here in the dark they are slowing down. I mean, it's not like light is the factor, right? That would be like the Zs have started to gain energy from the sun or something. Wouldn't that be the shit? Kryptonian zombies, strengthened by our yellow sun! Oh, joy!

Nah, couldn't be.

Kramer hinted that maybe the Consortium had been fucking with whatever the cause was that started all this. That's probably why the Zs up top are getting faster. Better living through chemicals!

I stop as my words echo through the pit. Fuck, I have got to be more quiet.

A couple Zs shamble towards me, and I move to the side while trying to watch my footing and look out for more Zs. I don't quite juggle the task correctly, and my foot hits a small hole, sending me slamming into the ground. My trusty forehead hits the dirt, because that's what my forehead likes to do, and the cut that had finally stopped bleeding starts up again.

Of course, the Zs smell the blood, and they groan and hiss, their rotten mouths opening wide, ready to get their snack on. The torch is still lit, since I saved that instead of saving my forehead, and I swing it at them as I try to scramble back to my feet. They both lunge at me, and I swing again, catching one of them across the legs where an old, ancient skirt still clings to the thing's desiccated skin. That skirt lights up like an ad-man after a six-martini lunch, and in a flash (literally) there's a lot more light as the Jack O' Z starts stumbling about this way and that. It bumps into the other Z, and the threadbare shirt that one still wears goes up as well.

This does not mean that I am out of the woods. Far from it. The flaming Zs get used to their new heated existence, and remember that lunch is right ahead. They each turn, their skin melting and dripping, and open their mouths wide for one hell of a hissing duet. I'm still not on my feet since the one arm thing really can be a handicap, no matter what the after school specials tell you.

I'm doing this scramble/butt scoot away from the flaming Zs (dibs on *that* band name!) when my back hits something a lot more solid than putrid flesh. I turn and look behind me, and am close to crying when I see the nice sized boulder.

"Yes!" I shout, and do a fist pump. Well, a torch pump since I sure as shit am not letting go of Mr. Torchy. The Zs moan loudly in return. "Fuck you guys!"

Now, here's the tricky part: how does one climb a boulder with one hand while holding a torch? And here I thought life in the pit was going to be easy.

I do have one option, and it is not an appetizing one, but one option is better than no options.

Taking a deep breath, and saying a silent prayer (I think), I open my jaw wide and grip the torch in my mouth. This wouldn't be so bad if the torch was made of wood or metal. But I have fashioned this particular beauty from a femur. An honest to goodness femur. Hurray.

It tastes about what you would expect a scorched Z's femur to taste like. Yes, it tastes just like an Arby's roast beef sandwich. It could use some of that Horsey sauce.

Femur torch in hand, gorge building at the back of my throat, I reach up and get a good hand hold, set my foot in an easy nook, and then heft myself up onto the boulder. Well, it takes a couple of hefts to get up top, but I make it just as the flaming Zs reach where I had been standing. Their hot and gooey hands claw at the rock, their mouths snapping and spitting.

"Kiss my non-flaming ass," I yell down at them. "I'm on a boulder and you're not! Neener neener!"

That's when I hear the hiss behind me.

The Z tumbles on top of me just as I spin about. I get the torch between us, jamming it up under the thing's chin to keep its very nasty looking teeth from trimming my eyebrows. The blood that still leaks from my forehead sends the monster into a frenzy, and I have to use every ounce of my strength to keep it from taking me out. Carefully, I scoot myself to the side, then shove up and to the right as hard as I can. It doesn't take too much strength since the Z is pretty emaciated.

The Z goes falling off the boulder, taking my torch with it as the thing's mouth makes one more play for my face. I stare in horror as my only light source falls about seven feet to the pit floor, then goes out as the Z rolls over on it and snuffs out its precious, precious flames. Sure, the two flaming Zs are still trying to get at me, but they aren't up on the boulder with me. If I move just a few feet away from the edge then I'm plunged back into semi-darkness.

After the surprise Z attack, semi-darkness is not very comforting. But, I guess it's better than total darkness. I should feel blessed. I do not.

Carefully, I feel my way across the boulder. I'm really hoping there aren't any more Zs up here. I doubt there are. I have a feeling that last one was someone that started off living, escaped onto the boulder, then got stuck up here and pretty much starved to death. That would explain why it was so easy for me to lift and toss. Too bad more Zs aren't as Karen Carpenter.

Okay, that was awful, even for me. I take that joke back. No need to rack up bad karma while fumbling about on a boulder in the middle of an ancient pit deep inside an old coal mine. I need positive universe points, not negative ones.

I reach the other side of the boulder and try to see what's down below me, but the illumination from the flaming Zs doesn't reach, and all I see is a whole lotta nada. I work my way back to the middle of the boulder and rest for a minute. It feels good to just lie here and look up into the emptiness above. I assume it's empty. Shit, there could be a whole nest of vampires hanging upside down watching me, for all I know. Not that vampires exist. That would be crazy talk. Zombies, sure, but vampires? Puh-lease.

Note to self: do not think of mythical monsters while trapped in the dark. That's just dumb. Stop being dumb.

I wriggle about on the boulder which, by the way, is not some smooth boulder you find at the top of a peaceful mountain. This is a coal miner's boulder, motherfuckers! It has ridges and grooves and really, really uncomfortable pieces that feel the need to jam themselves up my ass. So the wriggling takes a while before I can get even close to a semblance of comfort.

I lie there, listening to the moans and scraping from the flaming Zs, whose flames are slowly, slowly, slowly dying. And then gone.

I now understand what complete darkness is.

I didn't get it even when Oscar was first leading me down here, because there was always the hint of some type of light. Now? No hint. There is a distinct lack of hinting.

My eyes are wide open, yet I can't see anything. I place my hand right up to my nose, and it's as if it isn't even there. I wave it around, but all that does is shift my body so I have to spend the next few minutes chasing down a comfortable position again. I do, and it probably isn't long after that I fall asleep, even with the formerly flaming Zs' (such a great band name) moans echoing up to me.

***

There are no dreams, no nightmares, no thoughts whatsoever while I sleep. The only way I actually know that I sleep is that something wakes me up. I feel a light touch which, in the zombie apocalypse, is plenty of touch to bring me out of a sleep. I have the presence of mind not to panic and try to scramble away, since I know I'm up on a boulder in the pitch blackness, and any move could send me tumbling down to the Zs.

The Zs? Did they make it up to the top?

I listen, but don't hear the telltale hissing, or moaning, or shuffling.

What I do hear is a soft snuffling sound. Like a dog sniffing its food dish. There is no doubt that whatever touched me is also sniffing me. Jesus, are there animals down here in this mine? Did some possum work its way into the pit and is living off the scraps of those that don't make it? Great.

The snuffling gets louder until it is right next to my ear. I can feel something next to me, but the feeling I'm getting is that it's much larger than a possum. I can also feel warmth coming off it from its breath and body heat. And the distinct smell of ... BO?

So, it's a large possum with warm breath and body odor. That totally makes sense.

Then it licks me.

"Motherfucker!" I scream, and start swatting blindly in the dark.

"Ow! Hey! Stop!" a voice shouts.

A voice I recognize.

"Rafe?" I ask. "Is that you?"

"Short Pork? Holy shit, man! How'd you get down here?" Rafe replies, only inches from me.

"Fuck how I got down here. Did you sniff and then lick me?" I ask.

Rafe doesn't answer for a while then quietly says, "Maybe."

"You fucking asshole! You were totally going to try to eat me! You can take the canny out of Cannibal Road, but you can't take Cannibal Road out of the canny! You fucking piece of shit!"

"I wasn't going to eat you, honest," Rafe pleads. "I was just checking to make sure you were living. You know, like as in not a Z. I can't see shit, so I sniffed you. You smell like Z, by the way. Then I licked you, just to see if you tasted like a Z. Also, to see if you were warm."

"You could have just patted me down," I reply. "That's how you find out if a person is warm or not."

"Yeah, but I can't see you, and I was afraid I'd get my fingers bitten if I stuck out my hands," Rafe says.

"So you stick your tongue out instead? Because Zs don't eat tongue? There is a serious flaw in your logic, fucker."

"I don't have to explain myself," Rafe huffs. "You should just be glad I found you."

"Really? Why's that?" I ask. "You have some magic plan to get us out of here?"

"Well ... no," he admits. "But there's safety in numbers."

"Not if one of those numbers tries to eat the other one!" I yell. There is a distinct possibility all my yelling is bringing more Zs, but fuck if I care. The dude licked my fucking face!

"I wasn't going to eat you!" Rafe yells back. "It was a joke! God, you are such an asshole!"

"Better to be an asshole than a canny, any day," I say. "Fucking cannies. Why I agreed to let you people come with us on this convoy, I don't know."

"What the fuck do you mean 'you people'?" Rafe snaps. "You know, not everyone got to live in their fancy little subdivision after Z-Day. Some of us had to fight for every second of every day until we found someplace that was just a little bit safer than being out on the open road!"

"Whatever, dude," I snap. "You have no idea what life was like for me and my family after Z-Day. Life was not all block parties and barbecues. We lost a lot of people trying to defend our neighborhood from the Zs. Not to mention the bums that would come by and try to take what we'd built."

"Bums? What the hell are you talking about?" Rafe asks.

"Never mind," I say, realizing that I'd rather not think of the bums. Brenda Kelly went a little overboard when it came to keeping people out. There were more than a few needless deaths at her orders.

"What are bums?" Rafe pushes. "Homeless? People that didn't have any place else to go, so they looked to you for sanctuary? I've heard a few stories from some of the others. I know that Stuart used to be the triggerman and kill anyone that didn't just walk away from your precious subdivision. Fuck you, Short Pork. Say what you want about cannies, but at least we killed to survive. You just killed to hang on to your lawns and shit."

"Dude, there are no lawns in the apocalypse," I say, but without any real conviction.

The kid is right, we were not the best people towards the end there. Subconsciously, it's probably one reason I blew that place up. It stood for a world that could never be again, and wasn't exactly paradise pre-Z.

We sit there and fume in our own wrongness while more and more Zs gather around our boulder. No clue how many, but from the sound of it there are a lot. Looks like we aren't going hiking any time soon.

We probably give each other the silent treatment for an hour. I even manage to refrain from talking out loud. Or I think I do. No way for me to really know unless Rafe tells me, and that defeats the point of a silent treatment. So we'll assume I didn't talk out loud.

"How'd you find me?" I finally ask because I have a complete and total inability to keep from talking. "It's not like you can see down here. Where were you before you found this boulder?"

"Your torches lit this place up," Rafe says. "I could see you from like a mile away."

"Ha, funny," I chuckle.

"No, seriously, man," he insists. "This pit is huge. I was easily a mile away."

"That can't be true," I say. "You have no way to gauge that kind of distance. You think you were a mile, but you were probably only a football field's length."

"I used to hunt people for sport and survival, man," Rafe says. "I know how to gauge a mile. I was a mile away. Your torches were just bright dots in the distance."

"I only had the one torch until it got snagged by a Z I found up here," I reply. "The other lights you saw were the famous singing group known as the Flaming Zs." Rafe doesn't respond right away. "I said, the other lights you saw were the-."

"I heard what you said," he interrupts. "I just don't know what it means."

"I set a couple of Zs on fire, and they chased me here," I explain. "Me being me, I decided that the Flaming Zs would make a killer band name. But, alas, they weren't meant to last as a group. You know why?"

Rafe doesn't answer.

"Do you know why they weren't meant to last, Rafe?" I ask again.

"I don't think I want to," Rafe says quietly.

"Because they burned out!" I laugh. "Bam! Zing! Rimshot! Cue laugh track!"

"You are the most fucked up man I have ever met," Rafe states. "And I knew all the gang leaders on Cannibal Road. Barfly must have nearly killed you a million times."

"Barfly, bro? Nah, we were tight, bro. Like best bros, bro. He totally dug my sense of humor, bro."

"No, he didn't," Rafe says.

"No, he didn't," I admit. "He got tired of it, just like everyone else does."

Again, we sit there for a while with nothing to say. The Zs are getting louder and louder, so it's not like we're sitting in silence anymore. Their constant groans, and moans, and hisses are actually getting on my nerves. Up top you can hide in a shelter like a house or some other building. That shit will muffle their never-ending noise. Hell, even a car is better than this.

"Moan, moan, moan!" I shout. "Hiss, hiss, hiss! Fuck you!"

"That'll teach them," Rafe says.

"Hey, let me ask you something. Strictly for academic purposes," I say. "When we were giving each other the silent treatment, was I still talking out loud?"

"What silent treatment?" Rafe replies. "You haven't shut up since I got up on this boulder. At one point I honestly thought about jumping off and trying to make it against the Zs. You have some seriously fucked up shit inside your head, Short Pork."

"Don't call me Short Pork," I say. "I hated Long Pork. Short Pork is even worse. Just call me Jace."

"Only if you stop referring to me as a canny," Rafe counters.

"But you are a canny," I say. "That's the simple truth."

"Then you will always be Short Pork," Rafe says. "So get used to it, Short Pork."

"Knock it off," I snarl.

"Or what?" Rafe asks. "What the fuck are you going to do to me with one arm in the pitch dark? The second you try to hit me, I'll knock you the fuck out. I was a hunter, man. I can track with my ears."

"Who do you think you are? The Blind Swordsman?" I laugh.

"What the fuck are you talking about?"

"The Blind Swordsman," I say. "That old series of samurai movies? You never saw those?"

"Who the fuck watches old samurai movies? You must have been some nerd before the Zs," Rafe says, laughing.

"Listen, you little shit, while you were busy jerking off to the Pink Power Ranger, I was studying true cinema. The Blind Swordsman movies are classics."

"If you say so, nerd," Rafe laughs again. "Nerd Pork. That's what I'll call you from now on. Forget Short Pork, you are Nerd Pork forever!"

"Fuck off!" I yell, and take a swipe at him. My fist nails him across the chin, and he cries out. I hear some scraping against rock then nothing except for the Zs below. "Rafe? Dude? You still up here?"

"That's all I needed," he says as his fist hits me in the chest. His other fist catches me in the shoulder, and he adjusts fast and throat punches me.

I wish people would stop punching me in the throat. It makes it impossible for me to use my brand of sarcasm against them. I know sarcasm fu, yo.

Another fist to the throat, then one to my cheek. I try to hit back, but he stays out of my reach. I guess I should have thought it through more before picking a fight with a trained killer. He's no Blind Swordsman, but he did used to hunt people, like he said. I used to figure out how high to build fences, and how many rolls of razor wire we needed. We have different skill sets.

I decide the only way to win is to just not get hit, so I flatten myself on the boulder and cover my head with my arm. I hear his hands swinging above me, then I catch a solid thump right between the shoulder blades as he figures out my strategy.

"Knock it off!" I croak as I manage to squeeze a few words out of my damaged throat. It's not as bad as the last time I took it in the throat. "Fucking stop! I'm sorry!"

"What? What did you say?" Rafe asks, all out of breath from throat smacking me. "Did you say you were sorry?"

"Yeah," I reply. "I'm sorry, okay? I won't call you a canny again. Just stop hitting me. I'm done. All done. Let me lie here and just slowly die, alright? Give me that peace, at least."

"We're not going to die," Rafe says.

"How the hell do you know?" I snap. "There's no reason to think we'll live through this. No one can navigate a pit that's a mile long and doesn't have even a speck of light. Not while there're Zs shuffling about."

"That's not true," Rafe replies, and I can hear the grin in his voice.

"What? What aren't you telling me?" I ask. "Rafe, you little fucker, stop messing with me!"

"You'll see," Rafe laughs. "Just keep chatting, and then you'll see."

"I am so sick of this," I growl. "Why can't I catch one break? There are lots of other people I'd rather be with down here than you. Hell, Stuart and Critter are supposed to be down here. I could have bumped into them. Nope, I get the c-."

"Hey," Rafe snarls.

"I get the kid, was what I was going to say," I reply. I'm totally lying. I was gonna say canny.

"I know," Rafe says. "And you're talking out loud."

"Mother fuck," I grumble. Then I cock my head and listen. "Hey, Rafe?"

"Yes, Jace?"

"Do you hear Zs?"

"No, Jace, I do not hear Zs," Rafe replies. The smug is strong with this one.

"Why don't we hear Zs?" I ask. "Zs don't sleep, and they don't just walk away when there's two very loud meals just above them, out of reach."

"Maybe someone killed the Zs," Rafe says.

"What? Bullshit," I respond. "Who the fuck can kill a bunch of Zs in the pitch blackness of this pit? No one has those kinds of skills."

Rafe laughs a little more, and that's when I hear the scrape behind me and to my left.

I wheel about and strike out with my hand, but it's caught easily.

"Damn, Long Pork," Elsbeth giggles. "Ain't nobody whine and complain like you. Every single person in this pit can hear you."

"El? EL!" I yell, and try to hug her, but end up punching her in the boob. She punches me in the dick. That makes us even in El's world. "Ow. It's ... good ... to see ... you."

"Suck it up, and rub some dirt on it, Long Pork," Elsbeth says. "We've got a long hike before we get to the others."

"The others?" I ask. "What others? Critter? Stuart?"

"Oh, there's more than that," Elsbeth replies. "They been catching and bringing them in for days. Good thing I hung back once I knew they was tracking us."

"Wait? You knew these guys were around? And you didn't say anything?" I shout. "They have Greta, El!"

"I know, and we'll get her back, trust me," Elsbeth says, her voice sharper and more deadly than any blade could ever be. "They won't hurt her yet."

"Why the hell didn't you tell us we were being tracked?" I ask, still hurt by the thought that she let this happen.

"I was going to, then everyone started shitting and puking," Elsbeth says. "I wanted to wait it out then come tell you, but there was another distraction. Then you broke camp and left. I never got a chance. When I caught up, you'd left that farm, too." She grabs my shoulder and gives it a squeeze.

"Wow, I can't believe it's you," I say. "What are the odds you'd be down here with me?"

"Are you in trouble, Long Pork?" Elsbeth asks.

"Well, duh," I laugh.

"Then where the hell else would I be?" Elsbeth replies. "It's a full time job saving your ass."

"Well, I guess that's true," I say.

"We going now?" Rafe asks.

"Yes, we're going now," Elsbeth answers. "Did you lick him like I said to?"

"Yeah. He got really pissed," Rafe laughs.

"You guys suck," I say. "Totally suck."

CHAPTER EIGHT

There are quite a few things I'd rather be doing than walking through a subterranean pit in an abandoned coal mine while hundreds of zombies prowl around me in complete and total darkness. Shall I list them? Yes. Yes, I shall.

I'd rather be:

1. Eating glass out of a rhinoceros's asshole.

2. Placing my private parts in a blender and hitting the puree button.

3. Huffing Rush Limbaugh's farts after he's eaten six pepperoni and jalapeno pizzas from Pizza Hut. Deep dish, so they are nice and greasy.

4. Sharting while naked and singing the Star Spangled Banner in front of a black tie crowd at Lincoln Center.

5. Shitting out the undigestible glass I have eaten from previously said rhinoceros's ass.

6. Making sweet, sweaty love to Brenda Kelly.

Okay, okay, I went too far on that last one. Nothing would be worse than touching any part of Brenda Kelly's naked body. What? You think I am mocking the dead? Yes. Yes, I am. That woman deserves all the postmortem mocking she gets.

I would say I'm in a blind leading the blind situation, but I'd be a total idiot if I ever call Elsbeth blind. Sure, there is absolutely no trace of light in any way, shape, or form down here. Sure, the ground is pocked with holes and strewn with random rocks, boulders, and fissures. Sure, I only have one hand, and it's currently gripping one of Rafe's belt loops instead of holding a weapon (i.e. a rock) and getting ready to bash some unseen Z in the cranium. And sure, Elsbeth keeps giggling like a schoolgirl every time she kills a Z and clears our path.

But, it's Elsbeth. If I can't trust her to get my ass out of this frying pan, then I might as well lie down, curl up, and suck my thumb until the Zs find the Jace buffet.

"Dude, you have got to be quiet," Rafe hisses. "You're bringing them right to us."

"Don't worry about Long Pork," Elsbeth says. "He doesn't know how to be quiet. Hasn't shut up since I met him."

"Thanks, El," I say. "You really know how to defend a guy."

"Do I? Huh," Elsbeth replies. "I thought I was giving you shit. Did I do it wrong? Is there a better way to shit give?"

"Nope, that was fine shit giving," I say. "I have taught you well."

"I learned it from Charlie and Greta," Elsbeth says.

"Greta!" I nearly yell. Quite a few moans respond, and Rafe swears under his breath. "We have to save Greta!"

"You already said that back on the rock," Elsbeth says, and I hear the worry in her voice. "Your brain is slipping, Long Pork."

"That's what I have been saying," Rafe states. "You didn't want to listen."

There are plenty more Z moans, and I have to keep myself from freaking out. Not being able to see a thing is a little bit terrifying. Okay, who am I kidding? It's more than terrifying. I'd probably be shitting my pants if my asshole wasn't clenched so tight from fear.

"Seriously, man, you have to be quiet," Rafe growls.

"Don't worry about it," Elsbeth says. "It's easier when I know they are coming. Better than getting a surprise from behind."

I so want to make a joke about El's last statement, but the sounds of her crushing Z skulls, and then the issue of having to step over the fallen Zs, distracts me from a golden, sarcastic opportunity. Sometimes you have to let the perfect setup go for the greater good. That greater good being me staying on my feet and not falling over a dead Z. I want to clear that up in case there is any confusion. Greater good equals me staying on my feet.

"Can I gag him?" Rafe asks. "Please? You're used to it, but I'm not. This guy would have been Sunday dinner back on Cannibal Road."

"Fuck you," I snap. "You're fucking forgetting I survived Cannibal Road, bitch. I not just survived, but I escaped. With my family! So eat my shit, fuckhead!"

"You escaped because I helped you," Elsbeth says. A few moans, some hard thunks, a few thuds, I step over more Zs, Elsbeth continues. "I set it up so you could get that Bronco. I set it up so I was with the cannies by the quarry. I set it up so Barfly came after me, and you Stanfords could get away."

"But John had to shoot the fucker to save you," I say. "So don't think you're some superhero."

"I don't think I'm a superhero, Long Pork," Elsbeth responds. "I just think I'm the girl that has to save your ass all the time. Can't argue with that, can ya?"

"Nope, I can't," I say. "And I wasn't. I was arguing with Rafe here. Every point you made is valid. I just don't want Rafe to think he's better at surviving than me. He's the one that had to join up with our convoy to get away from that canny hell."

"Then why are we arguing?" Elsbeth asks.

"We aren't," I say. "Are we?"

"You people are so fucked in the head," Rafe says. "And considering the shit I'm in, I think I was safer back on Cannibal Road."

"Feel free to head on back, tough guy," I say. "Just go about fifty paces out, and hang a left. I'm sure you'll get there eventually."

"Fuck off, Short Pork," Rafe says.

"What's all this Short Pork shit?" Elsbeth asks. "His name is Long Pork."

"I didn't start it," Rafe replies. "That Critter guy did. He was making fun of Jace's little dick."

"Hey! Fuck you!" I shout.

More than a couple Zs groan in response. In fact, I might say quite a few Zs groan in response. And they are close. Like really close. Really, really, really close. I could probably reach out and touch-.

"WE KNOW THEY ARE CLOSE!" Rafe yells. "FUCK!"

"Wow," Elsbeth says as we suddenly stop. "I don't think he likes you, Long Pork. Should I kill him and let the Zs eat him so we can get away?"

"Wait? What?" Rafe screeches. "Are you fucking kidding me?"

"Yes," Elsbeth giggles. "I am kid fucking you."

"El, we are going to have to work on your syntax later," I say. "Sometimes it's cute when you switch words around. But, and I'm not criticizing, just giving some friendly advice, sometimes it's a little creepy. Kid fucking is creepy. Don't say that."

"See? Long Pork's brain is working just fine," Elsbeth says. "It's just his mouth that's the problem." She reaches out in the dark and pats my shoulder as if she can see me clear as day. "Thank you for the advice, Long Pork. Now I'm going to give you some, okey doke?"

"Okay. What is it?" I ask.

The patting on my shoulder turns to a tight grip, then she shoves me to the ground.

"Stay down and stay out of my way," Elsbeth says, and her voice is nothing but business. "You too, little canny."

"Little canny," I laugh. "Awesome."

"Fuck you too," Rafe says as he's shoved down next to me.

Now the fun starts.

And when I say "fun" I mean a paralytic fear bordering on a catatonic breakdown. Because, you know, complete and total darkness with zombies.

There are a lot of sounds happening around us. Many of them are easy to identify, such as the shuffling of Z feet, and the moans and groans associated with the Zs doing all the shuffling. And moaning and groaning. The Zs are moaning and groaning as well as shuffling. Which sort of brings that statement back full circle.

"Oh, shut up!" Rafe yells.

I don't respond to his rudeness because I am too busy listening to the action. I'm guessing this is what it's like to be a blind person at a Jackie Chan movie.

In between the sounds of feet shuffling are the sounds of precise steps. Now, these aren't as easy to hear, but since I have nothing better to do, I concentrate really hard. A step here, a step there, all the while there are plenty of thunks and thuds. Not to mention a few splatters and the occasional expulsion of trapped corpse gas. Z farts.

You know how the other senses get stronger when one sense is suppressed? Yeah, that's totally true. Z farts are the worst, man. You think you've smelled everything in the apocalypse until you can't see and your sniffer takes over, and all that gas that builds up inside a dead body is released into the air around you, and all you want to do is turn and puke, but you're afraid if you turn and puke you'll end up putting your hand in the puddle of puke because you can't see a fucking thing, which is what is leading to the heightened sense of smell in the first place and-.

"Shut up, Long Pork!" Elsbeth yells from my right.

"Can I shut him up?" Rafe asks.

"You shut up too, Little Canny," Elsbeth replies.

"Ha. Little Canny," I chuckle. "That is never going to get old."

A woosh goes by my head.

"Did you just try to punch me?" I ask. "You better watch it, Little Canny, or I'll beat your ass."

"Try it, fucknut," Rafe snarls.

"I just might!" I snarl back.

"Then do it!"

"Okay then!"

I don't get a chance to beat his ass since I am too busy screaming and thrashing about as a very rotten corpse lands in my lap. Guts and goo splash up on my face, and I'm instantly gagging and trying to wipe my lips off with my arm. Which doesn't do any good since my arm is just as goo covered as my lips. I just smear the gunk around, getting it up my nose and all down my neck. I can feel it dripping into my chest hair. And I have a lot of chest hair since I am so manly. Not much hair on my head, but plenty on my chest.

More guts and goo splatter across me, and I start to yell, then get hit with a third round, and the yell turns into the full on puke I was trying to avoid. Luckily, I'm not the only one. I can totally hear Rafe upchucking next to me.

"Dude, I think there's guts in my ears," Rafe says once he's done throwing up.

I still heave a couple more times before I'm through. "Better than up your nose, man," I whimper. "I'll never get the smell out. This is a nightmare."

"The nightmare is you two puking while I'm fighting," Elsbeth says. "Pussies."

Thunk and thud, thunk and thud. Over and over. I can't see Elsbeth fight, but I've seen her work enough to picture it in my mind.

She ducks a reaching claw and jams her blade into a Z's belly and out through its back. As she pulls the blade free, it severs the thing's spine, and it collapses onto the ground, joining dozens more she's already taken down.

A Z tries to grab her from behind, and she whirls and beheads it, then kicks the headless corpse into a group of five more, knocking them off balance, so all she has to do is come in fast with some quick stabs, and their days of shambling are done.

Elsbeth spins, like the homicidal dervish she is, and drops heads like a lawnmower taking down dandelion blooms in a long neglected lawn.

"Man, you really think you're some post-apocalyptic poet, don't you?" Rafe sighs. "I don't care how hot your daughter is, I'm gonna stay as far away from you as possible once we get out of here."

"That's the second best thing I've heard all day," I say. "Or night. Or whatever time it is. The first was Elsbeth's voice."

"Because she always has to bail you out of trouble?" Rafe sneers. I can't see the sneer, but I sure as fuck can hear it.

"Damn right because she bails my ass out of trouble," I agree. "I will admit that now. Listening to her shred these fucks without being able to see a thing is quite the life moment."

"Cram your life moment in your ass, Long Pork," Elsbeth says. "You're distracting me. Ow! My arm!"

"El? El!" I shout. "Did one get you? Are you bit? Oh, God, I'm sorry! I'll shut up, I promise!"

"Just kidding," Elsbeth laughs.

There are few more thuds and thunks, not to mention a couple stray splatters across my face for good measure, and then there's nothing but silence. Except for Elsbeth's heavy breathing. Damn, she sounds like a horse.

"You can be a dick, Long Pork," Elsbeth says. "I just saved you again, and you call me a horse. You're the horse, poop face."

"Good one, El," I say. "You can never go wrong with the poop face insult. And for the record, I didn't call you a horse, I said you sound like one. Also, for the record, that was supposed to be in my head, so it doesn't really count. I'll let you have the poop face this time, but next time it'll be a yellow card. No more warnings."

"What the hell is a yellow card?" Rafe asks.

"You know, from soccer," I say. "It's like a penalty."

"Soccer? I'm from Tennessee," Rafe says. "Soccer doesn't exist in Tennessee. Only Vols football."

"Yeah, I met some of those fans back in Knoxville," I say. "I have to tell you they got a little carried away. Supporting your team is one thing, trying to hang a guy is a whole other."

"Then I set them on fire," Elsbeth says, right next to my ear again.

"Jesus, El!" I cry, and nearly piss my pants. "Stop with the creepy sneaking up on me!"

"You didn't hear me sit down?" Elsbeth asks. "Maybe it was because you were busy jabbering like a stupid squirrel."

"I thought you liked my jabbering," I say.

"I was being polite," Elsbeth says. "Stella says I need to practice being polite more."

"And you decided to practice on me? While we're in a black pit? And you're fighting Zs blind?" I ask. "I think we need to practice timing next."

"Time to get up and move," Elsbeth says, and yanks me to my feet.

"Ow, fuck, El! Watch it!" I snap. "My leg still hurts!"

I literally don't see the hit coming. I do see bright flashes of light as my vision swims from the punch Elsbeth gives my thigh.

"How's it feel now?" Elsbeth laughs. "Still hurt?"

"Why?" I whimper.

"Pain helps you focus," Elsbeth says. "We need you to focus. Your smarty brain is all over the place. Can't have that anymore. The hard part is up ahead."

"Hard part?" I ask. "Little Canny? Did she say the hard part is up ahead?"

"I'm not talking to you if you call me that," Rafe replies.

"Yeah, I said the hard part," Elsbeth sighs. "Pull the Z guts out of your ears, Long Pork, and pay attention. There's no more resting. Now we move, and keep moving. Once we get to the pit, we don't stop. If you feel something grab you, kill it."

She shoves a rock in my hand.

"Wait, what pit?" I ask. "I thought we are already in the pit?"

"There's another pit," Elsbeth says. "It's a smaller pit, only four feet deep, but filled with trapped Zs. We have to get across that to get to Critter, Stuart, and the others. Once we get to them, then it's all easy peasy."

"There's a pit inside the pit?" I ask. "What is this? Some Russian doll nightmare hole?"

"Ain't no dolls, Long Pork," Elsbeth says. "Just Zs. Now, stay close."

"Hold the fuck on," I say. "If I have a rock in my hand, how the fuck can I stay close? I'll lose you guys in three seconds with my gimpy leg."

I scream as another hit to my thigh nearly sends me to the ground.

"FUCK!"

"Focus, Long Pork," Elsbeth says. I can tell her grin is ten miles wide. "You think you're getting lost, give that leg a whack and focus."

"I don't think that's how it works," I growl.

"It is now," Elsbeth says, her voice a little farther away. "So suck it up."

"Yeah, Short Pork, suck it up," Rafe mocks. "Ow!"

"His name is Long Pork," Elsbeth says. "No more Short Pork. He doesn't have a tiny penis. I've seen it. It's normal size."

"Jesus," I mutter. "When did you ever see my penis?"

"You get yourself knocked out and hurt a lot, Long Pork," Elsbeth says. "Everyone's seen you naked. Even Boyd."

"Who the fuck is this Boyd?" I yell. Far off I hear a reply from a whole lotta Zs. I kid you not with the whole lotta approximation. "Oh, never the fuck mind. Let's go."

I stand for a minute, waiting for word from the other two, then hear footsteps ahead of me.

"Did you guys already take off? You fuckers," I snap.

"I'm right here, Long Pork," Elsbeth says from my ear again.

"Motherfucker!" I yell and jump, dropping my rock on my foot. "Son of a bitch."

"Wait, if you're back there, then who's this here?" Rafe shouts back at us. "Oh, shit."

"He'll be fine," Elsbeth says as we listen to Rafe's struggle with what I am assuming is a Z. "Cannies are tough."

"No shit," I say.

There's a sound like a walnut cracking, then a loud splash followed by Rafe gagging and then throwing up some more. Elsbeth pushes me forward, and the stink of rotten Z brains is like a warm, wet, smelly blanket filled with, well, warm, wet smelly Z brains. Shut up.

"I can't believe you left me alone," Rafe says when we catch up to him.

"You lived," Elsbeth says, and taps me on the shoulder as she walks past. "Come on."

"I dropped my rock," I say. I cry out as a new rock impacts against my leg. "Thanks."

I pick it up and listen closely, making sure I keep my ear on Elsbeth's footsteps. They're easy to hear since she's making an effort to be heard. I think she's skipping. I listen a couple more seconds. Yeah, she's totally skipping.

I follow along for what seems like a decade past forever, my heart racing in my throat as every scuff and scrape echoes for a split second, then is swallowed by the immenseness of the pit. Or should I call it the big pit since we're heading for the small pit? Pit One and Pit Two? Kinda like Thing One and Thing Two. Would that make Elsbeth the Cat in the Hat? I could so see her as the Cat in the Hat.

"Long Pork?" Elsbeth calls back to me.

"Sorry," I say.

We keep going until I bump right into Rafe's back.

"A little warning," I whisper, sensing the smaller pit before us. It's easy to sense, it smells like Zs.

"Sit down," Elsbeth orders.

I do. I assume Rafe does too.

"Pay attention," Elsbeth says, and her voice loses her semi-innocent hick accent. "I'll go in first and clear space. When I say to follow, you follow. You do not hesitate, you do not pause, you just jump in and start smashing anything that tries to grab you. Keep a steady pace, and walk forward. Do not run, do not get off course. Steady and forward. Got it?"

"Yes, ma'am," we both reply. There's no other way to answer when Elsbeth sounds like that.

"Good," Elsbeth says. "See ya on the other side."

There're several loud crunches and then a thud as Elsbeth jumps into the small pit. The moans of the Zs amp up considerably until they're louder than my thoughts. That's loud, folks. Trust me.

It feels life fifteen or twenty minutes before I hear Elsbeth calling to us. She's quite a ways ahead, but I guess she knows what she's doing. She probably killed a bunch, but also wanted to draw the main horde with her to give us room.

"Follow!" she yells.

I jump into the pit and start swinging. I connect with one, two, three Zs, and send them falling away from me. I feel dead fingers claw at my clothes and have to wonder just how fucked we would have been if El didn't give us some breathing room. This pit is wall to wall Zs.

"My God," I say. "It's full of zombies."

I don't get a laugh from Rafe, but I wasn't expecting one. A good 2001 reference is for one's own amusement anyway. That's my philosophy.

Teeth clamp shut right by the side of my face and I whirl and strike out, caving in the offending Z's head with my rock. I have to say, having used spiked baseball bats, sharpened batons, and many other weapons, both one and two handed, since Z-Day, I have never given a good solid rock it's due. I shall rectify that.

Rocks rock.

Sorry. I couldn't help it.

A Z bumps right into me and we nearly kiss. So I head butt it, and then whack the fuck out of the thing with my new rock friend. Consent is important, especially during the apocalypse. Ain't no Z getting a kiss from me without at least a cup of coffee and a warm handshake. What does the thing think I am? Some end of the world slut? Puh-lease!

The Zs get thicker and thicker, and I'm soon sweating heavily, despite the chill in the pit. I'm also limping hard from my bad leg and starting to cramp in my good one from the extra work it's doing. I elbow a Z back, smash another in the face, kick a third, elbow a fourth, smash a fifth, kick, elbow, smash, kick, elbow, smash, smash, smash, smash.

Trip.

Shit.

I'm on top of a squirming Z, and I can't get up because my arm is twisted under the thing's back. Which also means my rock is under the thing's back. Not good. Very not good.

"El!" I shout. "I'm down!"

"Hold on!" Rafe says, only a couple feet ahead of me. "Keep talking so I can find you!"

"Never thought I'd hear someone say that!" I shout, then begin to sing Row, Row, Row Your Boat. It's the first thing that comes to mind.

A Z stumbles and falls across my back. I twist and send it rolling off, but a second one, and then a third one just do the same thing.

"I said talk, not sing badly," Rafe says, his voice coming from right above me as he pulls off one Z. "Which you can stop doing now."

I stop singing and am grateful Rafe yanks the other Z off. I try to roll to the side and free my arm, but the Z I'm on is all kinds of twisted, and I almost get my ear bitten off. The thing's teeth clamp down on the collar of my shirt, and I slam my head back again and again until there's nothing but the sound of wet pulp.

"I think you got it," Rafe says, helping me to my feet.

I bend down and start feeling around, but Rafe grabs my arm and pulls me away.

"What the hell are you doing?" he growls as he keeps pulling me.

"I lost my rock friend," I say.

"How the hell did you make it this far?" Rafe asks.

"Luck and charisma," I say. "Heavy on the luck part."

"My name is Elsbeth, not luck," Elsbeth shouts from way ahead of us.

"How can she hear that?" Rafe asks. "That chick is different, that's for sure."

"You have no idea," I say as we start battling our way through the Zs.

I don't get another rock friend, but with a lucky twist of my wrist, I snap off a Z's arm and start using that to whack a path through the never ending pit horde. I may accidentally whack Rafe a couple times, too, but he doesn't notice and thinks it's just Zs.

"I notice, shithead," he grumbles.

"Oh, sorry," I apologize as I take a Z's head clean off with one swipe of my Z arm friend.

"Everything does not have to be called your friend!" Rafe shouts. "Shut up! Shut up, shut up, shut up!"

"Shhhh!" Elsbeth calls back. "You'll let the Zs know where you are!"

I have no idea if she's kidding or not. Sometimes you just have to live with the mystery of El.

Inch by inch, foot by foot, smashed Z head by smashed Z head, we trudge through the pit, until I slam up against Rafe's back as he stops suddenly.

"Take my hand," Elsbeth says, and I drop Stanley.

That's what I've named my Z arm friend.

I reach up, and Elsbeth pulls me up out of the pit with one hard yank. And it is a hard yank. I didn't really need that shoulder to be connected. Shoulders are overrated.

"Don't be a baby," Elsbeth says.

"Was that out loud?" I ask.

"No, I just know what a baby you are," Elsbeth says. "So stop it."

"Right," I say, and step away from the pit to give Rafe room to get up. I don't go far, since I can't see a fucking thing. Basically, I stumble a little ways away and stand there with my dick in my hands.

Not literally. I do not literally have my dick in my hands.

Elsbeth gives me a shove in my chest and spins me around, then starts pushing me at the small of the back.

"Knock it off," I say. "I know how to walk."

"Not fast enough," Elsbeth says, her voice cold and hard. "Move. Now."

"Okay, okay," I say. "Calm down."

We get a few feet away, and I run right into a large boulder. My nose stings from the impact, but I don't feel any blood start to flow, so it's an impact that goes into the win column.

"Down," Elsbeth says just as the pit is illuminated by bright lights.

Elsbeth shoves me and Rafe around the side of the boulder, then clamps her hand over my mouth. Probably a good idea since I find myself blinking against the intense brightness while also looking right at Critter, Stuart, and about six of the cannies from our crashed RV. Critter and Stuart look rough, but not as bad as I feared they would considering how Reptile Jesus was talking.

I immediately want to say something to them, which is exactly why Elsbeth has her hand over my mouth. So I blink a whole bunch of times, hoping my Morse code isn't too rusty. Critter rolls his eyes and Stuart just shakes his head. I don't think I'm blinking what I think I'm blinking.

There are some far off screams, and the sound of several shotguns going off.

"Come and get 'em!" someone yells.

We all sit there and wait. I'm guessing we're waiting for the lights to go out. Never thought I'd be glad to be plunged back into pure darkness.

The sounds of Zs fighting over fresh meat is something you recognize instantly when living in the zombie apocalypse. That goes on for several minutes, intermingled with laughter and small talk from the shotgun assholes. Then the laughter and talking slowly subsides, and finally the lights go back out.

"Hey, Short Pork," Critter greets me from the darkness. "Wasn't sure we'd see you again. I figured that hissy fit you threw causing you to pout and go upstairs might have saved ya from gettin' captured. Guess not."

"It wasn't a hissy fit," I reply. "You were being a dick."

"It was a hissy fit," Stuart says. "And did you just try to tell me my lips are full by blinking in Morse code?"

"No," I say. "I was trying to say hello, and it's good to see you guys."

"Well, that's not what you said," Stuart says. "But it is good to see you."

"What now?" I ask. "It's great we can all be back together as one happy family, but how the hell are we going to get out of here?"

"Through the back door," Elsbeth says.

"This place has a back door?" I ask.

"Every place has a back door," Critter replies, his voice thick with smirkiness. "You just have to know where to look."

"It's not going to be easy for you, though," Stuart says. "There's some climbing involved."

"Climbing? I don't do climbing," I reply. "Not anymore."

"Ain't got no choice, Short Pork," Critter says. "You want to leave the pit, then you best be gettin' to the climbin'."

"You can't call me Short Pork anymore," I state.

"Oh, and why's that?" Critter asks.

"Because Elsbeth says so," I reply.

"Critter can call you Short Pork," Elsbeth says. "I just said that Little Canny can't call you Short Pork."

"Why the hell does Critter get to call me Short Pork?" I snap.

"Because he's Critter," Elsbeth answers.

"Because I'm Critter," Critter chuckles. "There're perks to bein' me."

"Why the hell do I put up with y'all?" I ask.

"Because you have one arm and can't take care of yourself," Elsbeth says. "Not that you were any better with two arms."

"He actually got into more trouble when he had two," Stuart says. "Losing an arm has slowed him down."

"It has," Critter agrees. "That's a fact."

"I'm sitting right here, assholes," I say. "I may not be able to see, but I can hear."

"Shhh," Elsbeth says. "You hear that? Zs are about done eating. We need to get out now before they come hunting."

Someone picks me up and starts walking my ass quickly away from the boulder. I'm guessing it's Elsbeth from the sure-footed way we're moving. Or at least she's sure footed, I keep tripping over every damn rock and crack on the ground. I'm not the only one; quite a few grunts and curses follow us as the group tries to keep up.

Bam. My nose hits a wall.

"You did that on purpose," I say.

"Huh?" Elsbeth replies, all bullshit innocence.

"You let me run into the wall on purpose," I repeat.

"Did not," she says, but isn't very convincing.

Then she takes my hand and presses it to the rough surface of the wall.

"Find a grip," she says.

I search until my fingers can curl into a depression in the rock a foot or so above my head.

"Got it," I say.

"Good," she says then sighs. "Find a place for your toes."

I jam the foot of my good leg into another depression then stand there feeling stupid.

"Okay, now what?" I ask, well aware that physics are not on my side.

"Climb," Elsbeth says. There's a tone of regret in her voice.

"You okay, El?" I ask.

"I will be when we're out of this pit," she sighs again. "Now, climb, Long Pork."

"Okay, but I'm not going far," I say.

I dig my foot in more, grip hard with my fingers, and pull. I lift off the ground and that's when I find out why Elsbeth isn't sounding so happy. She puts her hand right on my ass and pushes, keeping me from falling back down.

"Keep going," she says. "Move, Long Pork."

I don't want the sigh to turn into a growl, so I do as she says, and I move. One hand, one foot then the other foot, and a shove on my ass from Elsbeth. That's how I climb the twelve feet or so, and find myself crawling up over the lip of a ledge. I roll out of the way, and Elsbeth joins me.

"Don't stand up," Elsbeth says.

"Ow!" I cry as I slam my head into very hard rock. "Too late."

Elsbeth keeps us moving. She turns us right, left, right, right, left, then it's straight on forever. We're walking for so long that I think I'm going to pass out, but I dig deep and keep going. Hearing the voices of the others behind me helps as motivation. I can't quit with an audience.

I glance over my shoulder as someone cries out. It's one of the cannies, holding his foot as he jumps up and down. Looks like he stubbed his toe on a decent sized rock. Ouch.

Hey ... hold on. How can I see that?

I whip my head back in the direction we're moving, and realize that there's light up ahead. It's not much, but considering I've been a subterranean troll for probably twenty-four hours, my eyes treat the little bit of light as if it's a full fucking moon. Huzzah!

Of course, for there to be light that must mean we are getting close to the surface. Which, by the way, is freezing fucking cold. It only takes a couple of minutes for my enthusiasm at being sighted again to be replaced by my whole body shivering uncontrollably.

I'm not the only one. I look back again, and everyone is shaking and shivering. None of us have winter coats on, just shirts and jeans. We do have sturdy boots, so maybe we won't lose our toes once we get outside. Not that it matters, since we'll die of hypothermia well before we feel the effects of frostbite. Or not feel the effects. I guess you don't feel the effects until you start to warm up. Oh, God, I wish I could warm up.

Teeth chattering and my will to live slowly fading just like my body heat, I step from the rock tunnel we've been walking in and out into the open air. Kill me now.

"Huddle together," Stuart says. "It's the only way to stay warm."

He doesn't have to say it a second time. We all instantly get into the group hug mood. Somehow I'm on the outside, which sucks, but at least part of me is warm. I wish all of me was warm, but freezing beggars can't be cozy choosers. I should have that saying cross stitched and framed when we get someplace that has cross stitching and frames.

"What the hell are you babbling about?" Critter asks. He's who I'm pressed up against. "I don't think arts and crafts are the priority right now, Short Pork."

"We'll need to find shelter," Stuart says, his eyes scanning our surroundings. "Getting out of this weather is our priority."

"Can't we huddle in the mouth of the tunnel?" someone asks.

"It'll just take longer to freeze to death," Stuart says. "We need to find a place where we can build a fire. The last thing I want to do is start a fire in that tunnel with all of that coal dust. It could get a lot warmer than we want."

"Right," Critter says. "And we should take some coal with us."

"Are you fucking nuts?" I snap.

"What?" he replies. "It's just sitting there. Look."

He points back at the mouth of the tunnel at the various size hunks of old coal that litter the ground not covered by snow.

"I bet if we dig a little under that snow we'll find even more," Critter says.

"Fuck the coal!" I yell. "And fuck shelter! We need to go get Greta!"

"We will," Elsbeth says, her voice a steel that's colder than the weather. "Don't you worry, Long Pork. We won't leave Greta behind. But first, we get to shelter like Stuart says. We get warm, we survive, then we get Greta. That's the plan."

"That's going to take too long," I growl. "Who knows what they're doing to her in that compound!"

"Nothing yet," Elsbeth says. "Trust me, Long Pork. These ain't crazy crazies, but religion crazies. They'll break her first before they hurt her. That way they think they are doing good. Religion crazies have to think they're good before they do bad. Which, I guess, makes them crazier than crazy crazies."

"You'd know," Critter says, and holds up his hands. "Not an insult."

"I know," Elsbeth says. "I do know. That's why I said the words I said. Because I know. If I didn't know, then that would make me crazy too. I'm not crazy."

A few of the cannies look down at their feet. Sure, I can see how they think Elsbeth is crazy, but they would be very wrong. Sometimes that woman is the sanest of us all.

"Let's go," Elsbeth says, and breaks up the warm group hug. "We have some walking to do."

"Hold on, let's think this through," Stuart says. "We don't know where we are. We could end up wandering out into the middle of nowhere and never find any shelter."

"Didn't I say?" Elsbeth grins. "I already know where the shelter is."

"You what?" Stuart asks.

"I already know where shelter is," Elsbeth says, and waves us on. "Come on, or you people are going to freeze to death."

Stuart looks at me, and I know he catches the "you people" part. What the hell does Elsbeth mean by that? Isn't she going to freeze to death too? Pretty sure humans all freeze at the same temperature, give or take a few degrees due to natural insulation. Which, by the way, none of us have. Despite a few folks back at Whispering Pines, being hefty and having a layer of fat for warmth is not a luxury people get in the apocalypse. We're kind of all skin and bones.

Very cold skin, and very cold bones.

"What about the coal?" Critter asks.

"Don't need it," Elsbeth says. "No place to burn it."

"How will we stay warm?" one of the cannies asks.

"You'll see," Elsbeth says.

"El, you have to give us more information than that," Stuart says.

"Not really," Elsbeth says. "You'll like the place. It's cozy. And there's a fireplace. With wood. That enough information?"

"It's a start," Stuart says.

"A start's all you need," Elsbeth smiles, then turns and hikes off into the blowing snow.

We have no choice but to huddle together and trudge through the deep snow after her.

Even with the boots on, my toes go numb after at about twenty minutes of walking. Actually, every part of me is numb. I'm afraid that if someone yelled in my ear right now it would just snap right off from the shock. The same goes for my nose. I'm afraid to wipe the snot away from it. If I bump it too hard, it'll shatter and leave me with a hole in my face. Besides the hole in my face called a mouth. That's already there.

A few more minutes, and I think I'm going to collapse. I look ahead, and Elsbeth is hiking along as if it's a spring day, and the sun is shining, the birds are tweeting, and—.

"Shut up!" half the group grumbles at me.

"Sorry," I say.

"What's that?" Rafe asks, pointing up ahead. "Is that it?"

We shove through a winter-dead hedge and onto a front yard that is maybe half an acre across. At the far side of the yard is a good-sized farmhouse. The windows are boarded up, and the place looks solid, but we can all instantly tell that things aren't right.

"What happened here?" I ask Elsbeth as I break from the pack and push myself to catch up with her. "Doesn't look like Zs took the place down."

"They didn't," Elsbeth says. "This was a people fight."

As I get closer, I can see the bullet holes in the wood siding. There are scorch marks around the window frames, and I see a dark stain by the front door as we step up onto the porch.

"The stains are new," Elsbeth says. "The fire and bullet holes are old. The fight was a while ago. Don't know who won."

"What do you mean the stains are new?" Stuart asks.

He holds up a hand, and the group stops at the edge of the porch. Everyone is freezing, but all eyes are on the stains that are obvious blood. No one is in a hurry to get inside.

"Elsbeth? Where you done brought us, girl?" Critter asks.

"It's safe," Elsbeth says. "They're gone. They won't be coming back."

"El? What are you talking about?" I ask. "What is going on?"

"Nothing, no more," Elsbeth says. "Do you want to come inside and get warm, or stay out here and die?"

There are a few grumbles about getting warm, but it is far from unanimous.

"Take us in," Stuart says. "Might as well get the mystery over with."

Elsbeth nods and turns the doorknob. She opens the door wide and strides right inside.

"There's a wood stove in the kitchen," Elsbeth says, walking past a pair of closed doors. "We can sleep in there. Wood is out back."

I stop at the pair of doors, since that's where the trail of bloodstains lead to. Stuart is on one side of me, and Critter is on the other.

"Are you going to open them?" Rafe asks from behind us.

I glance down the hall and see Elsbeth watching us closely.

"You don't have to," she says. "The message ain't for you guys."

"Message? Dammit, El, now I have to open the doors," I sigh. "You know I'm not going to just ignore bloodstains leading to some message."

I take a deep breath, and shove the doors open.

We all stand there and stare.

Written in blood on the far wall are the words, "*Loyalty above all else.*"

Just like back at that other farmhouse. And just like back there, lying under the bloody words, are a couple of skinned corpses.

"Want me to start the fire?" Elsbeth asks. "It should be safe. This storm will keep the religion crazies from seeing the smoke."

"I don't know if those are the crazies I'm worried about," Critter says.

"No shit, man," Rafe agrees.

"We're gonna have to sit her down, and get to the bottom of this," Stuart says.

"Yeah, I know," I reply. "I'm really fucking looking forward to that conversation."

We all turn as one and look down the hallway towards the kitchen as we hear a wood stove door creak, and the sound of wood being loaded into it. The next thing we hear is Elsbeth whistling. I know the song instantly.

Wheels on the Bus.

Great.
Yep, really looking forward to that conversation.

CHAPTER NINE

Awkward.

That's the vibe in the farmhouse. Awkward.

All the cannies have tucked tail and moved themselves upstairs. They found some bricks outside, and heated those up on the wood stove, then booked it into one bedroom and proceeded to huddle up and cuddle up.

That leaves me, Critter, and Stuart downstairs in the kitchen with Elsbeth. Rafe is wandering around somewhere. We told him to keep watch, but I doubt he's doing that. He's probably licking the skinless corpses in the other room, the canny bastard.

"You really don't like Rafe, do you?" Stuart asks.

"Son of a bitch," I snarl, then point an accusatory finger at each of them. "Okay, you guys know there is something scrambled with my brain and are totally taking advantage of it. From now on you hold up a finger if I start talking out loud. Got it? No more letting me ramble on thinking I'm, well, thinking."

"Sounds fair to me," Critter says.

"Good," I say. "Now-."

Critter holds up a finger.

"What?" I ask.

"You're talking out loud," he smiles.

"I want to talk out loud," I reply.

"Then what's the use of the finger if it ain't gonna shut you up?" Critter chuckles.

"You're a dick," I say, then look at Elsbeth. "Okay, El, I think we need to talk."

"I don't," Elsbeth says. "Nothin' to talk about."

"Yeah, there kinda is," I say, and hook a thumb over my shoulder. "Two things, actually. They're both in that front room sans skin. That's worth talking about, in my opinion. Anyone else think so?"

"Just tell us what's going on," Stuart says.

"I'm saving your asses," Elsbeth replies. "That's what's going on. It's what's always going on. Everybody gets into trouble, and Elsbeth has to save your butts. That's how this works. I don't mind. I'd get bored if Long Pork wasn't always getting captured or talking us into a fight or-."

"Hold on, hold on," I interrupt. "Talking us into a fight? I never talk us into a fight. I usually talk us out of fights."

Elsbeth shrugs. "Then why are we always fighting?"

"Because bad guys won't leave us alone," I reply. "It's not my fault the evil villains of the world are attracted to us like fucking shit magnets."

Elsbeth shrugs again, but doesn't say anything. Critter and Stuart look at me, then back at Elsbeth. She still doesn't say anything, just sits there with her arms crossed. After a few minutes, Stuart stands up and claps Critter on the shoulder.

"Let's find Rafe and make sure he hasn't fallen asleep on watch," Stuart says. "We can check on the folks upstairs too."

"I ain't no canny babysitter," Critter says. "You all put me in charge, so I'm gonna use some of that power to announce I'm going to bed. I think there's a nice, dark closet I can cozy into. Don't wake me until we're ready to leave."

"Maybe we'll leave without you," I say.

"Wouldn't that be my lucky day," Critter replies as he and Stuart walk out of the kitchen.

"I think he means that," I say. "Not very nice."

"He always means it," Elsbeth says. "He thinks he's better off alone. He's wrong, because he's old and getting slow, but he likes to think he's still young. I'll miss him when he dies."

"Jeez, El, way to bring it down," I say.

"Bring what down?" she asks.

"The mood," I respond. "Not cool to talk about Critter dying. Sure, he's older than everyone, but he's a survivor. He'll probably outlive us all."

"Not all of us," Elsbeth says, her eyes filling with sadness. "I'll probably see everyone I love die first."

"Okay, okay, time fucking out, El," I say, and make a T with my hands. "Where is this all coming from?"

"I can't tell you," Elsbeth says. "Not yet. Right now you are safe. They won't touch you."

I decide to take a different track, and not play the back and forth game. Gonna have to circle around and see if I can get answers a different way.

"El? Where did you go? What were you checking on when we took off without you? And don't say you were tracking Kelvin's shotgun brigade. I don't buy that anymore," I say. "Not with those skinned corpses in the other room. Just give me some clue, okay? I'm your friend, remember?"

"You're my family," she says, but without her usual insistence and enthusiasm.

"Right, I'm your family," I agree. "And family is honest with each other."

"Not all family," Elsbeth says. "Some lie. Some keep secrets. Some change."

"You just described the human race, not just family," I laugh. "People are who they are, and yes, people do change, but it's what's in their hearts that counts."

"What if they have no hearts?" Elsbeth asks. "What if they are hollowed out, and can't return to the people they were? What if they are nothing but empty robots coming to kill, kill, kill?"

"Um, we aren't talking about us, are we?" I ask. "I mean, the Stanfords are a bunch of badass motherfuckers, but I don't know if I'd say we're kill-kill-killer robots badass. That might be overstating things."

"Not the Stanfords," Elsbeth says. "That's not who I'm talking about."

"Want to clue me in?" I ask.

"I can't," she says. "Not yet. Don't ask me anymore, Long Pork. It hurts my head to keep it all in."

"Okay, no problem," I say. "I certainly don't want to hurt your head."

I glance towards the kitchen door, my mind on the bodies in the other room.

"The only problem is I can't just forget about the naked corpses," I say. "Stuart, Critter, and everyone else are expecting me to get some answers on those. You have to admit, you'd be curious if you were in the dark."

"I'd beat the answers out of the person that knows," Elsbeth shrugs.

"Yes, yes you would," I nod. "But I can't really do that to you. So, help me out, and give me something to work with, El. Anything."

Elsbeth stares at me for a very long time. Those eyes of hers just drill right through me, like she's taking an X-ray. It weirds me the fuck out, but I know El is just being El. So I wait.

"It's a message to me," Elsbeth finally says. "It is for me to see, and me to deal with."

"Yes, but who are the people?" I ask. "Why did they get skinned?"

"Unlucky," Elsbeth shrugs. "Just like the other ones."

"The other ones? The ones back at the farmhouse by the barn?"

"Yep," Elsbeth nods. "I tracked the RVs, found those bodies too. There will be more. Probably lots more. Until I do what I have to."

"And what's that?" I ask.

"What I always do," Elsbeth sighs. "Kill them all."

"You realize you haven't really told me anything, right?" I ask. "You say the message is for you, but if you're with us, then the message is for everyone. You don't get to go solo on this. So, I'm going to ask for one favor, alright? Just tell me who you are going to kill. What all are you talking about?"

Elsbeth does her X-ray stare for a good five minutes. I can almost see the gears turning in her brain. I wait. Nothing else I can do. When Elsbeth needs space to think, you give her space to think.

"I'll tell you," she says. "But you have to promise that..."

Rafe comes skidding into the kitchen, his eyes wide and his cheeks bright red from being out in the cold. His hair and clothes are covered in snow.

"We have a big fucking problem," Rafe says.

"Yeah, you're interrupting us," I snap.

"No, dipshit, a bigger problem," Rafe says. "Stuart sent me to get you and Elsbeth. You'll want to come outside."

"Is the storm getting worse? It seemed like it was clearing up before," I say.

"No, it's getting worse, but that's not the problem," Rafe replies. "Just come see."

"We finish talking right after this," I say to Elsbeth. She just shrugs.

Dammit, I was so close. Fuck.

We get up and follow Rafe out through the front door. I keep my eyes averted from the skinned corpses and the bloody message. What am I saying? No, I don't. I totally peek. Yuck.

We get out onto the front porch, and the cold hits me like a freight train. Rafe is right, the storm is getting worse. The snow is blowing sideways, and it's like a sheet of white only a few feet from the porch. Jesus, this house will be buried before the morning comes.

"Fuck," I say. "We'll have to dig out."

"Shhh," Stuart scolds, then points.

It's night, but the snow is doing that reflective light thing it does, and there's this semi-blue glow to everything. I squint into the dim light and try to figure out what has everyone so freaked. All I see are a bunch of snow covered bushes out in the yard. Nothing else.

Then I realize the snow covered bushes are moving. At first I thought it was an optical illusion because of how the snow is coming in sideways. You know, like when you are parked, and the car next to you pulls out and makes you think you're moving? That.

"Zs?" I ask, huddling close to the others so they can hear me over the storm.

"Yeah," Stuart replies. "Shoulder to shoulder. Hundreds of them. Maybe thousands."

"Why isn't the snow slowing them?" I ask. "Shouldn't they be stuck until the sun comes out? There's no way their muscles can be working right in this."

"They ain't runnin' hurdles, Short Pork," Critter says. "They's just shuffling along."

"But that shouldn't be possible either," I say. "The snow is so deep they should be falling over on their faces."

"No shit. I went to take a piss around the corner, and almost walked right into the herd. It's like something is driving them," Rafe says. "Like cattle. Something is making them keep moving."

"Yes," Elsbeth says.

We all look at her.

"Care to elaborate?" I ask.

"No," she replies.

We stop looking at her. Elsbeth really is not helping her cause tonight.

"Maybe they'll pass by, and we can still get out of here in the morning," I say.

"Maybe," Stuart says. "Maybe not."

"Okay, well as long as that's settled," I smile. "I think I'll go back inside and try to feel my face again. This has been fun."

"Any chance I can keep watch from an upstairs window?" Rafe asks. "I really don't want to be out here."

"No need to stay out here," Stuart says. "They can't hear or smell us in this. We'll keep an eye on them, and stay prepped. If they change course and decide to come for a visit, then we'll need to make a run for it. With that many, this house won't last more than a couple of minutes. Storm or no storm, we'll be safer on the run than trapped in here."

"We'll all stay upstairs," Elsbeth says. "Watch every side. Better views up there. We see a break, then we go. May not get many chances."

"I'll tell the others to gather up whatever clothes and blankets they can find," I say. "This cold will kill us as fast as the Zs if we have to skeedaddle."

"Skeedaddle," Elsbeth giggles.

"I live to keep you smiling," I say.

"Inside," Stuart says. "We sleep in shifts. Try to get as much rest as possible."

"Sleep is good," I say. "I call firsts!"

"It'll keep him quiet," Critter says. "Finally."

***

Not a lot of sleeping happens.

The herd of Zs moves in closer and closer, tighter and tighter around the house. Instead of being able to take shifts so some of us can get some sleep, we all have to stay awake and watch out the windows, hoping for the Zs' numbers to slack so we can make a break for it.

Of course, this plan isn't exactly unanimous. The cannies would all rather just stay. I don't blame them, it is nice and toasty in the farmhouse now that the wood stove has really kicked in. There are those huge vents in the floor above the kitchen so the heat from there moves upstairs. It's a hard sell to say that going outside in the storm is better than curled up by the grate with some warm tootsies.

The thing is that more and more of the Zs are starting to get a little curious about the farmhouse. Most of them are annoyed it's in their way. Those are the spoiled Zs that think the whole world should be paved over and flattened for their ease of movement. Kind of like how all the retirees and developers felt about Florida, pre-Z. But a few of the Zs keep turning their heads and checking out the farmhouse like it may hold a little snack or two. Which it does.

Those are the Zs Stuart watches like a hawk.

"Six more," Stuart says, perched by a window facing east.

It looks like the herd is moving from east to west. Kinda like the Westward Expansion of the 19th century, just with less wagon trains and slightly more rotten body parts falling off.

"Four out here," Rafe says from a different window. "Two have stopped and are standing by the front porch."

"Let me see," Stuart says. He moves to Rafe's window and studies the Zs for a minute. "They're moving on."

"They always do," Critter says. "Storm's too strong for them to know we're in here."

"They'll know," Elsbeth says. "It may be a while, but eventually they'll know. It just takes one."

"She's right," Stuart says. "Once one gets curious enough to try to make it up the porch steps, then plenty more will follow."

"Plenty more," Elsbeth nods. "It's what they do."

"Yep, it's what they do," I say. "Thanks for the cheery reminder, El."

"No problem," she smiles. "I like to help."

Critter cackles at that, and half the cannies hiss at him to shut up. He doesn't take kindly to their hissing suggestions, so he starts bitching at them. In seconds the room erupts into a bicker fest. Awesome.

"Shut the fuck up now," Stuart growls. "Or I toss all of you out into the Million Z March!"

"That's a good one, Stuart," I smile. "That's a Jace worthy joke."

"Jace? You shut the fuck up too," Stuart snaps. "This is fucking serious. Not only do we have to deal with the Zs out there, but we have to figure out where we're going to go when we do see a break in the herd. We can't just run and wander. We need a direction, a goal. I'll be willing to bet there's another farmhouse somewhere, but where? These pieces of land can be hundreds of acres. We may have to hike for miles before we find another place to hunker down."

"We'll go to the bus," Elsbeth says. "I left it about three miles up the road behind a stand of trees. I covered it with brush so no one would see it. I bet it's just a pile of snow now. I can find it, though."

Raise your hand if you think all eyes turn to Elsbeth and stare at her with a healthy dose of "What the fuck?"

I hope all hands are raised.

"I got this," I say before Stuart explodes. "Uh, El? Are you telling us you've known about this bus the whole time, and are now just telling us because ... why?"

"I was going to tell you in the morning," Elsbeth says.

"Yes, that may be true," I say. "And I'm sure in Elsbeth logic that makes some kind of sense, but can you say specifically why you didn't just tell us right away?"

"Because you were all mad at me over the bodies," Elsbeth says. "The cannies don't trust me, Little Canny thinks I'm crazy, Stuart is always mad, and Critter is an old dick. Then you started in on me."

"Me? What did I do?" I ask.

"You doubted me," she says.

Ouch. That stings.

"You shouldn't doubt me, Long Pork," Elsbeth continues. "Family doesn't doubt."

"Well, that ain't true," Critter says. "My whole family doubted me my whole life. But I think you are confusing trust and doubt, little lady. My brother trusted me with his entire soul, but he still doubted every decision I made. You gotta learn to lighten up, and just take the lumps. That's what real family is about."

"I don't like lumps," Elsbeth says.

"Tough shit," Critter snaps. "Lumps is life, life is lumps. Get over it, and grow up."

"Can we get back to the bus?" Stuart says. "We don't need to do this family therapy session every time Elsbeth gets her panties in a wad."

"I ain't wearing panties," Elsbeth says.

There is a collective groan.

"What? They ride up my craw craw," Elsbeth says. "Hard to kill Zs and save Long Pork with panties in your craw craw."

"Okay, enough about your craw craw," I say. "I'm going to brain bleach that image right outta my noggin. El? The bus?"

"It's three miles away, due west," Elsbeth says.

"West?" I say. "That means you backtracked at some point."

"Backtracked? I been circling everyone the whole time," Elsbeth says. "Easy to do since that compound don't move none. I had plenty of time to map this whole place. I bet I could walk these farms blindfolded."

Considering that she got us through the pit in the pure darkness, I do not doubt her.

Watching Stuart's expressions as he tries to find words that aren't all shouty and pissed is pretty fun. I know he knows that getting angry at Elsbeth is like getting angry at a grizzly bear; it'll hurt you more than it'll hurt the bear. After a few seconds of some serious facial calisthenics, Stuart lets out a long, slow breath.

"Elsbeth?" he asks.

"Yes, Stuart?" she replies.

"Would you care to tell me what your whole plan was?" he says through gritted teeth. "Since it sounds like you had a plan, and just neglected to tell us."

"You didn't ask until now," Elsbeth states.

"Were you waiting for us to ask?" Stuart grumbles.

"No," Elsbeth says. "I was waiting for you to be nice. None of you have been nice. Except Long Pork. He's been nice. He was bugging me, but he was nice about it. Sorta."

"Panties in a wad," Critter mutters.

"I ain't got panties on," Elsbeth huffs. "I said that."

"Stop," I say, and hold up my hand. "Everyone just chill their bones a bit. We are all exhausted, and probably a bit traumatized. Emotions are high, nerves are frayed, bodies are run down. No one is thinking straight, and we're just going around in circles."

I look from person to person, but see only blank stares.

"Was that out loud?" I ask. "It was supposed to be."

"Yeah," Critter says. "We's just waitin' for you to continue. Everybody knows you gots more to say than just that."

"True, Crit," I nod. "I do. The gist of it is, we are all pretty freaked out by the bloody words and the skinned corpses. El has told me it's a message to her, but she won't say from whom and why. Right now, that doesn't matter. We drop it and focus on getting the fuck out of here without getting eaten or freezing in the storm. After that, we can deal with the other stuff. Everyone agreed?"

"Nope," Elsbeth says. "We don't deal with the other stuffs. *I* deal with the other stuffs. It's my stuffs. *Mine.* After we get to the bus, what we're gonna do is drive to the RVs and get Lourdes. She has the guns. Then we go to the compound, and save Greta. Maybe save some others if they haven't had their brains washed too long. Then keep going on down the road. That's my plan. It's a good plan. None of you have a better plan. I know that."

Stuart might be having a stroke. Or an epileptic fit. Or an epileptic stroke. Or it's bad gas. Or...

"I'm fucking pissed is what it is," Stuart snarls. "Because Elsbeth has not only held back info on a bus, but also knows where the rest of the convoy is!"

"Hey, what happened to holding up a finger when I talk out loud?" I whine.

Elsbeth points a finger at Stuart. "Should have been nicer and not treated me like a crazy. That's the lesson."

"There is no lesson!" Stuart shouts.

"Hey, guys," Rafe says.

"Not now!" Stuart snaps, then stalks over and gets right in Elsbeth's face. Bold fucking move. "El, I have been accepting of you since day one. I have fought by your side since day one. We have bled together. We have also rescued Jace's ass together more times than I can count."

"Six, I think," I say.

"Guys," Rafe says.

"Shut up, kid!" Stuart yells. "El, you are acting like a toddler. I would have expected this behavior from old Elsbeth, the one that still talked about Pa, and acted like she was a lost canny girl. But we all know that's not you. You're Carly Thornberg, and have skills and conditioning that most soldiers dream of. I know I do. So, cut the pouty little baby act, and suck it up. You may not want to wear panties, but it's time to put your big girl ones on, and join the team 100%! Do you hear me?"

"I hear you," Elsbeth says. "You're right."

"Guys, I really think—" Rafe tries to say.

"Shut. The. Fuck. Up," Stuart says, blinking at Elsbeth. "Did you just say I was right?"

"Yes," Elsbeth nods. "I'll put big girl panties on, and be part of the team. Just so you know, it may mean everyone dies horrible deaths because that's what's coming. Okey doke?"

"Yeah, I'm not alright with the horrible deaths part," I say. "Maybe we should let Elsbeth keep her panties off? If her going commando means we all live, then who are we to judge?"

"It's a metaphor," Elsbeth says. "Jeez, Long Pork, you can be dumb sometimes."

"What? I know it's a metaphor. I am well aware of when metaphors are being used. I am the metaphor master around—."

"Guys!" Rafe yells. "We have visitors downstairs, and I don't think they're here to tell us the good news!"

Everyone moves to the windows. That's a lot of movement. Even with the storm raging, we get more than a few Zs' attention. Undead heads creak on frozen necks, and chilly chins turn up to us. Not that it matters, we all see the horde of Zs that's broken off and is busy trying to climb the icy steps of the porch below.

"Poopy," I say. "Looks like it's big girl panties times all around now."

"Blankets, coats, weapons," Stuart orders. "Downstairs now. We go out the back, we go fast, and we don't look back. Any objections then?"

Everyone holds up a hand; there might be a few objections.

"Tough shit," Stuart says. "Let's move, people!"

***

So, apparently the cannies already scrounged the house for weapons. Good on them. Of course, the elephant in the room is whether or not they were going to tell us. I mean, they weren't thinking of keeping the weapons, waiting until Stuart, Critter, and I were asleep, and then butchering us were they? That would have really put a damper on survivor/canny relations.

I prefer to give them the benefit of the doubt, and think they were just being good, prepared canny scouts. Is that a thing? In this world? Yeah, I have a sinking feeling somewhere in the US there are canny scouts. I bet out West. What? You thought there'd be Canny Scouts in the South? Fuck you. Nope, I call the West. Probably Utah.

Since we're talking about it, I have to wonder what merit badges Canny Scouts would get? Skinning a victim? Proper preparation of the liver (with or without fava beans)? How you use human hide to make lampshades? To make fanny packs? To make Moleskin notebook covers? There would have to be an entire separate category for use of human hides. The possibilities are endless.

Everyone around me holds up a finger.

"Out loud?" I ask as we stand by the back door of the farmhouse, all crammed into the small kitchen. With the wood stove still going, it's downright toasty in this place. "Sorry."

"The second we hit the yard, we don't stop," Stuart says.

"You've already told us that," Rafe says, then shuts up fast as Stuart holds up the hatchets he has in each hand.

Weapons roll call!

Elsbeth, of course, has her blades. I think the things are like Thor's Mjolnir, they always come back to her. I mean, I assume those are the same blades. Fuck if I know anymore.

Stuart has those hatchets, and Critter has a nice, solid looking axe handle. Rafe is holding two aluminum baseball bats, while the cannies have various gardening tools, from hoes to shovels. One has a metal rake. I don't think that's practical, which I voice, but the guy won't listen to me.

Speaking of me, which is my favorite subject, I have a trusty, rusty crowbar. It's a sweet deal. One of the round, solid ones. Full size, too! Not one of those half bars, but a big one with the curved hook part. I love it so much. I can smash Z heads, and then jimmy open a safe later. I'm the shit.

As for clothing, we have as many layers on as we could find that would fit. Some of us look like the little brother from A Christmas Story, but it's worth it. Shit's gonna get cold. I have two blankets wrapped around me and tied off with rope. Didn't seem fair to waste long sleeved shirts on me when I only need one sleeve. You know what I mean?

"No stopping," Stuart says. "Elsbeth is going to lead. Follow her. Keep up. If you get separated then head due west. That's where the bus is."

"Behind trees," Elsbeth nods. "You'll find it."

"What kind of trees? Coniferous or deciduous?" I ask. Everyone glares. "What? It's good to know. I don't want to be hunting for a stand of cedars if it's behind some oaks."

"Trees," Elsbeth says. "Without their leaves."

"Deciduous," I smile. "Confers don't have leaves, they have needles, and you'd still see those because they don't drop off in the winter."

"Jace, shut the fuck up," Stuart sighs.

"Gotcha," I nod. "Let's do this."

Stuart shakes his head, tucks a hatchet under one arm, and yanks open the back door. His hatchet is instantly back in his hand as he bounds down the back steps and out into the dawning morning light. The storm is still pretty bad, so it could be ten in the morning and not actually dawn, but the clouds are so thick it doesn't matter.

Snow and wind whip against us, becoming like a first attack well before we reach the front row of Zs. I grip my crowbar, and hope I have nice, solid hits. This thing is made of heavy metal, and is going to hurt like fuck if I ding it. I don't think Rafe thought of that when he picked the aluminum bats. Those are the worst when it comes to arm vibrating dings.

Elsbeth and Stuart take point and rip into the herd of Zs, cutting a swath through the rotten parade. The snow darkens, and soaks up the black blood and liquids instantly. The other Zs close ranks and try to surround them, but I come at them with Critter and Rafe, and we keep Elsbeth's and Stuart's backs clear. I can hear the cannies behind us grunting and fighting, doing the same for us.

Which makes me wonder who is going to cover their backs? This fucking herd is thick, and we are barely twenty yards in when it looks like it will swallow us whole and never let any of us out. A scream on my right flank tells me that the cannies got the raw deal. Not that I care a ton. Allies? Yes. Cannies that were more than likely cheering at the top of their voices when my family was forced to run Cannibal Road? Very likely. I'm conflicted. Sorta. Not really.

Three Zs come at me from my right, and I take out the first one's knees with the crowbar, whip it up, and tear open the guts the of the second, get it stuck in the second's ribs, rip out the second's ribs, then bash in the third's skull, spilling brains all down its front. Bam! That's how you do that!

Oh, shit!

Two more try to take a bite out of my only arm, and I duck and throw my shoulder into them, knocking then down into the thick snow. One whack, two whacks. Their skulls crack, their bodies still.

I whirl around as I hear a snarl right behind me, and almost kill one of the cannies. Damn, that guys sounds just like a Z. I mean, he's all snarly and foamy at the mouth, and OH, FUCK! HE IS A Z!

Fucking A, that guy turned fast! What the fuck?

I'm able to get my crowbar up and block his mouth from clamping on my face. The bastard is so fresh that his muscles haven't been slowed by the cold. He's all ragey and thrashy and mean. I spin him about, but can't free the crowbar. Motherfucking fresh Z has the lockjaw goin' on. I try to kick him off, but all I do is get my wound singing. I'd almost learned to block it out, but leave it to me to figure out some way to fuck myself.

Stumbling backwards, I yank and yank on the crowbar, but the piece of shit Z won't let go. Dead hands grab at my blankets, and I shake them off, but there are only more to replace them. Why won't this fucker let go?

The guy's head explodes in a spray of bright red blood and grey brain as Critter slams his axe handle down on the fucker's skull. The crowbar comes free so fast I go flying back and fall on my ass. I'm nipple deep in snow and just start swinging wildly, taking out Zs at the knees, cracking femurs, ripping open long dead thighs, hooking them in the hamstrings. I hobble those bitches!

"Get yer ass up, Short Pork!" Critter yells as he grabs me by the neck and lifts.

He totally hits a nerve, and I shout as I scramble to my feet. I'd scream at him, but he did just save my life. I'll scream at him later. That fucking hurt.

I can barely see Elsbeth and Stuart ahead of us as the snow keeps coming down. I'm not from this area, and have been living in Asheville for years, so I haven't ever witnessed a Midwest blizzard like this. This shit is insane, yo. The flakes are huge, and they punch you in the skin like icy gauntlets. Every smack is a challenge to a duel, but there's no winning this test of honor. I just have to keep taking the smacks, and force myself to move.

More Zs, an endless sea of them.

My arm is nearly numb from swinging the crowbar and the constant, soul-crushing cold. Every time I lift the crowbar, I think it will be the last time, but then I get a little adrenaline rush from killing a Z, and I find the strength to lift again. This pattern goes on and on as we battle through the herd.

Rafe shoves me to the side and kills two Zs, then spins about, and kills two more behind us. Critter is on his side and crushes three, then lunges back to avoid a claw swipe by an uppity Z. He cracks that one's skull, then we hear the screams of another canny behind us. I look over my shoulder after shattering a Z's legs, and see there's nothing to be done for the screaming canny. That guy is a goner. His throat and chest are ripped into before I can take a step in his direction, even if I wanted to.

I don't want to. One of the many unspoken rules of the zombie apocalypse is you learn to let a lost cause die. That rule doesn't apply to me, though. I came into this shit a lost cause, so I'm grandfathered in.

In minutes, it's only me, Critter, and Rafe, with Elsbeth and Stuart well ahead of us. This is not good. I have a sinking feeling we three have only survived because the cannies were our death buffer. Now that they are Z chow, that leaves us as dessert. I'm suddenly claustrophobic, even though the herd hasn't gotten any thicker. Man, I can't breathe. I'm choking! I'm choking!

WHACK!

Hey, I can breathe again! Oh, wait, a Z had grabbed onto my blanket, and it was choking me from behind. Rafe broke his arm off, so the pressure's gone. Damn, I thought I was having a panic attack. Can't afford one of those while fighting for my life.

"Less talking!" Rafe yells. "More fighting!"

"The finger rule is still in effect while fighting!" I say. He flips me off. "Fair enough!"

A Z goes for Critter's shoulder, and I crush its head before it can bite down. Of course, it being me, the crowbar slips and nails

Critter in the shoulder, causing him to scream and turn on me, the axe handle raised.

"Z!" I yell, and point at the one at his feet.

"Fuck you!" he yells back and pushes forward.

Rafe and I are right behind him, turning in constant circles to keep from being taken down from behind. It's dizzying and exhausting, but that kind of describes the whole apocalypse when you think about it. Not that I have time to think about it! More whacking! More cracking! More smacking! More falling!

No, wait, not falling! Falling bad! Shit.

I'm down, and two Zs pile on top of me. More stumble over us, and suddenly the little light there is gets blocked by the Z dog pile that has chosen me to be the bottom. For the record, I'm a top. Wait, I should probably clarify that.

No time to clarify!

I jam the pointy end of the crowbar into a Z's eye socket, then another and another. I keep doing that, ducking my head to the side this way and that to avoid the ever-gnashing teeth. Always with the gnashing, these Zs! Oy!

I keep jamming and sticking and jabbing and gouging and screaming! There is a lot of screaming! So much with the screaming, I am!

What the hell? When did I turn into Yiddish Yoda?

More jamming and gouging, and then my shoulder can't lift anymore. The weight of the Z pile is too much, and I collapse, unable to keep my leverage. The fight has left me, and I lie here and wait for it all to end. And wait. And wait.

Why isn't it ending? Hello? Zs? Gimpy, one-armed dipshit here, ripe for the eating. Hello?

I count to one hundred, because that seems like a plan, and then start shoving Z corpses off me. It takes me a while, but I am finally free. And coated in Z gunk. This is not a bad thing. The herd parts around me since I now smell and pretty much look like them. I even swear some of them are giving me the stink eye, like I'm the slacker Z taking an unsanctioned break from the constant marching.

Oh, please, let me stay quiet.

I sort of work my way sideways out of the herd, stumbling a little this way, then a little that way, in a zigzag line that gets me to a field that adjoins the one we'd started in. The herd is much thinner, and I can turn on the normal human speed. Oh, who am I kidding? I'm so tired that my top speed is pretty much Z speed. Harder to attract attention, at least.

There is a long while of stumbling and limping before I come to a road. I can see the outline of the sun above me, just barely. So that would make that direction east? West? Wait? If the sun is above me then it's probably noon. That means I have zero idea which direction is which.

Fucking awesome.

So, I close my eyes, spin in a circle, fall on my ass, pick myself up, and point.

"That way," I mutter. "I'm going that way."

I must have been under that Z pile for a while, because I don't even see traces of footprints in the snow. Sure, the shit is coming down hard as ever, but there's no way footprints can fill up that fast. Can they? Again, my ignorance of Midwest weather is a bummer.

I walk like fifty miles before I hear a sound that isn't the howling of freezing ass cold wind. Okay, I probably walk maybe ten miles. Five. Two? One mile. I at least stumble along the road for one mile. You gotta give me one, man.

I look around, trying to figure out what the noise is, when I see two dots of light directly behind me. Headlights! Yes! Or no? Shit, I have no idea if those are good headlights or bad headlights. Fuck, fuck, fuck! I stumble to the side of the road and into snow up to my chest as I fall into the drainage ditch. I duck down and wait as the vehicle gets closer and closer.

Then it starts to go by, and I realize I have panicked for the wrong reason. It's a bus! It's the bus! And, irony not lost on me, it's a short bus. Of course it is.

I wave my hand and start yelling for it to stop, but it just rolls on by with Stuart at the wheel. I see Elsbeth's face, Critter's, Rafe's, all pressed to the foggy glass windows, their eyes searching through the storm. But they don't see me. Why would they? I'm buried in snow, down in a ditch, and the storm is not helping. Again with the fuck, fuck, fuck!

"FUUUUUUUUUUUUUUUUUUUUUUUUUCK!!!" I scream at the top of my lungs.

Brake lights come on, and the bus skids to a stop.

No way.

The side door opens and Elsbeth jumps out, her blades at the ready. She spins about, her eyes scanning the scene.

"EL!" I scream. "EL! OVER HERE!"

I wave the crowbar over my head, and that catches her attention. She sprints to me, then falls into the same ditch I'm stuck in.

"Hey, Long Pork," she smiles. "We lost you."

"And now you've found me. Thanks for that," I say. "Any chance you can help me get out of this shit? My scrotum is frozen to the insides of my thighs. It's not feeling so great."

"That is too much information, Long Pork," Elsbeth says, and uses her vastly superior physical skills to get us both out of the ditch. "I know all about too much information. Telling people about your frozen scrotum is too much information. Don't say it again."

"Words to live by," I smile, then look at the bus. "Short bus, huh?"

Elsbeth shrugs. "Critter thinks it's perfect for us."

"So do I, El," I smile as she helps me to the bus. "So do I."

CHAPTER TEN

I don't think Lourdes is as happy as I am with the hugging.

"You stink, Jace," she says as she shoves me away.

"Jace!"

"Dad!"

I run from the short bus and into the arms of my wife and son. Now, *they* are all about the hugging!

"Where's Greta?" Stella asks as she pushes me away and looks towards the bus. "Jace? Where is Greta?"

"We're going to go back for her," I say. "Don't worry."

"Don't worry?" she snaps. "Are you fucking joking? I'm fucking terrified! Why isn't she with you?"

"Too many shotguns," Elsbeth says as she comes up behind us. "Those guys like shotguns. Lots of shotguns."

"She ain't kiddin' there," Critter agrees. "Them's boys do like their shotguns."

"And their antiquated ideas of gender roles," I say. "Men get shotguns, women get chores. And total subjugation, apparently." I see the horror on my wife's face and wince. "Shit. That probably wasn't what you wanted to hear."

"Jace, you have to go get our daughter!" Stella yells.

"We're already on it," Lourdes says as she cinches a pack on her back and slings her M4 over her shoulder. "I have six men ready. If anyone wants to join, I won't argue."

180

"Six? Just six?" Stella barks. "That's not enough!"

"With my men, that's plenty," Lourdes says, and looks at the RVs that are circled together in a rest area parking lot. The snow is still coming down hard, but it looks like she's made sure the asphalt is cleared and there's sand and salt spread everywhere. "I can't risk taking more. Not if we have to deal with another herd."

"They aren't stopping," Stuart says to Stella. "I don't know why, but the Zs just keep coming. We'll go get Greta, but the rest of you have to be ready to move." He nods at the RVs. "Even with the vehicles, you can still get overwhelmed."

"We won't be long," I say. "We put a plan together on the way here. We'll get in and out before they even know what's hit them."

"Well, that ain't true," Critter grins. "They're gonna know exactly what hit them. They just won't know we're the reason. I love this plan."

"Jace? What do you mean we? You're going too?" Stella asks.

"Yeah, I need to," I say. "I think I know where Greta is being held, if she isn't in the Tomb."

"The Tomb?" Stella cries.

"It's just a mine," I say. "But I have to go so we can get to her right away. There isn't much margin for mistakes with this plan."

"Yet you always find those mistakes, Dad," Charlie says. "I better come with."

"You aren't going anywhere!" Stella snaps, and jams a finger into Charlie's chest. He winces and backs away quickly.

"Ow, Mom, knock it off," he complains.

"He re-injured his chest wound when we crashed," Stella says. She looks me up and down. "What about you?"

"Oh, you know me," I grin. "Not a scratch."

"His leg is fucked, and he can't keep his thoughts in his head," Rafe says.

"My leg is not fucked," I argue. "But the second part is true. The filter is pretty much gone. Adios. Kaput. Sayonara. Ta ta. See ya later, alligator. Hasta la vista—."

"We get the idea," Stella says. She looks me in the eye, and then nods. "Fine, but I'm coming with."

"No, you are not," Lourdes says. "I need you here in charge. You're the best for the job. Coordinate with the Fitzpatricks, John, and Reaper. Have everyone prepped and ready to run as soon as we get back or if a Z herd comes. I'm counting on you, Stella."

Stella opens her mouth to protest, then there's noise from over by the RVs. It looks like one of the cannies is in a shouting match with one of the Fitzpatrick brothers. Stella sighs, and shakes her head.

"Okay, I'll stay," she says. "But you keep my husband safe, Lourdes. I'm counting on you for that."

"I think you have the easier job," Lourdes says despite the shouting match escalating so that now Melissa and Mr. Flips are involved. I'm not sure if they are trying to break it up, or if they're taking sides. "See?"

"Go," Stella says to me. "Bring my baby girl back."

"Will do, love of my life," I smile. "That's a promise."

"Hey, Stella?" Elsbeth says as we all turn and head for the short bus.

"Yeah, El?" Stella replies.

"Keep everyone close," Elsbeth says. "Don't let them wander around. They need to stay close. Wanderers may go missing. Just sayin'."

Stella looks at me, and I shrug.

"Not a fucking clue," I say.

"Something we should know?" Lourdes asks Elsbeth.

"I just said what you need to know," Elsbeth sighs. "Weren't you listening? Why don't people listen to me?" She turns and steps onto the bus, still talking. "I have things to say, and no one listens. Then they get mad when I don't have things to say. They should listen when I do, not ask when I don't. Stupid people. Dumb, stupid people. Cannies listen better."

"So, El's all fired up," I say. I grab my wife and son one more time for a quick hug, then turn and follow Elsbeth onto the bus. "Fare thee well, family! I shall return triumphant and with our lost daughter! Count on me!"

Stella shakes her head and points a finger at Lourdes. "Not a scratch."

"How about I agree to bring him back with all limbs?" Lourdes asks.

"That'll do," Stella says.

"Yeah, good luck with that," Charlie says, following Lourdes onto the bus.

"Hey, get the fuck off," I snap. "You're staying here and helping your mother."

"Oh, come on," Charlie whines.

I tap him on the chest just like Stella did. He winces, and folds his arms across his chest.

"Charlie!" Stella yells. "Stop fucking around, and get over here!"

The shouts from the Fitzpatricks and the cannies get worse, and Stella turns on her heels, all her anger and frustration aimed at them.

"HEY!" she yells. "KNOCK IT THE FUCK OFF NOW, ALL OF YOU!"

"Don't let her kill anyone," I say to Charlie as Stuart starts up the bus. "She's in that kind of mood."

"Will do," Charlie says as the bus door closes.

I give a quick wave, then grab a seat. Right next to Critter.

"Wait, why aren't you staying?" I ask. "You're the official leader here."

"And miss this fight?" Critter laughs. "I can't wait to see what happens to that Kelvin asshole. Runnin' a God con on everyone. I ain't exactly religious, but that just pisses me off."

"It's not fake," I say. "The guy actually believes he's chosen by God. I'm not saying he isn't crooked and corrupt and playing everyone, but he does believe what he says."

"Then kill him if you get a chance," Lourdes says. "I know the type. He'll sacrifice everyone around him and then himself just to win. If he truly believes, he'll think his glory is in death, not life."

"Maybe," I say. "I'm pretty sure he likes life." I glance at Elsbeth who is sitting at the back of the bus, pissed and muttering to herself. "Plus, the guy seems to know a lot about the Consortium and Elsbeth's ninja sisters. There's more going on than just his cultish ways."

"What?" Lourdes asks. "How would some guy out in the middle of nowhere know about all of that?"

"He's ex-CIA," I say. "Or something like that."

"That makes no sense," Lourdes says. "What are the odds of us running into a company man?"

"What are the odds of any of this shit?" Critter laughs. "Lady, if you haven't noticed already, odds went out the window when the dead started standin' up and chowin' down. If you think there's such a thing as coincidence in this world anymore, then you ain't payin' attention."

"As much as I want to wrap a logic blanket around this," I say, "Critter's got a point. Half the time I think it's all out of our hands." I look down at Stumpageddon. "Or hand, in my case."

"You sure this is how you want to do this?" Stuart asks, looking at us in the rearview mirror.

"Only way in to that compound where they won't notice us," I say. "It sucks balls, but it's a sound plan."

"And we have flashlights now." Rafe grins, then looks at Lourdes. "Right? We have flashlights?"

"Plenty," Lourdes says. "And better."

"Then this'll be a breeze," Rafe smiles.

"Who is this kid again?" Lourdes asks me.

"A giant pain in my ass," I say. "But he knows how to fight. And I think he's as eager to get Greta back as I am." I shudder. "Not that I'm thrilled about that, but I'll deal with it when this shit is all over."

"It ain't ever gonna be over," Critter chuckles. "Ain't no one listenin'?"

"They never listen!" Elsbeth shouts from the back. "Assholes."

***

So, guess where we are? Come on, guess. GUESS!

"Dude, who are you yelling at?" Rafe cries, his hands covering his ears as we step off the short bus.

"Sorry. That was supposed to be my inside voice," I apologize.

"You failed on that one," Rafe says.

"Has he been this bad the whole time?" Lourdes asks.

"Yes," everyone answers. Well, everyone that's been with me the past couple of days.

"Should we gag him?" Lourdes asks. "We can't have him alerting the enemy to our presence."

"I don't need a gag," I say before Critter can answer. He'd love for me to be gagged. "I can stay quiet. I promise."

"But can you keep up?" Stuart asks as he racks the slide on his M4, slings it, then racks the slide on his 9mm, and holsters that on his hip. "You're favoring that leg a lot."

"That's because it hurts like a mother fuck," I say. "But it won't slow me down. Or slow any of you down. My daughter is in there. I plan on being the first friendly face she sees."

"Second," Elsbeth says. "My fault she got taken."

"How do you figure that?" I ask. "I'm her father."

"And I left the group because of..." She trails off, then kicks the snow with her left foot. "I shouldn't have left. The shotgun guys wouldn't have lived to take you. Any of you."

"Well, time to make up for that," Critter says as he pumps a round into his own shotgun. "Let's show these God fearin' idiots who they need to really fear."

"That's a good one, Crit," I say. "Wish I'd thought of that."

"Well, ya didn't, so shut up," Critter says as we trudge through the knee deep snow to the mouth of the pit's back entrance.

Dammit! I wanted you all to guess where we are, and there I go spoiling it.

Yeah, we're back at the pit. It's the only way in that isn't guarded. Well, not guarded the same way the compound is at the front of the mine. The pit's guarded, but only to prevent an escape, not to prevent an assault. And we be bringin' the assault, motherfuckers!

I can tell by the glares that that last part was out loud.

"I don't need a gag," I mutter as we switch on headlamps and flashlights and walk into the darkness of the pit's back tunnel.

He he, back tunnel. We are totally going into the pit's asshole.

185

Wait ... that's not funny. That means I'm going in an asshole. Dammit! That metaphor totally backfired. Sigh.

***

Once we are in the pit proper, Lourdes's men fan out, the flashlights on the barrels of their carbines and rifles going dark. Why do they go dark? Because Lourdes had a nice surprise for all of us when we told her what we are up against.

I feel a hand fumble at the side of my face, and suddenly the pit is illuminated by a greenish glow. Yay for night vision goggles! I knew that woman had some toys tucked away somewhere, I'm glad she trusts us enough to bring them out so we can all play.

The pit is completely different when you aren't fumbling about blind. I can see the various rock formations and boulders that dot the area. Rocks of various sizes are everywhere, and I quickly see just how lucky we were to even get out without tripping and breaking our necks. Gotta thank Elsbeth for that one.

Slowly, making sure we don't make too much noise, we work our way across the pit. Zs come at us, their hands outstretched like bad Frankenstein's Monster imitators, but we take them down with ease. Some rifle butts to the temples, axes through skulls, and my trusty crowbar caving in more than a couple of heads.

Why do I have a crowbar and not a gun? That's a fine question. For some reason, no one wanted me to have a gun. No pistol, no rifle, not even a sawed off shotgun. Something about my unstable mental state. Now, I am all about caution, but I don't see a connection with my verbal foibles and an inability to handle a firearm. I am a firearm handling motherfucker. I have to be one of the better shots in the convoy. And that's with my left hand!

Fuckers.

But, hey, I have a crowbar and it rocks, so I'm not complaining.

"Yes, you are," Rafe whispers next to me.

"Am I being too loud?" I ask.

"No, just mumbling a lot," Rafe says. "I think you've learned to keep the volume down."

Lourdes turns, and gives us the NVG bug eye glare. It's not so much a glare, since we can't see her eyes, as it is a sustained, silent chastisement. I'm married. I know what those are.

Shit, I take that back. Never let Stella know I said that. Dammit, now my brain is betraying me in even worse ways. Why, brain, why?

"I will kill you myself," Lourdes says.

"Sorry," I whisper.

We keep going.

We must get somewhere that Elsbeth recognizes, because she holds up a hand and pushes some of Lourdes's guys out of the way. She slowly moves to a large boulder and places her hand on it. A couple of Zs come around the side, but she snaps their necks and tosses them to the ground without even flinching.

"The landing is just ahead," she says, and then takes off.

"Elsbeth! Wait!" Lourdes calls out as quietly as possible, but Elsbeth is already out of sight.

We move around the boulder, and I can see the landing to the stairs about a hundred yards away. This is good and bad. Good we made it with only a few Zs to deal with; bad because there is at least six feet of rock to climb up to get onto the landing, and my leg is hurting way more than I'm letting on. I do not look forward to that climb.

We're fifty yards out when the pit turns into a blinding, migraine inducing, holy shit I think my retinas are on fire, hell. Someone just turned on the lights.

"Hi, folks!" a voice calls out from in front of us. I know that voice. Reptile Jesus. "Jace! Welcome back! And you brought friends! Here I thought you weren't a true believer. I have to thank you for having confidence in me enough to do a little recruiting while you were gone!"

We all yank the NVGs from our faces and scatter. The pit's lights are on, and we are out in the open, fish in a barrel.

"Where are you going?" Kelvin asks. "I'm hurt you're running away. I was going to read a couple of Bible verses, then we could have some graham crackers and milk. We do have some delicious milk here, straight from our own cows, you know."

"What is up with his accent?" Stuart asks me as we cower behind a small boulder that is a lot less cover than I'd like.

"I know, right?" I reply. "I think the guy is trying for a Southern preacher accent, but is ending up more with a shitty Kevin Costner as Robin Hood accent. Not good."

"I can hear you, Jace!" Kelvin yells. "And I spent a lot of time abroad, so I have picked up some subtle European nuances here and there. More than one woman has told me it makes me sound cultured."

"Like spoiled yogurt," I yell, and turn to Stuart. "Get it? Because yogurt is cultured with bacteria and I hate him, so I said the yogurt was spoiled and-."

"I get it, shut up," Stuart replies.

"How about I make you fine new folks a deal?" Kelvin yells. "You drop your weapons and come peacefully, and I won't leave you down here in the pit. I think that punishment has played itself out. Plus, you know where the backdoor is."

I snicker.

"Really?" Stuart growls.

"Sorry," I reply.

"I'm sorry, but I don't think we will be surrendering," Lourdes yells. "In fact, I'll be asking for your surrender. I will also be asking that you release all prisoners. You do that, and you get to walk away alive today."

"That ain't the deal," Critter hisses. "I want to shoot his ass."

"Yes, I have to agree with the old man," Kelvin responds. "That isn't the deal. The deal is you throw down your weapons, and I let *you* live. Not the other way around."

"You all have shotguns," Lourdes yells. "We have rifles and carbines. It's short range versus long range. We'll cut you down before we close the distance enough for your weapons to even be remotely effective."

"That's quite the assumption," Kelvin laughs.

"It's not an assumption," Lourdes says. "It's firearm basics."

"No, I agree with your assessment of the effectiveness of shotguns to rifles," Kelvin agrees. "But what I don't agree with is that these shotguns are our weapons against you. Our weapons against you are coming right now. You see, Ms. Torres, and yes, I

188

do know who you are, a simple fact about warfare is that it is nearly impossible to win when you are fighting two fronts. Or, in your cases, fighting your front and your behind."

"He he," I snicker. "Behind."

"Long Pork," Stuart snarls.

"What? I can't help it," I reply. "It's how I handle stress before shit gets crazy."

"Too late," Stuart says as he points behind us. "Zs!"

He's right. Here come the Zs. And it's quite a fucking lot of them. Looks like they're fresh too, which means they'll be limber and strong and really, really fucking hungry. That's not good.

"Whatever shall you do now?" Kelvin asks. "If you stand up and fight the biters, then you'll expose yourselves and we'll start firing. If you stay put, then the biters will overwhelm you, and it'll all be over before it begins. So, how about you lay down those weapons, put your hands in the air, and walk to my voice. Despite my ambiguous accent, I have been told I have a comforting voice. Would it be so bad to walk to such a voice as this?"

"Your voice is stupid," Elsbeth says. "How about if I rip it out for you?"

There's a scream, and the sound of shotguns discharging fills the pit. Lourdes and her men don't waste time with the Zs behind us, and stand and open fire at the shotgun men, moving quickly from their cover and towards the landing.

I, on the other hand, only have a crowbar and can't exactly sprint at the moment, so I keep my attention on the encroaching Zs. They'll reach me way before I can get to the landing, and that's assuming I don't get cut down by a shotgun on the way. So, it's Z fighting time!

I get up, raise my crowbar, and run at the Zs. Then I trip over a rock and fall flat on my face. Guess what? That gash on my forehead opens up again. Fresh blood pours as I struggle to stand. Guess what else? Zs love the smell of fresh blood.

I swear half the horde comes for my ass.

Fuck the crowbar, I'm bailing!

But instead of running to the landing, I run parallel to the front of the Zs towards the far wall of the pit. I see a boulder, and I have an idea. With the lights on, the pit looks so much smaller than I thought it would. Sure, I saw it when I was first brought down here, but you know how it is when you visit or travel somewhere the first time, it always takes longer and everything seems bigger. The magic has worn off for me, so it's not so imposing now.

I run (and by run, I mean quickly and painfully limp) as fast as I can. The Zs are getting closer and closer, and I know that if I just make it to the wall, I'll be fine. Why do I think this? Because, like I said, I have an idea.

All the Zs' attention is on me, and when I get to the boulder right by the wall, I clamber up it as fast as possible. Unfortunately, only having one hand, this means I have to let my crowbar go. No worries, I'll get it back when it's all over.

"Stuart!" I yell. "Now!"

"Now, what?" he yells back, fighting off a dozen Zs at once. "What the fuck are you talking about?"

I wipe my forehead and flick blood down on the ground. The Zs go completely apeshit and swarm over the fresh blood.

"Sitting ducks! Fish in a barrel! Turkey shoot!" I shout.

Stuart blasts a Z's head off, cracks another's spine, takes a third out at the legs, then crushes it's skull with a boot, and blasts another Z's head off. He looks over at me, and how the majority of the horde is surrounding my boulder, all eager to get at my sweet, sweet Jace juice. My blood. I'm talking about my blood when I say Jace juice.

Thankfully, I see Stuart smile.

"Critter! Rafe! On me!" Stuart yells as he turns his rifle on the horde of Zs. A horde that faces me, since I decided that being bait was my best chance of survival.

They say the best offense is a good defense. Is being bait defense, though? Is it offense? What would bait be classified as in warfare terms? Or professional football terms? Because I always think of that saying referring more to football than to warfare.

Stuart, Critter, and Rafe open fire on the horde and start cutting them down. I curl up in the fetal position and cover my head with my arm, since I'd really not like to catch any friendly fire. Not that my one arm will exactly save me from a bullet, but I like to be optimistic in these situations.

The gunfire is deafening, and my ears are ringing so much that it takes me a second to realize that it's finally stopped. I pull my arm away and peek over the boulder. Nothing but piles of Z corpses. The few that decided they didn't want to stand there and die, and instead turned and went after Stuart, Critter, and Rafe, are quickly being taken down by those three, melee style.

I glance at the landing and see blood and bodies everywhere. Lourdes and her men are climbing up onto the landing, having obviously out fought Kelvin's shotgun bitches. I do a quick count, and see that Lourdes didn't lose a single guy. My count also tells me that there are two important people missing.

"Where's Reptile Jesus and Elsbeth?" I shout.

Lourdes gets onto the landing and looks over at me. "Who?"

"Reptile Jesus! I mean Kelvin! The asshole that was talking! Where is he?" I shout.

"He ran!" Lourdes shouts back. "Elsbeth took off after him!"

"Oh! Okay!" I yell.

"Jace, shut up, and get down here," Stuart says.

"Right-O," I say, and slide down off the boulder. I start to walk past the Z corpses, then stop as I recognize a face. "Oh, wow."

"What? Who is it?" Stuart asks.

"Her name was Tara," I say as I kneel next to the young woman's body. I look at the others and realize I recognize a lot of them, and they are mostly all women. "Fucking A. The son of a bitch sacrificed his own followers to fill the pit." Then terror fills my guts. "Greta!"

I start tearing through the piles of Z corpses like a madman, hoping and praying I don't find my daughter. The others realize what I'm doing and help, but after a few minutes of searching it's obvious she isn't here.

"She's still up top," I say. "Come on."

I'd be lying if I say my climb onto the landing is graceful. So I won't say it is. With Lourdes leading once again, with me navigating the twists and turns, we sprint through the mine and get to the mouth just in time to see Elsbeth and Kelvin face off in the middle of the compound. I'd also be lying if I didn't say that it's a pretty cool face off. Kelvin has some skills.

Elsbeth sends a flying roundhouse kick at the man, and he actually catches her leg in midair and throws her to the ground. He drops a boot right where her head was a split second earlier, but Elsbeth is fast enough that she dodges, and answers by slamming a fist into his exposed crotch. But Kelvin only smiles and falls to one knee, planting it right in Elsbeth's chest.

"I always wear a cup!" he yells.

"That doesn't seem practical for everyday use," I say to Stuart. I shut up without him having to tell me.

Elsbeth responds by boxing Kelvin's ears, then whips her legs like a helicopter, throwing the man off of her while flipping to her feet at the same time. So fucking cool!

"You have a cup for your face?" Elsbeth shouts, then rams an elbow into Kelvin's nose over and over again. The man sort of sways for a moment, then tumbles over onto his side. "Didn't think so."

"Totally badass," I say as we all run up to Elsbeth. "I so wish I could have recorded that. Fuck TV when you have an Elsbeth around."

"Why would someone fuck a TV?" Elsbeth asks. "That would hurt."

"Funny," I say.

"No, painful," Elsbeth replies. "That's what hurt means, Long Pork. Not funny."

"No, I meant… Oh, forget it," I say, and look around the snow covered compound, then point. "Those are the women's trailers. Greta has to be in there."

While Lourdes and her men pick up Kelvin, and not so nicely, I may say, Elsbeth, Stuart, Critter, Rafe, and I all hurry to the cluster of trailers where I saw the women at earlier. We get almost to the first one when the door is kicked open, and out comes my daughter.

Only one problem: there's a woman behind her holding a pistol to Greta's temple.

"Let Kelvin go!" the woman yells. "Or I kill your girl!"

"You must be Jobeth," I say. "Kelvin spoke so highly of you the other day. He especially said what a kind and caring soul you are, doing God's work by making sure the ladies of the compound don't come to harm."

"He never said that!" Jobeth snarls. "He hates me!"

"Uh, then why do you want us to let him go?" I ask.

"Because he promised to take me with him!" Jobeth yells. "He said once we were done here he'd show me where—"

She doesn't get a chance to finish as her head explodes into a thousand bits of bone and brain. Greta screams, and runs her ass off over to us as all of a sudden the compound is filled with rifle fire. Huh, I guess they don't just have shotguns.

I wrap my girl in my arm and hit the deck as Elsbeth falls on top of both of us. Stuart's face is close to mine, and we cower there, a pile of survivors, while rifles, carbines, pistols, and shotguns blast the ever living fuck out of everything. I now know why dogs hate the Fourth of July. There is nothing worse than a fuck ton of bang bangs going on when there is absolutely nothing you can do about it.

The gunfire starts to slacken, and I feel Elsbeth's weight lift off me.

"Get up, Long Pork," she says, and pulls me up.

She smiles down at Greta and pulls her up too, then gives her a huge bear hug. Greta's eyes about pop out of her skull from the hug, but I don't think she minds too much.

"Come on," Elsbeth says, and tugs us back towards the Tomb, which I am now going to just call a mine, since Reptile Jesus can't make me call it the Tomb anymore. "We're leaving."

"Wouldn't it be easier to go out the front?" I ask, then duck as gunfire erupts again in that direction. "Oh, right."

We get to the mouth of the mine, and then stop. It's pretty obvious we aren't going out the backdoor.

"Why are you giggling?" Greta snaps. "This isn't funny, Dad."

"Backdoor," I snicker, then stop as I get that teenage girl death glare. "Right. Not funny."

"What's goin' on?" Critter asks as he and Rafe come up behind us. "Why ain't we goin' in?" He looks at what we're looking at and frowns. "Well, fuck me. That ain't good."

There's a whole lot of smoke coming from the mine. Yeah, I'm thinking that shooting guns in a place filled with combustible coal dust was not the best thing to do. Looks like the backdoor is on fire. Kinda like the next day after eating Thai food.

"Dad!" Greta shouts. "Stop giggling! It's fucking creepy!"

"I was just thinking that…" I start, then see that none of the faces around me give a shit what I was thinking. "Sorry."

"We go out the front," Elsbeth says. "Only way."

We all turn and see Lourdes and her men pursuing the last of Kelvin's guys. But I don't see Kelvin anywhere. He must have gotten away from them. Oh, no, wait … there he is.

Right by the compound gate. Hey, he's opening the gate. How nice of him.

"It is God's fate!" Kelvin yells as he throws open the gates. "I know that now!"

After throwing open the gates, he throws his hands in the air.

Instead of making a bold escape, Kelvin has decided that a bold sacrifice is the plan of attack. Once again with the best offense is a good defense. Hmmm, I still don't think I'm using that right.

You remember that massive herd of Zs we fought through to get away from that last farmhouse? Yeah, it's found the compound. And it's bursting through the gates, all hungry mouths and clawing hands. Some of those mouths and hands rip into Kelvin as he just stands there, his arms and face raised to the sky.

"Slaves, be willing to serve your masters! Do this with all respect!" he shouts. "You should obey the masters who are good and kind, and you should obey the masters who are bad!"

Well, that's one way to go out. Hey, looks like some of the Zs get to find out if Reptile Jesus tastes like chicken.

"Oh, for fuck's sake," Greta says, and covers her face with her hands. "Will someone make him stop?"

"Girl, if we could do that we would have a long time ago," Critter says as we stare at the hundreds and hundreds of Zs that stream into the compound, all heading right for us.

CHAPTER ELEVEN

Choice isn't exactly your friend when you're facing the numbers we are. It isn't like before when we fought our way through the Z herd from that farmhouse. That was a risk, and one that paid off because we were only cutting across. We weren't actually fighting the whole herd, but just the few we needed to fight to get from one side to the other.

Here, now, is a whole other melon. That's a saying, right? A whole other melon? I don't know. Fuck it. It's a saying now.

You see, what we're facing is the entire herd, coming right for us. There's no cutting through, because that would be like traveling from a shark's mouth all the way out its anus. It can be done, but you sure as shit aren't going to be alive at the end of that journey.

"Come on," I shout. "I have an idea!"

"That isn't comforting!" Stuart shouts back.

"Just follow me, dickhead!" I yell, and limp off towards Kelvin's cluster of trailers. "I know where the safe room is!"

I know they don't really trust my judgement at the moment, but no one argues, and they all follow quickly behind me. I glance to the side and see Lourdes watching us.

"Come on!" I yell. Yelling is good because then she knows to rally her folks on us and get to the trailers. But yelling is bad because it also lets the Zs know which way we're going. "Poop."

We get to the trailer cluster, and Rafe is the first one to the door. He yanks it open, and then half his back explodes out at us in a spray of spine and fluids. His body does a brutal pirouette, then collapses at my feet as I look up and see Maury standing there with a high-powered rifle in his hands. I guess that answers who started all the shooting.

The world slows down. Maury's finger starts to press down on the rifle's trigger again just as a blur shoves me out of the way and flies through the trailer's door. I hear a gunshot, and even feel the heat of a bullet whiz past me, but luckily I feel no pain. Well, other than when the world speeds back up, and I don't get my hand out in time to stop my fall. Forehead and ground meet once again. Those two should get a fucking room.

I roll over and watch as Maury tries to get the rifle up in time to block Elsbeth's blades, but he doesn't stand a chance. None of us say a word as Elsbeth literally dismembers the man before our eyes. Limbs fall away, clothes fall away, ears, lips, nose, all fall away until all that's left is a stump of a man lying in a huge pool of his own blood. He tries to say something, but Elsbeth doesn't give him a chance as she jams a blade through his mouth and out the back of his head.

She looks back at us, rage filling her features.

"Little Canny," is all she says.

Critter and Stuart help me to my feet, and we look down as Greta is on the ground, cradling Rafe's head in her lap. His mouth is open, and he's trying to say something, but Greta puts a finger to his lips, and he stops. She leans over and kisses him on the forehead, the nose, then the mouth. He gets a smile halfway finished before the life leaves his eyes.

"Shit," I say. "I think I'm going to miss that kid."

"Yeah," Critter says.

"What are you people waiting for?" Lourdes yells as she and her men reach the trailer. Then she stops as she sees the scene. "Oh. Fuck."

"Nothing we can do," Greta says, tears filling her eyes as she gently gets up from Rafe's body and looks at me. "Where's the safe room?"

"This way," I say, and move past Elsbeth and the many pieces of Maury. "Back here."

I show them into Reptile Jesus's torture room, then turn around.

"You coming?" I ask Elsbeth.

She doesn't answer, just steps out of the trailer for a second. The unmistakable sound of a blade sliding through a skull reaches my ears, and I realize what she's doing.

"Thanks," I say to her. She still doesn't answer, just follows me into the torture room.

It's a little cramped with all of us in it, but the sound of the door latching and all the locks clicking into place tells me I made the right choice.

"Now what?" Critter asks. "We just stay in here until the herd goes away?"

"Uh ... yes?" I reply. "I wasn't thinking of an exit plan, just a stay alive for a few more hours plan."

"Weapons check," Lourdes says to her people. They comply, and all sit their asses down and start stripping their carbines, quickly going over them and cleaning them with their field kits.

It's kind of hypnotizing to watch, but that effect goes away as soon as the trailer begins to rock. The whole thing shifts at an angle, and then the pounding at the door begins.

"Looks like the Zs found Maury," I say. "I wasn't counting on that."

I can tell everyone would like to look at Elsbeth, but we all know better than to do that. It's not her fault, and if even one of us gives her a look like it is, she'll lose her shit. The last look on her face was not a judge Elsbeth look. It was more like a *let's leave Elsbeth alone because she's in a bad* place look. You learn these things when the woman saves your ass a few times.

The trailer keeps shaking, and the undead hands keep pounding. What do we do? Well, what can we do? We stand there and stare at the one way in and one way out, watching the heavy door shudder in its frame.

You see, this is the flaw of so many structures. Everyone thinks a solid door is how you keep a room secure. They put all kinds of locks on it, drill in braces for heavy bars, even use chains, but they forget about one very simple architectural fact: a door is only as strong as the frame around it. You can have a door made of fucking diamond, and it doesn't mean shit if the frame is made of goddamn particle board!

And that's exactly what the doorframe around this door is made of. Goddamn particle board. Okay, well, the frame itself is made of two by fours, but the walls are particle board. And the walls are connected to the frame. So we stand here, watching as the paint next to the door begins to crack and splinter. Then the wood that isn't really wood and more like wood stuffs (it's the Velveeta of wood!) begins to show through the paint and old plaster.

Yeah, it looks like the Zs are coming in, invited or not. How rude! Fucking rude Zs! I fucking hate rude Zs!

"We all hate rude Zs, Jace," Stuart says. "You can stop saying it over and over."

"I'm not saying it on purpose," I reply. "You think I like having the contents of my thoughts just spewing out of my mouth without my consent? It is no fun, trust me."

"No shit," Critter says. "It ain't no fun for us neither."

"Move to the back wall," Lourdes says. "Get behind us, and stay tight. We'll try to fight off as many as we can for as long as we can."

"Save some of them bullets for us," Critter says. "I ain't going out as Z food."

"Bullshit," I snap. "We're getting out of this. There is no way I have come this far to die with all you fuckers in Reptile Jesus's rumpus room. Not fucking happening!"

"Then what's your bright plan, Short Pork?" Critter asks. "Come on now, you have to have a plan, right? All that thinkin' happenin' up in that big brain of yours, there must be a plan. Enlighten us, Short Pork. What is it?"

"Don't call him Short Pork," Elsbeth says. "His name is Jace Stanford."

Critter looks over at Elsbeth, but she doesn't look back at him. Her eyes are focused on the door and the cracking walls around it. For one second, I think Critter is going to say something to her, but the man is way too smart to do that, and he just nods.

"Fine," Critter says. "Jace, what is yer plan? Huh, Jace? Ya got a plan or not?"

I have to give him credit, he doesn't back off. He may not be calling me Short Pork, but he's still gonna bust my balls.

I shake my head, and put my back against the wall.

"No, I don't have a plan," I say. "This was my plan. Get us in here and away from that fucking herd. That was as far as I thought. I was sort of hoping some of you professional killers would have a plan. Maybe take a page from the soldier playbook and take over."

"We're trapped in a small room with only one door, Jace," Lourdes says. "There's not much to work with."

"There's not much to that door," Stuart says. "It's going to come down in a couple minutes as soon as the walls around it give way."

I start bonking the back of my head against the back wall, over and over, as an act of frustration. It's something I used to do when I was a kid and got sent to my room, which happened a lot. I'd sit on my bed with my back to the wall, and bonk my head against it until the sound drove one of my parents nuts. They'd come whipping into the room, ready to yell at me, but I'd stop, and just be sitting there all innocent and shit. Didn't stop them from kicking my ass, but it did confuse the hell out of them. I don't think they ever figured out what was making the noise.

But my childhood bedroom wall was made of real materials, not like this stupid trailer wall. When I bonked my head on my old wall, it sounded solid, it had resonance. When I bonk my head on this wall it's all hollow and empty. It's a pitiful, stupid wall.

Wait ... it's a pitiful, stupid wall.

"Backdoor!" I shout. "I found the backdoor!"

Then I giggle.

"Jesus, Dad," Greta sighs.

"And Jace has now gone cuckoo," Critter says. "There ain't no backdoor, dumbass." He looks at Elsbeth. "Can I call him dumbass?"

She just shrugs, her eyes still on the one door, her blades ready at her sides.

"You're right, Crit," I smile. "There ain't no backdoor. Not yet." I turn and pound my fist on the wall I had just been leaning against. "But we can make one pretty fucking fast."

"Son of a bitch," Stuart says. "He's right. The brilliant moron is right."

"Um, that probably didn't come out the way you meant it to," I say to him.

"No, it came out exactly how I meant it to," Stuart says, then steps forward, lifts his leg, and slams his boot against the wall. A crack appears instantly. "Come on, folks. Let's get to work."

We do.

Boots, the butts of rifles and carbines, even fists, start working on the wall. In minutes we have trashed it completely, and we all stare at what's on the other side.

"I could have gone my whole life without seeing that," Greta says.

Apparently, on the other side of Reptile Jesus's torture room is Reptile Jesus's sex room. I shit you not. There's every kind of sex toy imaginable on the shelves that line the wall. There's also some very interesting equipment that I am not going to even try to figure out. I recognize the sex swing hanging from the ceiling, but that's about it.

"Looks like Kelvin wasn't so much God's voice as he was God's pervert," I say. "Not too surprising, really."

Elsbeth walks over and picks up a giant dildo. I do mean giant. The thing is like two feet long and eight inches wide. Giant.

"I could kill a man with this," she says, and tucks it inside her coat.

I really hope she means she could beat a man to death about the head and face with it. If she's talking about another way to kill a man with it, then I do not want to even go there. Please, brain, don't take me there.

Dammit. My brain takes me there.

"You know, while we're here, I should pick something up for Stella," I say.

"Dad!" Greta yells. "Yuck! That was out loud!"

"I know," I smile. "I couldn't help saying it."

"Looks like we gots another wall to go through," Critter says. There's a loud splintering sound from behind us. "And we best be hurryin'!"

I look back, and see hands and fingers start to work their way around the torture room's door as it breaks away from the walls. We've got like seconds before they get through and come for us.

No one has to say a word, we just move. We shove the sex machines out of the way, and then grab onto the shelves holding all the dildos. They're bolted to the wall. Great.

Lourdes and her men start ripping at the shelving, cracking shelves and tearing out supports. Dildos, vibrators, strap-ons, cock rings, ball cuffs, you name it, it's all flying this way and that. It's raining sex toys!

We finally get down to the wall, at least enough of it that we can squeeze through once we rip the thing open, but it may be too late. There's a huge crash and the trailer shudders as the torture room door comes free. We spin around and watch as the herd tries to jam itself through the opening. There are too many Zs, and they get stuck against each other.

Which is where the shitty walls come back into play. The particle board bends and stretches from the pressure of the herd, then the whole wall gives way, and here they come!

I just start picking up sex toys and throwing them at the Zs. Lourdes and her men are a little more practical, and all take knees and open fire while Stuart, Critter, Elsbeth, and Greta work on getting through the wall.

I throw some spiky thing (honestly, I have no idea what it is) at a Z, and it lodges right in the monster's mouth. Booyah!

It doesn't slow it down though. No booyah!

Lourdes and her guys have a little more luck as they choke the hole we made in the wall with Z corpses. There are so many of them that it gets clogged in no time, giving her and her men time to reload while everyone else keeps working on the wall.

"How's it coming?" Lourdes yells.

"It'd probably come pretty fast with this sucker," I say as I waggle a particularly girthy (Girthful? Girthtacular?) dildo about. "Damn, do I feel inadequate."

"Don't you always?" Critter cackles.

"Hey, less mocking and more, uh ... what rhymes with mocking that means breaking through a wall?" I say.

No one responds. I could use a pocket thesaurus. No, wait! One of those rhyming dictionaries that poets use. If we live through this I am totally snagging one of those from the next library we pass.

"No, you're not!" Greta yells. "That's the last thing we need!"

Everyone agrees quickly. Oh, sure, they respond to that.

The mound of dead Zs begins to tumble into Reptile Jesus's dildotorium. Then the Zs behind start to climb over their fallen comrades, and it looks like we're done for unless we get through the next wall.

"We know!" everyone shouts.

The amazing sound of crunching particle board comes from behind me. I turn, and nearly split my face in half as I grin at the sight. I can actually see snow falling! This wall leads outside! Huzzah!

Critter, Stuart, Elsbeth, and Greta keep working at widening the hole, as Lourdes and her men get back to the shooty shooty they do so well.

I just keep throwing dildos at the Zs. It's really all I can do since I only have one arm, and I lost the crowbar in the pit. Which is now a pit of fire. That could so be a country song. I lost my crowbar in the burning pit of fire. I need to remember that.

"Come on!" Stuart yells as they get the hole big enough to step through.

He sticks a leg out, then yanks it back in faster than I've ever seen him move.

"What's wrong?" I ask. But the answer shows itself quickly. "Oh, fuck."

Holes in walls, no holes in walls. Doesn't make a bit of difference when Reptile Jesus's entire cluster of trailers is surrounded by a Z herd. The ones coming from the torture room? That's just the welcoming committee. The real party is happenin' outside. Awesome.

"Fuck!" Stuart yells, and just starts firing into the herd, killing every Z he can.

It doesn't even make a dent in the numbers. There are easily a few hundred out there. And now that they know there's food through this convenient hole we've made for them, they want to be in here. Ain't no party like a Z herd trying to get inside a sex room trailer party! Hey! Ho!

"Daddy!" Greta yells. "What now?"

"I don't know, baby," I say, and take her in my arm. I kiss her forehead. "Just close your eyes, sweetheart. It'll all be over soon."

"Oh, fuck that," she snaps, and shoves me away. "I am not going out like some lame dork in a Roland Emmerich disaster movie."

Did my baby girl just make a Roland Emmerich reference while facing down certain death? Yes, she did! I couldn't be more proud! That's my girl!

"I'm out!" one of the PCs yells.

"Me too!" another shouts.

"Same here!"

"Out!"

We huddle up together as Zs come at us from inside the trailer, and Zs come at us from outside the trailer.

Then there are no Zs outside the trailer. I shit you not, folks. One second there are Zs, and the next second there's an RV.

Wait? An RV?

The side door opens up right into the trailer.

"Get your asses in!" Buzz yells. "We don't have much time!"

No time is needed. We basically teleport our asses into that RV. Buzz slams the door shut just as the Zs reach the RV, and undead hands smack against the side, while undead mouths moan with some serious disappointment.

Pup is driving and he floors it, sending all of us tumbling to the floor of the RV as it rockets forward through the herd of Zs. I don't think he lets up off the gas until we're turned around and barreling out of the compound, splitting what's left of the herd right down the middle.

"Damn, guys," I say. "That was some serious rescue shit right there. Thanks."

No one says anything; they all just stare at me. Except for Greta, who has her face buried in her hands.

"What?" I ask, then look down at what I'm holding. "Oh, hey, check it out. I snagged one after all."

I waggle the silicone dildo at everyone and laugh.

No one laughs with me.

"Put the cock away, Jace," Stuart says. "None of us need to see that right now."

"Stella's gonna be stoked," I smile.

"DAD!" Greta shrieks, gets up, and goes to the back of the RV.

"Oh, grow up," I call after her. "You're alive, aren't you? There are worse things than your dad joking about giving a dildo to your mother."

"Not many," Buzz says. "You should really put that away."

I toss the dildo aside and turn to Buzz.

"Thanks for playing cavalry," I say, holding out my hand. He looks down at it, then over at the dildo. "Dude, it wasn't used. At least I don't think it was. Hmmmm, anyone got some hand sanitizer?"

"Shut up," Stuart says, and pushes me out of the way. Buzz shakes his hand. "Stella send you?"

"Of course," Buzz says. "And Melissa. As soon as you folks left, they started conspiring. Good thing, too. We found the short bus, and then saw smoke coming from that tunnel. We would have been here faster, but we had to circle all the way around to find the compound."

"Your timing was perfect," Stuart says.

"Almost," Elsbeth says. "Little Canny."

"Who?" Buzz asks.

"That Rafe kid," Critter says. "He didn't make it."

"That's too bad," Buzz says. "I didn't really know him, but he seemed like a good kid."

"He was," I reply. "He actually was."

There's a few nods in agreement, then the RV goes quiet as we all settle in for the ride back to the convoy. I go and sit down next to Greta and wrap my arm around her.

"I'm glad you're safe," I say.

"No dildo jokes," she says.

"No dildo jokes," I reply. "I'm just here to hug on you."

"Okay," she says, and leans into me.

We sit like that for a while.

"But that room was pretty crazy, right?" I say, unable to help myself. "I mean, did you see all that shit?"

"I have no idea why Mom's stayed with you," Greta says. "I would have ditched your ass the second I saw the first Z."

"Nah, you love me just the way I am," I smile. "Think of how dull and boring the apocalypse would be without me?"

There are a few sighs of longing from everyone.

"Hey," I snap. "Not cool, people. You're ruining a tender moment between a father and his daughter."

"You ruined it a long time ago, Daddy," Greta says, but she leans in tighter. "But, yes, the apocalypse would be boring without you."

No one argues with her, so I'll take that as a win.

Pup has the heat on full, and soon the RV is one toasty, while pungent, vehicle. I drift off with Greta leaning into my shoulder, and I couldn't be happier.

***

I wake up with a start as I hear yelling, and I realize the RV has stopped. Greta is still against me, but she wakes up just as fast, and we look around at an empty RV.

"Get your fucking ass down, now!" I hear Lourdes shouting. "You move slow and steady, asshole!"

There's some more shouting, and then a gun goes off.

"OK!" a man shrieks. "Please, just stop pointing the guns at me! Please! I'm a doctor! I'm not one of those people! I'm not going to hurt anyone! I'm a doctor!"

"Yeah, you already said that, dipshit!" Critter yells. "And I've met some seriously evil doctors, so don't try to pull one over on us!"

"You have three seconds to climb down from there! THREE!" Lourdes yells.

"I'm climbing! I'm climbing!"

Greta jumps up and races for the RV's door. "Stop! Don't hurt him! Stop!"

"Greta? Get back in there," Lourdes orders. "You don't need to see this."

"I said to fucking stop!" Greta shouts as I scramble up and follow her out into the snow. It's not falling anywhere near as hard as before, but it's still falling. "I know him, dammit! Put down your guns!"

"Greta?" a voice asks from above us.

I look up and see a man wrapped in all kinds of blankets and coats. Only his eyes are showing, and his eyelashes are nothing but icicles.

"Hey," Greta smiles up at the man. "What the fuck are you doing up there?"

"I hopped on as you were leaving," the man says. "I was stuck on top of the infirmary trailers, and when you drove by I took my chance. Nearly fell off at that last curve. I guess some of your people heard me thumping around up here."

Greta turns to Lourdes and glares. She is almost the spitting image of a pissed off Stella, and Lourdes actually flinches at the look.

"Put down the guns," Greta insists. "He's a friend."

"From that compound?" Stuart asks, a shotgun to his shoulder. "Greta, I think you're confused. There are no friends from that compound."

"He is!" she snaps, and points a finger at him. Then she steps in front of his shotgun. "You going to shoot me, Stuart? You going to blast a hole right through my head like a Z? Because you'll have to if you want to get to him."

"Who is he?" Elsbeth asks.

Funny, it's the first time anyone thinks to ask that. Leave it to Elsbeth to get to the point.

"Jimmy," Greta says, and I hear something in her voice I am none too pleased with.

She likes this guy.

"Dr. James Stenkler," the man says. "I was the doctor back at that compound. I checked Greta over when they brought her in."

"He saved me," Greta says.

"Greta, we saved you," Lourdes says, looking around at all the people holding firearms still pointed up at the man. "This guy was part of those crazies. He didn't save you. He may have convinced you he did, but he didn't. It's normal for hostages to-."

"Oh, shut the fuck up, Lourdes," Greta says. "I'm not some Stockholm Syndrome bippy twat. If I say he saved me, it's because he actually saved me. Some of the men came sniffing around for a new piece of ass, and he kept them from taking me. Told them I had syphilis and crabs, but it did the trick."

"Do you?" Elsbeth asks. "Because those are bad things. Never eat someone with crabs. They get stuck in your-."

"Oh, Jesus," I snap. "That's enough, El."

"Just shit fucking with you, Long Pork." Elsbeth laughs, then sheaths her blades and walks back into the RV. "Get him down. We should keep moving. We can't stop like this anymore."

Everyone looks from the man on the RV, to Greta, then back to the man.

"Come on, Jimmy," Greta says. "They won't hurt you."

"I'm not so sure about that, G," Dr. Stenkler says.

"G?" I say. "Excuse me? You do not get to call my daughter G."

"Oh, sorry," the man apologizes as he scoots to the end of the RV and climbs down the back ladder. "You must be her father, Jace. Good to meet you. G, or, uh, Greta didn't stop talking about you."

"How the fuck is he calling you G when he's only known you for two days?" I growl.

"He saved my life, Dad," Greta says. "He can call me Bunny Nuts, if he wants to."

I point a finger at the guy. "You call her Bunny Nuts, and I cut ya."

"Get in the RV!" Elsbeth yells from inside.

"Later," I say to Greta as Lourdes and her guys grab Dr. Stenkler and roughly shove him up into the RV.

"Whatever," Greta says.

***

We get going again, and I stare at Dr. Stenkler as he unwraps himself from his bundle of blankets and coats.

"You must have known you'd need to bail if you had those ready," I say.

"We always kept lots of blankets in the infirmary," Dr. Stenkler replies. "Plenty of other supplies, but those are gone now. Too bad. I'm sure you and your people could use them."

To say I'm surprised by how he looks is an understatement. He can't be more than thirty.

"What kind of doctor are you?" I ask. "Pediatrics? Learning by being?"

"I'm twenty-nine," he says. "I know, I'm young. I'm used to it. I graduated med school at twenty, and rushed through my residency at Northwestern Memorial. That's when the plague hit."

"Plague?" Elsbeth asks, finally taking an interest. "No plague. Just Zs."

"Yes, well, the phenomenon had to occur somehow," Dr. Stenkler says. "It spreads and acts like a typical plague, so that's what it should be classified as."

"Listen, Doogie, it's a fucking nightmare, is what it is," I say. "That's what it should be classified as."

"Plagues are nightmares," Dr. Stenkler smiles.

I'm not a sexist pig, but I'm pretty sure all the women in the RV just melted when he smiled. Fucker, with his dark hair and dark eyes and dimple chin. He has a beard, and I can still see the dimple. Smile away, bitch! You're in my world now! We'll see how long you last!

The guy stares at me, then looks around like he's waiting to be attacked.

"Uh ... okay," Dr. Stenkler says. "Sorry. I know you don't trust me, but there's no reason to get personal about it."

"Fuck," I sigh. "That was out loud, wasn't it?"

"Yep," Greta says. "Good one, Dad. Can you be more embarrassing?"

"Do you really want to ask that question right now?" I reply. "There is a dildo in this RV somewhere."

"You didn't mean to say all that?" Dr. Stenkler asks, wisely ignoring my dildo comment. "Have you had many of these involuntary outbursts?"

"Yes," the whole RV replies.

"Fuck all y'all," I say. Then, "Yes."

"It's getting worse," Stuart says. "He pretty much thinks it and says it now. It was funny at first, but by now it's just annoying."

"And a little scary," Critter says. "I seen a lot of crazy people in my time, and he's starting to top the list. He may get on our nerves, yet he's handy to have around sometimes. But he'll stop bein' handy if he can't shut up!"

"Gee, thanks, folks," I frown. "The warm and fuzzies are just overwhelming."

The guy starts patting himself down, and Lourdes has a pistol in his face before he can get halfway down his chest.

"Just looking for my pen light," he says. "Sorry."

Lourdes reaches into his coat and pulls out a white pen light. "What do you need it for?" she asks.

"I was going to do a couple of quick tests," Dr. Stenkler says. "Just check some simple neurological responses. It'll help me diagnose what's wrong with him."

"Um, I don't have a boo boo, Doogie," I say. "If there is something wrong with me, then it's beyond your pediatrics degree."

"I'm not a pediatrician," he frowns.

"Then why'd you say you were?" I smirk.

"I didn't. You did," he replies.

"He's right, Dad," Greta says, sounding a lot more worried than I'd like. "You called him the pediatrician. It wasn't funny."

Dr. Stenkler reaches for the pen light. "May I?"

Lourdes looks at me, and I nod. "Why not?" I say. "But shoot him if he tries to do a rectal exam."

"Deal," Lourdes says.

"Thanks," Dr. Stenkler says. "Now hold still, and do exactly as I say. If my requests are confusing, or you can't do them, then let me know right away."

"So, what kind of doctor are you?" I ask as he scoots forward and takes me gently by the chin, shining the light back and forth from one eye to the next.

"Neurosurgeon," he says. "Third youngest in the country before the plague."

"Third youngest?" Critter laughs. "The others must have still been suckin' their mommies' tits when they graduated."

"Exactly," I laugh. "Good one, Crit."

I sit there and let the guy do his thing while everyone watches. So glad I can be the in-flight entertainment.

***

Stella grips my hand as we sit together with Dr. Stenkler and Dr. McCormick in front of us, while Stuart and Elsbeth hang back, keeping an eye on our new addition while he explains what's up with my brainpan. We're all in the very back room of one of the RVs while the convoy moves on. Elsbeth insisted we break camp and hit the road, even with the weather still pretty bad. Mt. Vernon was mentioned, as was hunkering down for the winter, but she left zero room for argument. So we hit the road.

The RV is stiflingly warm, but I can't help shivering as Dr. Stenkler lays it all out.

"There is no way I can know for sure without some major tests," Dr. Stenkler says. "But my guess is he has some severe lesions on the brain from all the concussions he's suffered over the years. The bleeding could be bad, or could just be localized enough to affect his verbal control."

"Will he die?" Stella asks, straight to the point.

"Stella," Dr. McCormick soothes. "He's not going to die."

"But lesions mean he's bleeding from the brain," Stella says. "That's not good."

"He's not hallucinating, not having issues with phantom smells or sounds, so I rule out a tumor," Dr. Stenkler says. "That would be way worse than lesions. We'll keep an eye on him, and start logging the time and frequency of his outbursts. If they stay consistent, then I think he's in the clear. The lesions shouldn't get worse."

"But if they aren't consistent?" Stuart asks. "Sorry. I shouldn't interrupt."

"Answer the question," Elsbeth says to Dr. Stenkler.

"I don't know," the man replies. "Like I said, I need to run way more detailed tests, and I can't do that in an RV. I need a fully equipped neurology department."

"We'll find one," Stella says, looking up at Stuart. "You will help us convince Lourdes and Critter to find one. The next big city, we find a hospital, hook up a generator, and run some fucking tests."

"If we can," Stuart says. "It depends on the situation."

"Depends on the situation?" Stella roars.

Everyone, even Elsbeth, flinches.

"Hey," I say quietly, and grip her hand hard enough that I know it hurts. She doesn't let on at all. "Chill, baby. We can't jeopardize everyone's lives so I can get some polaroids taken of the inside of my skull. Stuart is right, we stop when and if we can. It does depend on the situation."

Stella wants to reply, but the tears start, and she can't. I take her in my arm and glance at everyone else. They get the idea and start to filter out. Except Elsbeth, who just stands there until Stuart grabs her by the shoulder and yanks her with him.

"He could be lying," Stella sobs. "We don't know this guy! He's a liar!"

"Dr. McCormick quizzed him," I say softly. "So did Kramer, not that I trust that assfuck. They both say he's legit and knows what he's talking about."

"But he could be wrong," she counters, her words pretty much lost in hiccups.

"Yeah, he could be," I say, and then just press her to me.

I don't know how long I hold my crying wife, but I can say it isn't long enough. It can never be long enough.

CHAPTER TWELVE

St. Louis is a ghost town. There aren't even any Zs around, just burnt down buildings and streets that look like someone took a giant chainsaw to the asphalt and went all Leatherface. It's not a good scene. The giant arch is even gone. We see some of it sticking up as we drive past, but the thing is demolished.

Landon Chase, our resident tech asshole, tweaked the radios so we have some private, scrambled channels. This means Lourdes can bark orders at everyone over the radio to keep eyes open and be ready for an ambush.

In addition to barking, she also complains about how we have to keep detouring to get around the cracked roads. She's all ambush this and ambush that. But it never comes, and we get past St. Louis and suddenly we are in the West, even if we couldn't see the great arch that is supposed to represent the Gateway to the West. Arches telling you where you are is so old world, man.

The weather doesn't exactly play nice as we travel. More snowstorms, more brutal cold. How the fuck did the settlers survive on the plains before space heaters?

A particularly nasty storm comes down on us about fifty miles outside of St. Louis. Lourdes and Critter want to have us stop and circle up, but Elsbeth refuses and throws such a fit that I am actually worried she's the one with brain lesions. Needless to say, but I'll say it anyway, Lourdes and Critter reluctantly give in, and we keep going, pushing through the storm.

It's harrowing, but the clouds do break eventually, and the sky is insanely clear. I don't think I've ever seen such a vast sky before. It just keeps going in all directions.

So does the herd of Zs we run into.

"We can't drive through that," Lourdes snaps over the radio. "Can someone explain that to Elsbeth? We need to stop and figure out a different route."

"She's right, El," Stella says. "We can't force our way through. And we need fuel. We're going to stop for a couple of days and hope the herd clears out. We resupply, and then get back on the road."

Elsbeth doesn't argue with Stella, but she sure makes it known she is extremely put out by it, thank you very much.

We find a small town about twenty miles off the interstate, and huddle up the RVs next to a library. The walls are solid concrete block and brick, and there're only a few entrances. Plus, the books burn easy and keep us warm. I hate burning the books since they are now an endangered species, but warm is warm, people.

I find a rhyming dictionary, and am very pleased with myself, until there's a vote that it should be taken away from me. The vote is unanimous. Fuckers.

Melissa and her brothers take a team out to scavenge the town for food, water, and fuel, while Lourdes, Stuart, and Critter spread out maps of the region and see if they can find a way around the giant herd of Zs, and still keep us on course.

"Our options are limited," Lourdes says. "We're in flyover territory now. There just aren't the arteries that we're used to in the East." She plops her finger in the middle of the map. "We go up or we go down here. But there's no guarantee that there aren't more herds either of those ways."

"Why are they so thick here?" Charlie asks as he leans back in a chair and kicks his feet up on a table. He's salvaged a bunch of books, and he taps his toe against the stacks as he watches the navigational brain trust decide our best course. "We never saw herds like this in Asheville."

"Not until the Consortium herded them up to us from Atlanta," I say, holding Stella close to me in a blanket to keep warm. "Maybe others had the same warfare idea, and things got out of hand?"

Elsbeth snorts from a few tables away.

"Yes, El?" I sigh. "Would you like to contribute to the conversation?"

"Others," Elsbeth says. "Yeah, there are others."

"Come on, El," I say. "Will you please tell us what's going on? You know something, and you are risking all of our lives by keeping us in the dark."

"Don't matter," she shrugs. "In the dark, in the light, not a damn thing you can do. If they strike, then they strike, and you all probably die."

"We all die?" I ask. Everyone is listening, but they know me and Elsbeth well enough to stay quiet, and let me take lead. "You aren't counting yourself in that? Can you tell me why?"

"They won't kill me," she says. "They want me. I won't let them take me, so I'll probably die fighting, but you all will be dead way before that."

"See? Now we are getting somewhere," I say. "They strike, we die, you live. Now, how about we fill in the details a little? Maybe get more specific on the nouns? When you say 'they will strike', what 'they' are you talking about?"

"You know," she says.

"Really, El? If I knew, then why would I ask?"

"Because you're afraid of the answer," Elsbeth says. "You'll be pissing in your panties."

I slam my hand down on the table, making everyone jump.

"Dammit, El! Stop fucking around!" I shout. "Who the fuck are you talking about?"

"My sisters," she says, a smug look on her face. "How're your panties?"

I will admit there might be a little leaking in my panties. Fuck. Hearing Kramer mention it before was one thing. But hearing Elsbeth finally confirm it?

It means we're fucking dead.

I look around the library, and my feelings towards the temporary sanctuary turn on a dime. This isn't a sanctuary, this is a crypt. We're just corpses that haven't died yet. Fuckerty fuck.

The looks on everyone's faces tells me they are having the same thoughts. Unless…

"Was I talking out loud?" I ask. There are some nods. "Sorry."

"You ain't wrong, Long Pork," Critter says. He doesn't call me Jace as Elsbeth had ordered, but she doesn't seem to care anymore. Well, it was nice while it lasted. "Those psycho ladies catch up, and they'll cut us down before *any* of us get a chance to piss in our panties."

Stuart looks at the maps, looks at Elsbeth, looks back at the maps, and then looks at me.

"Jace," he says. "What're your brain's guts saying to do?"

"My brain's guts can't exactly be trusted," I say, and tap my temple. "They're on their period, remember?"

"Dad, that's just gross," Charlie complains.

"Life is gross, son. Life is gross," I reply, then sit there for a minute and think.

Everyone knows my headspace is fragile right now, so they actually wait and let me think.

"We do nothing," I say. "We keep going like we have been, and do nothing."

"That doesn't help," Stuart sighs.

"I honestly don't know what else to do," I say. "Seriously, how do we stop a team of killer ninja chicks? If El wanted to, she could wipe us all out right now by herself. Just imagine half a dozen Els. We're fucked, y'all."

"There're seven," Elsbeth says. "That's more than half a dozen. Half a dozen is six."

"Yes, thanks for the math lesson, El," I say. "But that's not the point."

"No, but it's true," Elsbeth says. She stands up and claps her hands, then laughs. "You people are stupid. You have the answer, but none of you want to see it. Turtles. You are all turtles. Hiding your heads in your shells."

"I've been called worse," I say. "Still not the point. Wait, what do you mean we already have the answer?"

"I've been waiting for you to figure it out," she says. "But you don't. Too busy getting captured. Too busy waiting for me to save you. No time to think and see what's right in front of you."

She turns and looks over at Dr. Kramer, who sits all by himself in a corner of the library, his eyes locked onto the exchange.

"Hello," he says, and waves.

"Motherfucker," I sigh.

Stuart starts to speak, then stops and shakes his head.

"Dammit, she's right," Critter says, catching on too.

I get up and walk over to Dr. Kramer, with Stuart, Critter, Stella, and Lourdes right behind me. Elsbeth hangs back, and pretends to check out Charlie's stacks of books. Smart ass.

"Hello, Doctor," I say as we stand in front of him. "You said that Camille knows all about your conditioning of these girls, right? And is probably using them to track us?"

"Did I?" Dr. Kramer frowns.

"Yes, asshole!" Stell yells. "You did!"

"Hmmm, that was a long time ago," Dr. Kramer says. "I say many things just to appease your aggression." His eyes fall on Stella. "Especially hers."

"Suck my dick, fuckface," Stella says.

"Yes, thank you, baby," I say, and pat her shoulder. "That helps."

I sit down next to Dr. Kramer, and lean in close. I know I stink, he knows I stink, hell we all stink, but that doesn't stop him from wrinkling his nose.

"You could use a bath, Mr. Stanford," Dr. Kramer says.

I ignore him. "Can you fix them? Undo the conditioning that is forcing them to follow Camille's orders?"

"Forcing? Oh, no, Mr. Stanford, you misunderstand my entire life's work," Dr. Kramer smiles. "The beauty of what I have done, is it forces them to do nothing they don't want to do. If they want to come kill you all, then that's unfortunate, but out of my control to stop."

"Bullshit," Elsbeth coughs.

We all turn, and she's pointing to herself.

Of course, it is bullshit. El broke the conditioning. But how did she do it?

"You said you bumped your head," I say to Elsbeth. "You bumped your head, and then Pa found you, and he changed you."

"Bingo was his name-o," Elsbeth says.

"Wrong rhyme," Charlie says. Elsbeth glares. "Your version is cool too."

"There is a way to fix them," I say. "But we have to capture them, and do a little bumping on their noggins."

"Oh, I would advise against that," Dr. Kramer says. "What happened to Ms. Thornberg was a complete accident. Even if you manage to capture the girls, being able to reverse the conditioning physically would take the knowledge of a skilled neurosurgeon. Where are you going to…?"

"Yeah," I smile, and glance over where Dr. Stenkler is sitting and chatting with Greta.

Chatting with Greta. Sitting and chatting with Greta. Sitting really close to her and chatting. A twenty-nine year old man and my teenage daughter are sitting close and chatting.

"Jace? Chill," Stuart says, and grips my shoulder.

"That was all out loud, huh?" I ask.

"No, but the look on your face says it all," he replies.

"I'll go get him," Stella says, and marches over to break up whatever is happening between my teenage daughter and the twenty-nine year old man. Teenage daughter and twenty-nine year old man. Sitting and chatting.

"Okay, that's out loud," Stuart says. "Maybe go hang back and rest some? We're all pretty sure we know where you're going with this."

"I'm good," I say. "I'm totally good."

"You sure?" Stuart asks.

"I'm sure," I say as I watch Dr. Stenkler come towards us while Stella stays with Greta and has a nice little talk, mom to daughter.

"What do you need?" Dr. Stenkler asks.

I look at Dr. Kramer and smile. "I believe you were about to say we will need a skilled neurosurgeon, but where will we find one? Guess what, Doc? We have one of those. Now, how about you spill the beans, and tell this guy everything you know on how to reverse the conditioning."

"You can't reverse the conditioning," Dr. Kramer says.

The blur that rushes past me is Elsbeth shaped, and the next thing we know Dr. Kramer is dangling with his feet several inches off the floor. Elsbeth has her hand around his throat and holds him up. Then she lowers him slowly, and pulls him in close.

"You will be honest," she says. "You will be helpful. You will do what they want and stop confusing them."

"You can't reverse the conditioning," he gasps. "But you can cut off the influence. If they decide not to kill you, then it'll be of their own free will."

"But they could still decide to kill us, right?" I ask.

"That's up to them," Dr. Kramer says. "I can't help with that."

That's believable. We all know Elsbeth. We live because she lets us live. No doubt there.

"Fine," I say. "El? Drop him." She does. "Dr. Stinkler?"

"It's Stenkler," Dr. Stenkler frowns.

"Not anymore," I grin. "Didn't you hear? We all get shitty nicknames in the apocalypse?"

***

We stay in that library for a day as Dr. Stenkler grills Dr. Kramer on everything. I understand about ten percent of what they talk about. The rest makes my head hurt.

Which seems to be the new thing. The talking out loud thing lessens, but debilitating headaches increase. I hardly notice when we get back on the road and finally reach Kansas City after a few days of skirting the mass Z migration.

"Well, the asshole wasn't lying about this," Stuart grumbles as we stand and stare at the hole that had once been Kansas City. "If anything, the guy downplayed the destruction."

"Nuke?" I ask Lourdes. "Is that what did this? I mean, look at it, it's just a crater."

"No nuke," Lourdes says. "We'd be sick from radiation poisoning by now. And there'd be singes of the blast where we're standing. No, I think when we get closer we'll see it was a lot of smaller explosions that cleared out the city."

She's right. We get the convoy rolling again, and the closer we get the more the ex-city looks like a teenager's pizza face, all pocked with craters and shit.

There really aren't words for what we witness. And that's saying a lot, coming from me.

Nothing but total destruction. It makes St. Louis look like a simple remodel. KC? It's just plain gone.

"I guess the Combine didn't know how to play nice," Critter says. "They either pissed off the wrong people, or they got in the worst bicker fight ever. Don't matter none which way now. They's just plain gone."

See? Even Critter agrees with me. Just. Plain. Gone.

"So we head on to Boulder?" I ask, looking over at Critter and Lourdes as the scorched Kansas landscape rolls by outside the RV. "Go to the Stronghold?"

"For now," Lourdes says. "But we have to also consider what's behind us. At some point, we may need to dig in and get ready to defend ourselves. That point could come before we reach Colorado and the Rockies."

We all know what she means by what's behind us. No matter how fast we move, which isn't all that fast considering how blocked the interstate and other roads are, the Z herd is going to catch up. That's just reality. They don't have to stop and hunt for fuel or food, they don't have to sleep or deal with crazies. Hell, they eat crazies!

And there're also the sisters coming. Elsbeth can't say where they are, but I'm almost certain she feels them somehow when they are close. I let everyone else worry about moving forward and about the Z herd, while I keep my attention on Elsbeth and that sisterhood sixth sense.

***

The days roll by, the plains keep going, and it's almost like we don't make any progress at all. Then after eight hundred years of being stuck in this stinky RV, as we lead a bunch of other stinky RVs, we see a sign that gives us just a little hope.

"Welcome To Colorado," the sign says. Well, kind of. It's sort of ripped in half and semi-melted, but we figure out the full message without a problem.

"Aren't there supposed to be mountains?" Charlie asks.

"You can't see them from here," Lourdes replies. "We have a couple hundred more miles to go before we can start catching a glimpse."

"A couple hundred? Fuck me," Charlie sighs.

"You all see that?" Critter asks as he points out the windshield. "Tell me that isn't what I think it is."

We drive past the welcome sign, and Lourdes moves up front with a pair of binoculars. She studies the horizon for a minute, then hands the binoculars to Stuart.

"Shit," he says. "Another herd. Looks bigger than the one we passed. Where are they all coming from?"

"Two thirds of the population of the US is behind us," Charlie says. "I bet they're migrating to find food. The East Coast has been picked clean."

"Maybe," Lourdes says. "Doesn't matter. We'll deal with them when we get there." She grabs a radio and calls one of the other RVs. "John? You seeing this?"

"Roger," John replies. "I'm estimating five or six thousand."

There are a few gasps in the RV.

"That's what I see too," Lourdes says. "Pass the word that we stay the course and move forward. We have at least a few hours before we catch up to them. Keep your eyes peeled for a spot to hunker down and strategize."

"Will do," John replies. "Out."

I can see Elsbeth is not happy with the hunker down part, but we have no choice. We are the meat in a Z herd sandwich. No going back without dealing with a shit ton of Zs, and no going forward without dealing with a shit ton of Zs. Limited supplies, getting low on ammunition, and about to jump out of our own skins from being trapped in these RVs for so long, options aren't exactly a luxury we have.

So, I'll take the luxuries I do have: friends, family, a badass killer always having my back. I push away the thoughts of my brain lesions, of crazy ninja chicks, of Z herd sandwiches. I let go of the constant feeling of anxiety in my gut as we continue our flight away from the Consortium and towards something we don't even know still exists. I lean back against the wall of the RV and decide that at the next stop, I'm going to grab my wife, find someplace private, and show her just how much I love her while I have the chance. That's a luxury I do have, and I plan on taking advantage of.

"Gross," Greta says, and I blink and look around. Oops, out loud again.

"Shut the fuck up, Greta," Stella says, and squeezes my hand. "I'll take that luxury if my man is wanting to give it."

"Damn skippy," I grin, and kiss her.

Hey, you know what? Maybe talking out loud isn't so bad after all.

"Yes, it is," everyone says.

Fine. Whatever. I don't care.

Man, people in the zombie apocalypse can be so mean sometimes.

Jake Bible lives in Asheville, NC with his wife and two kids. Jake has a record of innovation, invention, and creativity. Novelist, short story writer, independent screenwriter, podcaster, and inventor of the Drabble Novel, Jake is able to switch between or mash-up genres with ease to create new and exciting storyscapes that have captivated and built an audience of thousands.

He is the author of over a dozen novels, including the bestselling Z-Burbia and Mega series for Severed Press.

Find him at jakebible.com. Join him on Twitter and Facebook.

CHECK OUT OTHER GREAT ZOMBIE NOVELS

Z BURBIA
by Jake Bible

Whispering Pines is a classic, quiet, private American subdivision on the edge of Asheville, NC, set in the pristine Blue Ridge Mountains. Which is good since the zombie apocalypse has come to Western North Carolina and really put suburban living to the test!

Surrounded by a sea of the undead, the residents of Whispering Pines have adapted their bucolic life of block parties to scavenging parties, common area groundskeeping to immediate area warfare, neighborhood beautification to neighborhood fortification.

But, even in the best of times, suburban living has its ups and downs what with nosy neighbors, a strict Home Owners' Association, and a property management company that believes the words "strict interpretation" are holy words when applied to the HOA covenants. Now with the zombie apocalypse upon them even those innocuous, daily irritations quickly become dramatic struggles for personal identity, family security, and straight up survival.

ZOMBIE RULES
by David Achord

Zach Gunderson's life sucked and then the zombie apocalypse began.

Rick, an aging Vietnam veteran, alcoholic, and prepper, convinces Zach that the apocalypse is on the horizon. The two of them take refuge at a remote farm. As the zombie plague rages, they face a terrifying fight for survival.

They soon learn however that the walking dead are not the only monsters.

CHECK OUT OTHER GREAT ZOMBIE NOVELS

900 MILES
by S. Johnathan Davis

John is a killer, but that wasn't his day job before the Apocalypse.
In a harrowing 900 mile race against time to get to his wife just as the dead begin to rise, John, a business man trapped in New York, soon learns that the zombies are the least of his worries, as he sees first-hand the horror of what man is capable of with no rules, no consequences and death at every turn.
Teaming up with an ex-army pilot named Kyle, they escape New York only to stumble across a man who says that he has the key to a rumored underground stronghold called Avalon..... Will they find safety? Will they make it to Johns wife before it's too late?
Get ready to follow John and Kyle in this fast paced thriller that mixes zombie horror with gladiator style arena action!

WHITE FLAG OF THE DEAD
by Joseph Talluto

Millions died when the Enillo Virus swept the earth. Millions more were lost when the victims of the plague refused to stay dead, instead rising to slaughter and feed on those left alive. For survivors like John Talon and his son Jake, they are faced with a choice: Do they submit to the dead, raising the white flag of surrender? Or do they find the will to fight, to try and hang on to the last shreds or humanity?

CHECK OUT OTHER GREAT ZOMBIE NOVELS

VACCINATION
by Phillip Tomasso

What if the H7N9 vaccination wasn't just a preventative measure against swine flu?

It seemed like the flu came out of nowhere and yet, in no time at all the government manufactured a vaccination. Were lab workers diligent, or could the virus itself have been man-made? Chase McKinney works as a dispatcher at 9-1-1. Taking emergency calls, it becomes immediately obvious that the entire city is infected with the walking dead. His first goal is to reach and save his two children.

Could the walls built by the U.S.A. to keep out illegal aliens, and the fact the Mexican government could not afford to vaccinate their citizens against the flu, make the southern border the only plausible destination for safety?

ZOMBIE, INC
by Chris Dougherty

"WELCOME! To Zombie, Inc. The United Five State Republic's leading manufacturer of zombie defense systems! In business since 2027, Zombie, Inc. puts YOU first. YOUR safety is our MAIN GOAL! Our many home defense options - from Ze Fence® to Ze Popper® to Ze Shed® - fit every need and every budget. Use Scan Code "TELL ME MORE!" for your FREE, in-home*, no obligation consultation! *Schedule your appointment with the confidence that you will NEVER HAVE TO LEAVE YOUR HOME! It isn't safe out there and we know it better than most! Our sales staff is FULLY TRAINED to handle any and all adversarial encounters with the living and the undead". Twenty-five years after the deadly plague, the United Five State Republic's most successful company, Zombie, Inc., is in trouble. Will a simple case of dwindling supply and lessening demand be the end of them or will Zombie, Inc. find a way, however unpalatable, to survive?